PRIVATE EYES' FIRST CASES
MADE PUBLIC!
Brand-new tales featuring beloved detectives

In Stuart M. Kaminsky's "Snow," the eccentric Inspector Rostnikov follows a trail of blood to a brutal crime in the cold climes of Russia. . . .

Shocking secrets rise from the ashes when Laura Lippman's brash detective Tess Monaghan investigates a suspicious house fire in "Orphans Court". . . .

Praise for the FIRST CASES series:

"No fan of the contemporary private-eye genre will want to miss this wonderful collection."
—*Booklist*

"Suspenseful and provocative. An ingenious anthology." —*Atlanta Journal Constitution*

"Smashing concept . . . . lection of classic sto. . . . . *News*

FIRST CASES,
Volume 3

New and Classic Tales
of Detection

EDITED BY

Robert J. Randisi

A SIGNET BOOK

SIGNET
Published by New American Library, a division of Penguin Putnam Inc., 375
Hudson Street, New York, New York 10014, U.S.A.
Penguin Books Ltd, 27 Wrights Lane, London W8 5TZ, England
Penguin Books Australia Ltd, Ringwood, Victoria, Australia
Penguin Books Canada Ltd, 10 Alcorn Avenue, Toronto, Ontario, Canada
M4V 3B2
Penguin Books (N.Z.) Ltd, 182–190 Wairau Road, Auckland 10, New Zealand

Penguin Books Ltd, Registered Offices: Harmondsworth, Middlesex, England

Published by Signet, an imprint of New American Library,
a division of Penguin Putnam Inc.

First Signet Printing, December 1999
10 9 8 7 6 5 4 3 2 1

PUBLISHER'S NOTE
These stories are works of fiction. Names, characters, places, and incidents
either are the product of the author's imagination or are used fictitiously,
and any resemblance to actual persons, living or dead, business establishments,
events, or locales is entirely coincidental.

CONTENTS

v

INTRODUCTION

Our aim with these *First Cases* anthologies has been to give readers a first or second look at some of the more enduring characters in our genre. While the first two books were thematic—hard-boiled and cozy—this book combines the two and goes beyond.

We present bestsellers—Tony Hillerman and Anne Perry; a *Black Mask* legend in Talmage Powell; the mother of the modern female P.I., Maxine O'Callaghan; modern masters and multi-award winners like Lawrence Block, Stuart M. Kaminsky, and John Lutz; some stars who got started in the 1980s, such as Jerry Kennealy, Les Roberts, and Gar Haywood; and some of the brightest of the new breed from the 1990s, Dana Stabenow, Wendi Lee, Janet Evanovich, and Laura Lippman.

We have twelve reprints and two stories written expressly for this book. Laura Lippman has allowed us to print her first Tess Monaghan story, and in something of a coup, Stuart Kaminsky takes us back to the early days of Porfiry Rostnikov's career.

All in all, this has the look of our most complete *First Cases* book and, we hope, not our last. Please, read and enjoy.

—Robert J. Randisi
St. Louis, Mo.
March 1999

INTRODUCTION

HER DAGGER BEFORE ME

A Lloyd Carter/Ed Rivers story

Talmage Powell

FIRST APPEARANCE: *This story*

Talmage Powell is one of the last pulpsters. He has published five books in his Ed Rivers P.I. series, but the character debuted in this story in the July 1949 issue of *Black Mask*, albeit under the name of Lloyd Carter. It's an honor to reprint this story here, from one of the masters of the "Black Mask" school.

CHAPTER ONE

Cold Meat

I had been on a divorce case, shadowing a man most of the night before, so I didn't do anything about the screaming telephone for the first few seconds except try to swim back down in the sticky molasses of sleep and wish whoever was calling would go away.

The phone kept snarling. After a minute I was wide awake and in that state going back to sleep in the muggy, noonday Florida heat was out of the question. I heaved myself on the edge of the bed and shouted at the phone, "All right, I'm coming!"

The apartment was sodden with heat; I've been in Tampa a long time but I never got used to the heat.

While I'm padding toward the phone, I might as well tell you who I am.

The name is Lloyd Carter, age forty-four. I'm beginning to add an inner tube around my middle, and I don't like to be kidded about the way I'm starting to bald on the crown of my head. I live in a rundown apartment on the edge of Tampa's Ybor City. The bed is lumpy, the furniture old. It's just a place to sleep. I got in the private detective business twenty-one years ago. I never intended to make it a lifetime career, but I guess now I will.

I've never married, which is maybe what put the pickles in my disposition. I had a girl when I was young, in New York, that I might have married, but she ran off with a punk I was trying to nail. He was cornered in Indiana by state police, made a run for it, but a fast freight got in the way of his automobile. She was in the car.

New York wasn't the same after that, and I came south. I've been with Southeastern Detective Service over sixteen years . . .

I picked up the telephone.

"Lloyd?"

It was the old man's voice. Henry Fayette, who ramrodded Southeastern, should have retired a long time ago. He's seen too much of the seamy side of life streaming through his agency. It's in his voice. But he never could retire because he's a spender and is always scratching hard to keep the wolf at arm's length.

"Lloyd," his tired voice said, "I want you to come to the office right away."

I didn't argue. He'd known how late I'd worked last night. If he hadn't had to call me, he wouldn't have.

I went in the bedroom and dressed. Baggy slacks, sweaty sport shirt. And the knife under my left armpit. I'm naked without the knife. My work puts me across the tables now and then from Ybor City characters.

The only weapon some of those lads understand is a knife.

I was going to have to get my laundry out today. I wrote a note for the girl, left it on the kitchen table. I opened the ice box, drank a pint of beer, and headed for the office. The heat was terrible. Already beads of sweat were like a film of hot oil all over me.

The agency's offices are in a sagging brick building that was young when Tampa was young, on the lower end of Franklin Street. I opened the door to Henry Fayette's office. He was behind his desk, a tall, gaunt, rawboned gray man in a gray tropical suit. He stood up. The girl sitting at the end of his desk watched me cross the office. Without looking directly at her, I sized her up.

She wasn't exactly plain, but she wasn't beautiful, either. She was tall and slim, with nice enough figure and face and rather drab brown hair. Just a girl who could lose herself in a crowd, with a sort of hungry look on her face that might mean she was hungry for food—or love. Her clothes, white linen frock and bag, indicated she had enough money to eat regularly.

The chief introduced us. Her name was Allene Buford.

"Lloyd," Henry Fayette said with a small, tired gesture of his hand, "Miss Buford wants us to do something about her stepmother and a chap named Buddy Tomlinson. You might repeat the details, Miss Buford, to Lloyd as you told them to me."

She sat on the edge of her chair, hands in her lap, and gave me the details. Her voice was calm, even, but it was belied by the cold fire deep in her eyes.

It was about the average sordid mess. This Allene Buford's father had been a fairly wealthy man. Allene's mother had died ten years ago, and her father had remarried six years later, all of which was normal enough. But the sordid part began when the old man died. In his will, he left provisions for Allene to have an income, not too large. The bulk of his fortune, Emagine Buford, Allene's stepmother, was to hold until the girl was thirty—seven years from now.

"My father seemed to have some foggy idea that I wouldn't be capable of handling almost a million dollars until I was at least thirty."

"And what happens then?" I asked her.

"Emagine is to come into two hundred thousand. I am to have the rest of the money." Her face tightened, and I leaned back with a sigh, knowing that now we were getting around to the sordid part.

Emagine Buford and her stepdaughter had come south for the winter, to St. Petersburg, the resort city across the bay from Tampa. She had joined the throngs, a woman who had outlived her responsibilities. Who had nothing but time, money, and restlessness on her hands. She'd met Buddy Tomlinson. From Allene's description, he was one of those boys who had perpetual youth, a husky physique that, at forty-five, was still trim, a disarming smile, coal-black hair, and one of those little-boy faces.

The fact that she was almost fifteen years Buddy's senior hadn't worried Emagine any. "She's like a schoolgirl," Allene said, "with her first beau. She's buying bathing suits and evening gowns and seeing Buddy Tomlinson constantly."

"And where do I enter? What do you want me to do?" I looked at her over the flame of my lighter as I touched it to a fag.

Allene looked steadily at me. "I want you to mark up Buddy Tomlinson so he'll never be handsome to any woman again!"

A second or two ticked away. She saw the old man about to speak. "Of course," she said, "I know you can't be hired to do that. But I know Buddy's trying to marry Emagine. He has plenty of chance of success. My money is melting away fast in her keeping, and if Buddy marries her, there won't be anything for me when I'm thirty!"

"Could Tomlinson and Emagine manage that?" I asked the old man.

"You know anything can be managed with enough money and the right lawyers," he stated flatly.

"But it's my money!" For the first time a bit of panic showed in Allene's face. "He was my father; he made the money. Now it's my money! You can't let them do that to me!"

"Will you wait outside for a minute, Miss Buford?" Fayette asked. The girl looked at him, then got up and went out of the office.

"Lloyd," Fayette said when she had closed the door behind her, "I want you to drive over to St. Pete with her. This is a sort of personal thing with me. I've known Emagine Buford for a long time. She used to live in Tampa. Then she went north to work, met and married Ollie Buford. Since she's been back in Florida I've visited her a time or two at her place in St. Pete. That's why the girl came here to us, I guess.

"Emagine's going through a phase in her second childhood, to my way of thinking, but I don't want anything to happen to her. I want her to have a chance to wake up. See what kind of man Tomlinson is. See if he'll scare. Then scare him."

"I'm flat," I said.

He grimaced, pulled out his wallet, hesitated, and handed me the lone twenty from the worn leather sheath. "Use my car. It's parked in back of the building. See Buddy Tomlinson, phone me back, and take the rest of the day off."

I said thanks. When I left his office, he was punching tiny holes in his desk blotter with the tip of his letter opener . . .

The girl rode with her head slightly back, catching the breeze that blew in the gray sedan. Her hair rippled. Her lips were parted a little as she looked out over the bay. "Tomlinson has a beach place," she said. "On Coquina Key. We'll probably find him there."

That was about all the talking we did. But I kept looking at her. She wasn't beautiful. Yet there was—something.

Coquina Key isn't the real name for the island, but we'd better call it that. It's one of that long chain of islands west of St. Petersburg, all connected by bridges and causeways, that separate Boca Ceiga bay from the Gulf of Mexico.

We drove through the snarled, slow traffic of St. Petersburg, took the Central Avenue causeway, stopping once at the toll gate and then driving on across the white, four-lane parkway that had been pumped up out of Boca Ceiga bay. Then we were on the keys.

The islands are a lot alike, long fingers of land stretching north and south for miles, but just wide enough crosswise to separate Boca Ceiga from the Gulf. Where they're settled, the keys are built up heavily, with cabanas, frame boathouses, frame cottages, and a development here and there of bungalows. But in the unsettled stretches, the islands are desolate, white sand and shell and, closer to the boulevard, grown over with weeds, scrub pines, cabbage palms, and palmetto. Over the whole put a vast blue sky, torrid sun, surround with sparkling blue water and whispering surf on the white beaches, populate with easy living people, put a fleet of fishing boats in the inlets, with a fine cabin cruiser at a private pier on a private beach here and there—and you've got the picture.

Toward the lower end of Coquina Beach we turned off the boulevard on Sunshine Way. The street was wide, white concrete, curving gently toward the cluster of squat bungalows half a mile down the island. It looked like a brand new development, the white land so clean it was barren. Here and there small Australian pines and royal palms had been set out.

Buddy Tomlinson lived in the CBS—stucco over cement block—near the end of the street. The whole row of houses was painted a light pink. I opened the car door. Allene opened hers.

"Hadn't you better wait out here?"

"No," she said, "I'm coming in."

I shrugged and we went up the walk together. I rang the chimes on the oak-stained door. Nothing happened. In the bungalow next door I could hear warm laughter, and in the background a radio playing softly.

I rang four times in all. Then I walked around the side of the bungalow and looked in a window. I looked away quick, closed my eyes for a second. The first thing I saw when I opened them was Allene's profile. She was standing close to me, looking through the window, as I had done.

"He's dead," she said calmly.

I didn't ask if it was Buddy Tomlinson crumpled in there in the living room. The description fitted like a glove. Allene had her wish. He'd never be beautiful to any woman again.

"Well," Allene said, "we won't have to worry about him any longer." Then her eyes rolled up in her head.

Her face was very white. And before I had time to think, she was keeling over.

I caught her, carried her out to the car. There was a half empty pint in the glove compartment. I figured that ought to bring her to. "You," I told her limp form, "are one hell of a funny sort of dame!"

I was tilting the pint bottle to Allene's lips when a nearby male voice said, "Anything wrong?"

I looked at the bungalow that was next door to the one in which Buddy Tomlinson lay dead. I remembered the music and casual laughter I'd heard.

Now the music was silenced. A man and woman stood together just outside the screen door of the bungalow, on the small, hot flagstone terrace. I noticed the screen door behind them was one of those fancy jobs with a huge, white silhouette of a flamingo on it.

The man and woman were watching me warily, thinking, no doubt, that Allene and I were a pair of drunks out celebrating.

There was just one word for the girl standing on the terrace: sleek. She was wearing a white playsuit that was startling against her dark tan. She had a sultry looking face, with wide, red lips. Her hair was midnight black, cut with bangs. She was holding her hands at her sides in a sort of theatrical way, the way models do, pointing very slightly outward.

The man beside her was tall and athletic, dressed in an expensive T-shirt that was a riot of colors, cream-colored slacks, and tan sandals. His arms and face were freckled, his hair a crinkly, close-cropped, light blond mass on his head.

He and the girl watched as I took the bottle from Allene's lips. Allene sat up, mumbling a groan. Her lids fluttered. "I'm all right," she said weakly, shaking her head.

I got out of the car. The strapping young blond experienced a tightening in his face. To put him at ease, I said, "The lady simply fainted."

"That's too bad," the girl in the white playsuit said. "Is there anything we can do to help?"

"Phyllis!" the man said, obviously annoyed.

"Oh, they're all right, Baxter!" she said crossly. Then to me: "We saw you carrying the girl to the car. We thought you might be drunk!" She giggled and made dainty, studied gestures with her hands. They were graceful long hands. She probably realized it. She probably made use of them with every word she said.

"Do you know the man next door?" I asked.

"Buddy? Sure," Baxter said. "But Phyllis and I haven't seen him around since we came in from our sail, if you're looking for him—"

"I'm not looking for him," I cut in. "Have you got a phone?"

Baxter frowned. "Yes, here in the living room."

"I'd like to use it."

Baxter looked annoyed. Phyllis told me to go ahead. They followed as far as the doorway, stood there, while I phoned. Maybe Baxter was afraid I'd carry off the ivory bookends on the table near the phone.

The Gulf beaches are not incorporated in the City of St. Petersburg, which allows the beaches to sell alcoholic beverages on Sunday and a later curfew for their nightspots. So I put in a call to Sheriff Ben Aiken. What I told him jarred a few morose curses out of him, and he said he'd be right out.

When I turned from the phone, Phyllis' hands were fluttering about her throat. Baxter's face looked tight—and somehow mean.

"Buddy Tomlinson is dead?" Phyllis said, as if it was simply too, too horrible for her to realize.

I was in no mood for details, and simply nodded. I went back out to the car and sat down on the running board on the shady side and lighted a cigarette. "Can I have one?" Allene said. I gave it to her.

"What will they do with him, Lloyd?"

"Take him to an undertaking parlor. I think Doc Robison has got the corner on that trade for the county."

"I wonder who killed him?"

"I wouldn't know." I didn't particularly care. I sat and smoked chain fashion, and at last Ben Aiken arrived.

There were two other men with Ben, but they were just faces. He was the whole show. He was a big, fat man, with a lot of gut hanging over his belt. His pants were even baggier than mine and his shirt was pasted to his big, sloping shoulders with sweat. He had a large, florid face with a tiny button nose in the middle of it, and a sweating bald head.

I sat there in the open door of the car, watching the house. I couldn't see much, but I could hear Ben and the other two men working inside. Shortly the county coroner drove up. He was swallowed by Buddy Tomlinson's bungalow.

After a while, Ben Aiken came out. He came over to the car, questioned Allene and me. I told him the short, simple story of my finding Buddy Tomlinson. To keep myself clean, I told him why Allene had hired me. She was sitting on the car seat behind me, at a higher level, of course. When I brought her stepmother's name into it, the toe of her shoe bit in my spine.

Aiken got nothing more out of her. He questioned the couple from next door. Phyllis' last name was Darnell. She had been married, she said, but was a divorcee. Baxter's full name was Baxter B. Osgood. Yes, he and Phyllis both had seen Tomlinson. No, they hadn't seen him since yesterday afternoon when they'd all been drinking at the Pelican Bar and Grill, half a mile down the beach. He and Phyllis had had a morning date to go sailing. They'd sailed and swam and come back here just before Allene and I rolled up.

When he'd finished with them, Ben motioned me off to one side. "You got any ideas on this thing, Lloyd?"

"No, I'm off it. I was supposed to warn Buddy Tomlinson off Emagine Buford. Now Buddy doesn't need it."

"You think the gal is holding anything back?" He cut a side glance at the car where Allene was still sitting stiffly.

"If she's holding out on you, she's holding out on me, too."

Ben sighed and mopped his face. "May be one of them long drawn cases. I got to trace this Buddy Tomlinson backward, find out who he was, where he's been keeping himself, in whose company, and so on. I might find a motive somewhere along the line.

"Funny kind of kill. You didn't get a good look in there, did you, Lloyd?"

I hadn't. But I didn't say anything. I just stood passive and let Ben get it off his chest. I knew that in talking it in his confidential whisper, he was setting the details in his mind.

"Nothing in the whole bungalow had been hurt—except Tomlinson. You saw the wound in his face, Lloyd. He was shot in close. The side of his right palm was mutilated. Looked like somebody was threatening him with a gun. He made a grab for it and the shooting started."

"What does that give you?"

"Nothing much. It must mean he was shot with a revolver. Don't need to tell a man like you that an automatic won't fire with pressure on the killing end of it. Ejector won't work, gun won't cock, gun jams up. We're hunting the slug. From Tomlinson's cheek looks like a thirty eight. So maybe when I find out where he's been keeping himself, who he's been seeing, I might find out somebody who owns a revolver like that."

"You need me for anything else, Ben?"

"I guess not."

"Then I'm going back to Tampa. I'll drop the girl in St. Pete. She'll probably want to talk with her stepmother."

"She won't have much privacy," Ben grinned. "There's a phone in Tomlinson's bungalow and I'm gonna have city Homicide look in on Mrs. Emagine Buford." He mopped his face some more. "Hell to work in this heat. I'll see you around, Lloyd."

I got in the car and drove off. The last I saw of the scene, Baxter Osgood and Phyllis Darnell were still standing on Osgood's flagstone terrace, watching Ben Aiken waddle his way into the Tomlinson bungalow. Somehow, they looked scared.

I drove Allene to the Morro Hotel, in the northeast section of St. Pete. The drive along Tampa bay was wide, beautiful, lined with fine houses and hotels. A few boats were out sailing on the bay, the small, white triangles of their sails tilted over in the light breeze.

The Morro was built like an old Spanish castle. When I braked before it, I saw a black car at the curb. Allene saw it, caught her lip between her teeth. She turned her face to me as she got out of the car. "I'd like to see you again sometime," she said.

I looked at her for a minute. "I'll phone you this weekend."

She closed the car door, went running up the wide, palm-lined walk. She was staying here at the Morro with her stepmother, but I didn't know the phone number and I decided I didn't like to thumb through the phone books. It was just as well. I was twenty years her senior.

I drove back to Tampa and went to the office. The old man wasn't there and I mumbled talk with the girl behind the reception desk until he came in. He went into his private office and I told Fayette everything that had happened. His chiseled, rawboned face looked gaunt. He sank behind his desk. "What'd you find out about Tomlinson?"

"Nothing, except that now he's just a dead pretty boy. It ain't our case. I'll see you tomorrow."

I caught a bus and rode up through the squalor of lower Nebraska to my apartment. I bought a twenty-five-pound block of ice at the icehouse on the corner, carried it up to my apartment. I put the ice in a dishpan, set the dishpan on a center table in the bedroom. I plugged in the electric fan and set it behind the pan, so that the air was blowing over the ice, over the bed.

I sat down on the edge of the bed. The air was cool and good for a second or two, until I got used to it. I reached under my left armpit and pulled out the knife. It was long, keen, and gleaming with a six-and-a-quarter-inch blade. I knew what was bothering me, now.

A living, breathing, feeling man had been killed.

I slung the knife. It flashed, struck the doorjamb, stood out from the wood, quivering.

I flopped over on the bed and went to sleep.

It was a hell of a hot day.

CHAPTER TWO

Knife for Hire

I didn't sleep long. I woke with a mouthful of cotton, sweat drenching me, a heat-thickened pulse pounding in my head. I ran my tongue around my gums, realized that somebody was knocking on the door. As I went to answer, I plucked the knife from the doorjamb, put it back in its sheath under my armpit. I looked at my watch. It was 4:40 in the afternoon.

When I opened the door, Phyllis Darnell had her hand raised to knock again. She'd changed from the white playsuit, wearing now a yellow silk dress that really set off her complexion, lazy black eyes, and midnight hair.

"Oh!" she said, as if the opening of the door had startled her. She made vague gestures in the air with her hands. If it hadn't been for that way she had of using her hands, she'd have been a very beautiful woman.

"You wanted to see me?"

"Yes, Mr. Carter. Are you busy?"

"It depends. I guess you want to hire a detective?"

"Why do you say that?"

"Well, my looks didn't bring you here, did they?"

Ice flaked in her eyes. "No, your looks didn't bring me here. Are you going to ask me in or not?"

"Why not?" I held the door wide. When she came in and I'd closed the door, I said, "You care for beer?"

"No."

"Well, excuse me a moment. Make yourself at home."

She followed me out to the kitchen. I opened the icebox, counted the bottles of beer. The girl who'd come in to clean while I'd been out had been thirsty again. I opened a bottle of beer, killed half of it, said, "I'm listening."

"I really don't know how to begin, Mr. Carter. I really don't!" She wrung her hands, real fright coming to life in her eyes. "It's very awkward."

"I've heard awkward things before. Sit down. Iced tea?"

She shook her head, then nodded. "Yes, I'll have a glass of tea."

I put water on to boil.

"How'd you find me, Mrs. Darnell?"

"I asked that sheriff. From the way he talked to you when he arrived at Buddy Tomlinson's bungalow, I knew you were a detective. He told me where you worked, where you lived. You weren't in your office, neither was your boss, and the girl at the reception desk."

"Okay, okay. I guess you wanted to talk to me about Tomlinson?"

"I—yes—no. I mean, in a way I did." She glanced about the kitchen as if seeking a way out, a way to stall. "I see the water is simmering, Mr. Carter."

So it was. I took the battered aluminum pot off the flame, dropped in a tea bag, chipped ice and put it in a glass, and poured the tea over it. I set out cream, sugar, and scratched in the back corner of the icebox for the lone, wilted lemon there. Slicing the lemon, I said, "Why don't you just tell me straight off? Why beat around the bush? Buddy Tomlinson has been murdered and it's put you on the spot somehow. You want me to remove you from said spot. All right, what is it?"

The way she whitened beneath her deep tan gave her the appearance of wearing a heavy coat of dark powder. Her hands were trembling. "I—I really don't know what to say. I really don't."

I set the tea before her, sat down across the table, and finished my beer. Then I just sat there, not speaking, not moving.

When the silence began to eat away her nerves, she said shrilly, "I lied this morning! I'm married—but I'm not a divorcee. And I had every reason in the world for wanting to kill Buddy Tomlinson!"

She began to cry softly. She took out a wispy handkerchief, made dabs at her eyes.

"I really hate to say this. I really do. You see, Mr. Carter, I have a husband in Augusta, Maine. But we're not divorced, and never intend to be. I really don't know how I'm going to explain this to you. Oh, I've been a fool! I can hardly explain it to myself.

"I love my husband deeply and I am sure I mean more to him than life itself. I won't try to excuse myself. But every year I take a vacation, to Florida, the West Coast, South America, or Cuba. My poor, trusting husband! His business keeps him tied to his desk, but he insists that I might as well escape a few weeks of northern winter every year. It's on these trips that I present myself as an unmarried woman or a divorcee. That way one interests a better class of men, than if one admitted being a married woman. Somehow that way it always seemed in my mind to cheapen my husband less."

She was looking down at her hands, momentarily quiet in her lap, waiting for me to speak. To condemn her, maybe. I opened another cold beer and didn't say anything.

"Drink your tea," I said.

It wasn't very good tea, but she drank it gratefully. I finished my beer and said, "Buddy Tomlinson was one of those men?"

She nodded mutely.

"You certainly made a mistake about classifying men in his case!"

She shuddered under the sentence as if it was a blow of my hand, but she continued to look silently down.

"How'd you meet Tomlinson?"

"Through Baxter Osgood. They seemed to be close friends. Baxter Osgood owns a small beer garden on Coquina beach. I was there one night—he introduced me to Buddy."

"And you were promptly swept off your feet."

"You aren't a woman. You didn't know Buddy Tomlinson," she said in a stricken voice. "Now he's dead, and the letters have disappeared."

"You made the mistake of writing him some mush notes?"

Her face flooded red. "He was in Bradenton for a week. He begged me to write him every day. He was so sweet, so boyish." Her voice thickened with a violent anger; her hands played on the tabletop. "Something I said must have caused him to suspect that I wasn't really divorced."

"Can you recall what you might have said?"

"I—No. One night—just before he went down to Bradenton—we drank quite a bit. I was drunk, when he took me to my hotel. I must have talked of my life in Augusta."

"Afterwards he wanted money for the letters?"

She nodded again, swallowing in such a way her throat constricted with the action. "I gave him almost five hundred dollars—but he didn't give me the letters back. I knew then that I was in a deadly game, that my life in Augusta depended on what I did. I hoped to wheedle the letters out of him. Now he's dead. Can't you see what might be the results, if those letters come to light? My husband's life ruined, a possible murder charge against me. Mr. Carter, you must help me. I can't afford to be drawn openly in this kind of mess."

I opened a third beer. She was in a jam, all right. If those letters had been worth five hundred before Buddy Tomlinson's death, now they were worth every nickel she could lay her hands on, and somebody evidently knew that. If the police had discovered the letters, they'd have taken her in for questioning by this time. I said, "Any idea who Tomlinson might have boasted to? Who might have known about those letters?"

"No—unless it's Baxter Osgood. I don't think he makes all his money out of that beer garden he owns. I think there was something more between him and Buddy than mere friendship."

"Business deals?"

"Perhaps."

"All right," I said, "I'll do what I can to help you. But get one thing straight. This is murder. Contrary to what the public thinks, private dicks don't like to get mixed in murder. If we have to wade through murder the cost is high."

"I know," Phyllis Darnell said. "I'll pay."

"I'm not worrying. After all, I'll have the letters, won't I?"

I ushered her out, showered, and went over to Mac's garage, where my coupe had been laid up with a ring job. Greasy, limp from the heat, Mac had just finished the job. He wiped his hands on a piece of waste and told me the old crate was ready to roll. I made arrangements to see him on the fifteenth and drove down to the office.

The old man was locking his private office, getting ready to leave for the day. I told him to unlock again, explained the case.

He unlocked the door, walked across his office saying, "A murder case? I don't like it, Lloyd. I never liked a murder case."

"I know."

"The official boys have everything to work on a murder case, labs, organization, everything. A private agency small as ours ain't equipped for it."

"I know."

I opened his desk drawer, took out the .38 police special that always nestled there. I pulled out a corner of my shirttail, tucked the gun in my waistband, and tucked the shirt back in over the gun. You'd never know it was there. A box of loads was in the corner of the drawer. I dropped a handful of them in my pocket.

The old man was already on the phone, talking long distance.

I sat down and smoked until he finished.

He pushed back the phone, shadows over his raw-boned, gaunt face.

"Ben Aiken's glad we're going to cooperate," Fayette said.

"That's good. He give you much?"

Henry Fayette nodded, his frown deep and sour. He jabbed at his desk blotter with his letter opener. "This Buddy Tomlinson was quite a guy. Convicted once in Miami on a larceny charge. Charged once with blackmail in Baltimore, Maryland, but got off for lack of evidence. Nabbed once in Brownsville, Texas, for being mixed up in the marijuana racket, but beat that rap too. Miami had his whole previous record.

"Tomlinson came to St. Petersburg almost a year ago in company with an unknown woman who can't be located. There's nothing on the St. Pete blotter against him except a charge of driving intoxicated, for which he was fined.

"He was killed between twelve midnight and one o'clock last night, which means that he lay in his bungalow during that time without being found. The murder gun has not been located, but Aiken has got him an important witness. Guy by the name of Baxter B. Osgood. He the one you met over there?"

I nodded. "Osgood owns a beer garden on the beach. He lives in the bungalow next to Tomlinson's. An athletic, freckled, blond guy. He could be plenty mean, I guess."

The old man traced a pattern on the desk blotter with the opener. "Osgood says he was awakened last night about twelve thirty. Says he dreamed a backfire woke him, now realizes it must have been the shot in Buddy Tomlinson's bungalow. Osgood says his bedroom window faces the Tomlinson house, and that from that window he saw a woman leaving Tomlinson's bungalow. There was a bright moon. You know that moon at the beach, turning night into day. Osgood recognized the woman by the red swagger coat she was wearing, and her hat. The hat had a couple of tail feathers sticking up out of it."

Fayette flung the opener on the desk; his face was gray. "Dammit, I told you she was an old friend of mine." Accusation flamed on the old man's face; then he shook his head as if clearing it. "I'm upset. I can't blame you. I got no reason to blame you, Lloyd."

"You mean the woman Baxter Osgood recognized leaving the Tomlinson bungalow is Emagine Buford?"

Fayette nodded. In his quiet, flat voice he said, "Ben

Aiken's jailed her—charged her with first degree murder."

I whistled softly. It didn't help the old man's feelings any.

It was pretty late in the day to do anything much, but Fayette insisted on driving over to St. Pete, to talk to Emagine Buford. We took my coupe. The thing I wanted out of this case was those letters of Phyllis Darnell's. That's what we'd get paid for. But the letters were somewhere in the pattern of Buddy Tomlinson's death, and I knew we were going to have to sift through that pattern to find them. I didn't like a damn thing about the case.

It's only half an hour's drive from Tampa to St. Pete by way of Gaudy Bridge, and it was still daylight when we got in the Sunshine City, though the sun had dropped in the Gulf, leaving behind it vast streamers of crimson and gold in the western sky.

We wasted fifteen minutes talking over the case with the St. Pete men. Then we went back to Emagine Buford's cell.

She had been crying, and her face was swollen, but even so you could see that she had been a raving beauty in her day. As Allene had said of her stepmother, Emagine was well preserved, slim, with a small, unlined face, and hair dyed to a nice shade just darker than auburn. She didn't look a day over a young forty.

She managed a smile when the old man entered her cell. "It's unfortunate that you have to visit me here, Henry."

Fayette said, "We want to help you. This is Lloyd Carter. Mrs. Buford, Lloyd."

We each said it was a pleasure, and Emagine sank

on the edge of her cot. She looked at the old man
with hope and trust. They talked for two minutes. She
wasn't able to tell us a thing more than the county
men had. She had been home asleep, she claimed,
when Buddy Tomlinson had been murdered. She
hadn't seen him since the night before his death. She
spoke of him with a mixed tenderness and hot, new-
born hatred.

The old man told her that we'd do our best, and
we left her.

That was that, for my money. Outside headquarters,
Fayette mopped his face with a big red bandanna and
said we might as well eat.

We went to eat.

It was just after 8:30 when I got back to my apartment house in Tampa. The place had no garages, so
if you owned a car, you left it at the curb. I locked
the coupe, and walked in the apartment house. I was
halfway up the flight of stairs when the door opened
in the lower hall and my landlady's nasal drawl came
to me, "Is that you, Mr. Carter?"

I bent over the stair railing, looking down the hall.
She was standing in her doorway. "There's a woman
in your apartment," she said. "Said she had to see
you. I let her in to wait."

She slammed her door.

I went on up the stairs, down the hall, and opened
my apartment door. Allene Buford stood up when I
entered.

She'd turned on the small lamp over near the corner, and the soft light silhouetted her. I remembered
her as I'd first seen her in the old man's office earlier
in the day: not plain, but not beautiful either. Now,
with the light behind her like that, a light not bright
enough to glare at her or to show up the room in

which she was standing, she almost made the grade.
She was almost beautiful.

"Are you mad at me, Lloyd?"

"For coming here? I don't think so."

"I'm glad," she said in her calm, colorless voice.
She took a turn up and down the room. I closed the
door and stood watching her. "I couldn't stand it in
the empty hotel room any longer," she said. "I thought
I hated her, Lloyd, but she was so pitiful when the police
came and took her."

She came over closer to me. "Emagine and I never
got along, but when she was gone I sat in the room
there in the Morro for a while, remembering the fights
we'd had. The things I'd said to her. I couldn't stand
the room any longer. I called one of the St. Petersburg
detectives. He didn't know you, but had a buddy who
did. So I got your address and drove over."

A moment of silence passed.

"Lloyd, will you take me someplace?"

"Where would you like to go?"

"Any place there's some music, a glass of wine,
something to eat."

She caught my arm. "Lloyd, they won't send her to
the electric chair, will they?"

"I don't know."

"But what if she didn't do it?"

"It looks pretty much like she did. Murder is a
funny thing. Sometimes cops flounder around a lot on
a murder case, because they haven't got direction. But
once they get direction, once they know what they're
looking for and who it's to be used against, they usually dig up evidence."

I sensed a shudder rippling over her.

"Let's go have that glass of wine."

We went down, got in the coupe, and drove over

to Club Habana, a small, quiet place with Cuban music, fair wines, and fairly good food.

I sipped a beer, danced with her, watched her eat her dinner. She ate the spicy Cuban food as if she'd been too nervous and distraught to eat before. Now that she'd let down, she'd discovered she was famished. But that other hunger, that longing in her eyes—it was still there when she'd reached her coffee. It had been there always, I guessed, lonely, without an anchor.

We danced a few more times. We talked for a while. She told me about her hometown, her girlhood. "I was walled off," she laughed, "by high walls of greenbacks." She reached over and clutched my hand. "I feel much better now, Lloyd. I think I'd better go back to St. Pete. But tomorrow—couldn't we do something then?"

"I dunno, I—"

"Show me Florida, Lloyd! Not the Florida the tourist sees, but the backways, the way the swamp people live, the farms, and villages."

"Sometime," I said.

She didn't take her hand off mine. She leaned toward me, her mouth parted a little, the soft, blue light of the Cabana glinting faintly on the tips of her teeth. I could see a pulse beating in her throat and the almost invisible sheen of perspiration on her forehead. Very softly the band was playing a tender Cuban love song.

I kissed her softly on the lips. She leaned back, said quietly, "Thank you, Lloyd." Then she gathered her handbag, stood up, and we left the place.

She said she'd take a taxi to St. Pete, and I deposited her in one, and drove on back to my apartment.

The heat was still like a blanket, even though the night was a bit older. I had a cold beer in the kitchen.

Cold beer was the only thing I'd ever found to help against the heat, but even that was a losing contest. The beer didn't keep you cool long enough.

I wondered if I'd ever get used to Tampa heat.

I went in the bedroom. The ice I'd put in the pan on the center table that afternoon had long since melted, but the fan was still running, sending a stream of sluggish hot air over my face. I didn't lay down. I simply sat on the edge of the bed, trying to get my thoughts straight. I couldn't go to sleep, so I got up and went back down to the coupe.

I started the motor, let it idle for a minute. Then I pointed the nose toward St. Pete and Coquina Key.

It was a little after 11:00 when I rolled down the boulevard on the island. A huge moon bathed Coquina Key in silver light. White surf broke against the beach, and out in the water, moon rays lay in a great elongated splash, a pool all their own. Stars were out by the millions in a sky that was pure black velvet.

I braked in the business section of the Key. It was pretty grubby, most of the buildings of frame wooden construction, a cluster of boathouses down at the inlet, along with some bait houses. Cabanas and cottages were stacked over the area, close together. Everything there was dark, except for a bar, a chicken-in-the-basket place, and Baxter Osgood's beer garden.

CHAPTER THREE

Kill One, Skip One

The beer garden was crowded with people in rumpled sport shirts and slacks and cool cotton dresses. It was hot, smoky, wet and rank with the odor of beer, turgidly alive with sluggish conversation and the rasping of a jukebox. I bought a beer at the bar and asked if Baxter Osgood was around.

"I'm right here," Osgood said, practically at my elbow.

I turned around to look at him. He moved up to the bar beside me, sat down on a stool.

"I saw you come in, Carter."

"The beer isn't cold," I said.

"No? Why don't you buy someplace else?"

"I couldn't—not the product I'm in the market for."

"No?" he said again. "What is it you're wanting to buy?"

"Letters," I told him.

He watched the dancing for a few seconds. "I don't know what you're talking about."

"I know you don't, Mr. Osgood."

"How much are you paying for this product?"

"Enough—but not too much."

He yawned against the back of his hand. "I've got to run over to the house for a minute. Like to come along—just for the ride?"

"Sure," I said. "I'll come along, just for the ride."

We went outside. His car was angle parked at the curb, a blue convertible. We got in, and he drove down the boulevard, turned off on Sunshine Way, braked before his bungalow.

"Every time I look at the house next door," he said as we got out of the car, "I think of Mr. Tomlinson."

"Too bad about Mr. Tomlinson, but I understand they've got the woman who killed him."

"I thought you might be interested in it—say in an academic way."

"Not even in an academic way."

"Just in letters, huh?"

"You said it."

He keyed open the front door. The house was like an oven; he turned on lights, opened windows, threw the switch on an attic fan. Cooler night air began to rush through the place.

Osgood walked over to the kneehole desk, stuck a cigarette in his mouth, and picked up a box of matches that was on the desk. He turned halfway back toward the desk, dropped the matches on it, and opened the drawer and pulled the gun, all in one liquid motion.

He laughed faintly. The gun was leveled at my middle.

"Well," I said, "every man is entitled to one mistake."

"Yes—one."

He came halfway across the room toward me. "Turn around, Carter."

I stood still, and he jerked the gun up. His words didn't bother me—the sudden message in his eyes did. I turned around.

He came up behind me as if to frisk me. He hit me on the crown, where I'm starting to bald. I don't remember much after that.

I think I tried to get out of the house. Common sense tells me I tried to pull Henry Fayette's .38 out of the waistband of my pants. Putting it together later as it must have been, I think I crawled as far as the kitchen door and passed out for a moment, and he must have unlocked the kitchen door and dragged me outside. I tried to stir on the powdery sand of the backyard. He hit me again, on the back of the head.

The next thing I sensed was a slow melting of black nothingness into a quivering curtain of heavy gray fire, if there ever was any such thing, against the walls of my eyeballs. As the black faded, feeling came in to take its place. My head was a pincushion of pain; my heart was laboring; and I was sucking in mouthfuls of cool, clean air. It was very early morning.

Ten or fifteen minutes later I sat up slowly. I was still in Baxter Osgood's backyard. I stumbled to my feet, staggered to the kitchen door, opened it. The old man's gun had still been in my waistband. Now it was in my hand. I intended to fix Osgood so he'd never beat another man again. In my state, I was no match for a fever-ridden midget, but that didn't occur to me. I had a gun, I was on my feet, and Osgood deserved every damn thing I could dish out.

But he wasn't in the house. The place was pretty well messed up, with drawers pulled out and stuff strewn over the floors. I decided he'd grabbed a few valuables and skipped. Then I looked out the window, saw his convertible still parked on the edge of the street. I tried to make sense out of it, but didn't feel up to it.

As the anger burned out of me, I didn't feel up to anything. I went in his kitchen, started some coffee making. I looked in his refrigerator. Two bottles of beer were in it. I drank both of them.

I followed the beer a few minutes later with two cups of scalding black coffee. I ate a piece of bread and butter, a slice of cheese, and followed that with another cup of coffee.

I went to the living room, opened the front door. My head was still aching and spinning like crazy. I wondered if I had a concussion. The sun was just over the lip of the earth in the east, rising in that burst of orange and crimson you see nowhere but in Florida.

Low in the air, over the edge of the beach, a cluster of gulls were wheeling and screaming.

I did a double take at that group of gulls, stared at

them a few seconds, then went stumbling toward the strip of beach as fast as I could go.

Baxter Osgood was lying on his face, the water almost lapping the tips of his upflung hands. He'd been shot in the right temple, and near his hand lay a .38 caliber revolver.

I squatted on my heels beside Osgood's body and tried to figure the way it had happened. He'd left me in the backyard, entered the house to get something. Somebody had arrived.

He and the somebody had walked down here, and the somebody utterly without warning had shot him, then with panic gnawing, the somebody had wiped the gun, pressed Osgood's prints on it, and left it where it might have fallen from his hand. I was pretty sure the gun was the same that had killed Buddy Tomlinson.

It was just a hunch, but granting the hunch, and granting that Ben Aiken fell for the suicide picture, Aiken would conclude that Osgood had killed Tomlinson because one of their shady deals went sour, then in panic had killed himself.

There was one other point. The murderer evidently hadn't known I was in the backyard. My coupe wasn't at Osgood's house, but up at his beer joint. There was no other evidence that I was lying in the backyard unconscious when the murderer had called on Osgood.

I turned Osgood over, remembering the way his bungalow had been searched. I patted his torso, his waist.

The money belt was one of those jobs that blends right in with the body lines. If you weren't careful, you could search him and miss it. I tore his shirt open, took the belt off him.

Osgood's belt contained five thousand dollars in

money and a few sheets of paper that upon reading I knew were the letters that Phyllis Darnell had written to Buddy Tomlinson.

I went back in the house and phoned Ben Aiken.

An hour after that, a small crowd of people was gathered in a room in St. Pete's old, sun-baked city hall.

They all looked at me when I entered. I had my head bandaged, three aspirins under my belt, pile drivers still in my skull, and a feeling like a wad of cotton in my throat.

I looked over the silent room. Ben and a city dick were there, along with a stenographer, who was a big, brawny man. Henry Fayette was standing beside the chair that held Emagine Buford, who'd been taken from her cell. Allene Buford stood near the windows, and Phyllis Darnell stood with her back to the wall near Emagine's chair.

I tossed Phyllis Darnell's letters on the scarred table. Her gaze rabbitted around the room, her hands fluttering to her throat. "Go ahead," I said, "and pick them up. My boss will render you a bill later. For my money, you're a dirty little tramp, Mrs. Darnell, but Ben has agreed to keep the letters confidential. Not because of you—because of that poor devil up in Augusta, Maine."

"Then you know that I didn't kill Buddy Tomlinson? You really do know!" Phyllis held her hands pressed tight against her throat.

I looked at Allene. She took a step or two toward me. That wad of cotton fluffed out in my throat. "We know who killed Tomlinson and Osgood both, don't we, Allene?"

She stopped, then began moving again, circling around the room. "Are you joking with me, Lloyd?"

"I wish I was. I wish it more than you know, though maybe not for the reason you think. You knew Tomlinson had a good chance of getting his hands on the Buford money through Emagine, unless something was done about him. You went to his bungalow, maybe planning to kill him, maybe not. But you did kill him. Osgood saw you leaving. You were wearing Emagine's hat and coat, and he thought it was Emagine at first. But when he heard her story, he was inclined to believe it and guessed it had been you.

"You had killed Tomlinson to hold on to your money, Osgood reasoned. If Emagine went to the chair, it would not only leave you clear, Allene, but would remove her as the last obstacle between you and the Buford fortune. It looked sweet from where Osgood sat. He dug you for five grand, but when you'd had time to think, you knew it was no good. It would never be any good as long as Osgood was alive. So you killed him too.

"When I found Osgood dead on the beach, I started trying to think of the whole thing as he would have thought. You were the only answer, Allene. You were the one who could have easily gotten Emagine's hat and coat. You had motive. And I'm afraid they'll pin it on you. There must be some of your fingerprints on the five grand I took off of Osgood. There'll be so many more things when they start looking and digging, Allene."

She looked from face to face, her hands knotted at her sides. Then she wheeled and lunged for the door. But the knife was quicker. The knife flashed in my hand, thudded in the door, close to her face. It paralyzed her. It paralyzed everyone in the room. She came to life first. She grasped the knife and pulled it from the wood. "You'd do this to me, Lloyd?"

That wad of cotton in my throat choked me.

"What else could I do?" she whispered. "I'd never had but one thing in a lousy life—that money. That damned filthy Buford money—and now I was going to get cheated out of that. I didn't mean to kill Buddy Tomlinson. I only wanted to scare him. But he grabbed at the gun—and it went off. I thought that if I hired a detective to warn Buddy away from Emagine, Buddy's body would be found and no one would ever think I had known he was dead. I thought that would take suspicion from me, and once Buddy's body was found, the detective would have no more to do with the case.

"After that, it seemed easier. It was much easier to kill Osgood. Yes, killing gets easier all the time—"

She sliced the word off with the knife. A spasm crossed her face, telegraphing a wave of horror over the room. A little cough bubbled in her throat.

I had never thought she'd use the knife for that. I'd only wanted to scare her, to bring her up at the door before Ben and his men began pulling guns. I'd wanted her to stop, to think. To talk. To cop a plea. To live.

She had saved my life. It was the only possible way I could have saved hers.

But she'd used the knife on herself.

I caught her in my arms as she crumpled, laid her gently on the floor. The scene in the room was breaking apart, people moving, converging on her. Her eyes flickered open. "Why couldn't it have been different, Lloyd? Why couldn't you have showed me Florida— the—part—the tourist never sees?"

Tears welled in her eyes. A spasm shuddered over her.

I stood up, fighting the moisture in my eyes. Distantly, I heard Emagine Buford say, "In a way, I'm not surprised. She was always sort of—"

"Shut up!" I screamed.

Somehow I got out of the room. I walked down the corridor outside, not seeing its walls, not feeling its floor under my feet.

Only remembering. That longing that was almost pain. That terrible, pitiful hunger. Even death hadn't erased it from her face, and I knew at last why Allene Buford had never been quite beautiful . . .

A CHANGE OF CLIENTS

A Delilah West story

Maxine O'Callaghan

FIRST APPEARANCE: *This story*

Maxine O'Callaghan is generally acknowledged as the "mother" of the modern female P.I. This story, published in 1974 in *Alfred Hitchcock's Mystery Magazine*, predates the first appearance of Marcia Muller's Sharon McCone in *Edwin of the Iron Shoes*. While Ms. O'Callaghan is proud of this distinction, she defies anyone to call her a "pioneer." When asked what she thinks of being called that she replies, "Don't!"

Ms. O'Callaghan was honored for her twenty-five-year-old P.I. series at Eyecon '99, the Private Eye Writers of America Convention.

I got to bed at two in the morning, too exhausted to resist the nightmare: a cliff lashed by wind-shattered sea spray, Dana Point glittering below, Jack walking into a trap . . .

The telephone jerked me awake, shaking and sweating.

"Wake up, Delilah," Rita chirped. "Got a live one for you."

After three days spent tracking a runaway through the L.A. jungles, I was in no mood for cheerfulness. I squinted against bright sunlight and muttered mild obscenities.

"Now, now," Rita reproved, "you want to be a successful female private eye, you gotta grab the clients when they come along. Write this down. Craig Zarath." She added an address and directions. "Be there at one o'clock and he says to bring a suitcase. It might take a few days."

"Rita, you know I like to see clients in my office."

She laughed. "Honeychile, you really are asleep. Zarath, I said—as in Zarath Construction. You have time to brush your teeth if you get moving."

"Here I thought I was on my own," I said nastily, "but actually I'm working for my answering service."

"I have to keep you on your toes or I don't get paid, speaking of which—"

"I'm going, I'm going."

I hung up the phone and rubbed aching temples. Every monotonous, ear-splitting hour of the previous night still throbbed, but at least the dream was gone. I showered, swallowed aspirin, and plugged in the percolator while I packed, dressed, and checked the contents of the leather bag that serves as briefcase and purse. Jack had given me the bag when we opened the agency.

Quickly, I suppressed memory and drank the stomach-jarring coffee. It helped. My head cleared a little as I drove west on the Newport Freeway and thought about Zarath Construction. I knew the company specialized in pseudo-Spanish subdivisions. From their proliferation in southern Orange County, I guessed the company was big and probably growing bigger.

Leaving the freeway, I followed Rita's directions toward the coastal hills to Zarath's house. The best California modern with angular lines that looked all glass, it blended into a wild hillside. The Pacific gleamed on the horizon. It was a safe bet that Zarath owned a chunk of surrounding land as a buffer against the urban sprawl he helped to create.

The driveway circled and offered parking beneath a second-story deck, mounted on massive concrete posts, which jutted over a deep ravine.

Taking a deep breath, I ordered myself to concentrate on the job. I sure wasn't adjusting to widowhood. West & West Detective Agency was just me now—regardless of what it said in faded gold leaf on the office door in Santa Ana.

A heavyset maid let me in, took me to the den, and asked me to wait. I blinked and sat down. Against a wallpaper suggestive of tawny African velds, big cats stalked the room in poster-size photographs: leopards snarled and unsheathed razor-sharp claws; a lion devoured the broken body of a gazelle.

My empty stomach quivered. I was grateful when Craig Zarath finally arrived, looking right at home with the rest of the predators. He had a hard body, sleek hair, a face dominated by a bony nose, and black eyes that blended pupil with iris. I imagined him mainlining Essence of Chauvinism every day before breakfast.

He stood an inch too close and pressed my fingers while he said, "Delilah West." ·

Females usually dropped left and right, I presume, but I just sat down and waited politely.

Without wasting any more charm he said succinctly, "I want you to watch my wife."

"I don't take divorce cases—"

"It's not that. During the next week, I need somebody competent around because I'm afraid she may try to harm herself."

"Suicide? Why me? Sounds like a good nurse—"

"She'd spot one a mile away, and don't suggest commitment. Margaret's not insane."

"You have household help?"

"Just Consuelo and she's only here half days. Well?"

At least it would be a change from unwashed bodies and acid rock, and considering the condition of my bank account I really couldn't afford to be choosy. Still, I stalled by asking, "Why are you particularly concerned about this week?"

"Two years ago my wife was involved in an automobile accident. She was driving; our infant son was killed. Naturally she blamed herself. She had a rough year and then when I thought she was pulling out of it she tried to drown herself. That was right around the anniversary of Jimmy's death. I simply don't want to chance another episode like last year. There's not a lot I can do but I would feel better if you were here to keep an eye on her."

"You seem to have a lot of confidence in me."

"I checked out your background. Swim team and gymnastics in college; policewoman; well-trained." His eyes did a complete job of assessment. "You look perfectly capable to me—among other things. Half your fee now as a retainer, Mrs. West."

His idea of a retainer did a lot to blunt my curiosity. I took it and let him press my fingers again before he finished his briefing.

Ostensibly I was helping him at home with an overload of office work. He had form letters and reports as a cover. His assumption that I typed raised a few Lib-type hackles, but I bit my tongue.

"Margaret doesn't go out much these days," he told me. "If she does, follow her. Lord knows what she'll try."

"Any relatives? Friends?"

"No relatives except a few distant cousins. Since the accident, she's cut herself off from her friends."

Prickles of uneasiness had sprouted on the back of my neck. I didn't like any of this. Somehow Zarath impressed me as the type who didn't give a damn about anybody except himself. He looked past my left ear and said, "Margaret." I knew then that I was right. He didn't love his wife.

Tiny and gaunt, she had an unfocused look in her bruised eyes and dull brown hair curling around a thin face that remained sallow beneath a suntan.

"Margaret, you promised to take a nap." His voice was even but edged with ice.

"I can't sleep."

She was strung out on something; her unsteady bee-line for the bar told me what. After a slug of vodka, she noticed me sitting there and horror twisted her face. "You brought her here," she whispered. "No, Craig—"

"Mrs. West is from the temporary agency," Zarath cut in smoothly.

Another jolt of vodka steadied her slightly. She tried to rearrange her face into a smile.

"Since my hours are going to be irregular," Zarath went on, "Mrs. West will stay here for a few days. Show her the guest room, will you? I have to go to the construction site." His nod included both of us as he left.

Margaret took a pair of sunglasses from the pocket of her terry robe; it was a relief when her eyes were covered. "I didn't mean to be rude," she said shakily.

I said something reassuring but she wasn't listening. Her eyes fastened on the photograph of the lion and she seemed cold sober as she said, "I hate this room."

"The pictures are a bit scary," I agreed, "but good. Who's the photographer?"

"Craig. I suppose if he'd lived when big game hunting was fashionable he'd have mounted heads. Instead of that he hunts with a camera. Or else a tranquilizer gun. A friend of his works for the zoo and Craig goes collecting specimens with him. He talked me into going along once." She shivered at the memory and turned away. "Please excuse me, Mrs. West."

Any further attempt to get close to her was ended for the moment. I sighed and found Consuelo to ask about my room. It was next to Margaret's, sharing the deck that projected over the ravine.

I noted the drop down the boulder-strewn hillside and my apprehension grew. Obviously I couldn't be with Margaret every minute. She could slash her wrists, gulp a bottle of pills, or blow her brains out—all with me in the next room. It was senseless for Zarath to hire me as a watchdog. I told myself it was his money.

Still the doubt nagged all afternoon as I did the feigned work and answered a few calls on Zarath's business line in the den. Once I managed to slip into Margaret's room. It confirmed my pessimism—bottles of sleeping pills, razor blades—the only thing missing was a gun and I guessed there was one in the house somewhere.

I finally ran out of lame excuses to check on Margaret and paced the den, feeling right at home with the feline menagerie.

Not for the first time did I ask myself what I was doing cooped up in a place I didn't want to be, worrying about people I didn't know. It was fun when Jack and I were a team, but now . . . I could go back on the police force, I suppose. I hear they even let women do something besides hand out parking tickets. Maybe . . .

While I brooded, Consuelo worked like a grim whirlwind and left after preparing dinner. Margaret paced her room—I assumed it was definitely her room; there was no sign of male occupation—or else she lay on the deck with her sunglasses pushed up across the top of her head and her face bared to the sun. Once I heard muffled crying through the door that stayed closed despite my efforts.

Dinner was something less than sparkling. Zarath made polite conversation, nothing more. Margaret drank steadily, and her pale eyes watched him with despair.

I'd made up my mind by then that she needed a doctor more than a bodyguard and to hell with the fee. I told him so.

"I hired you to watch Margaret, not to give me advice," he said coldly. He was on his way out and I'd caught him with his hand on the doorknob. "Anyway, we've spent a fortune on psychiatrists. It didn't help."

I tried again. "Maybe if you took her away—"

"Impossible. Oh, look here, I'm not heartless, but I've watched my wife degenerate from a lovely woman to the verge of alcoholism and suicide. Maybe you're right. It didn't work before, but as soon as I can manage it I'll take Margaret on a trip."

I ought to have been reassured but, as the kids say, the vibes were bad. I wandered restlessly around the house until a crash from Margaret's room sent me flying upstairs. She had tripped and fallen—not surprising considering her intake of alcohol that evening.

She mumbled her thanks as I helped her to the bed. "You're good to me, Delilah. I thought at first you and Craig—but I was wrong—that was somebody else. I was wrong?"

"Yes," I said firmly. "It's strictly business."

Tears slipped down her cheeks. "It was wonderful once; Craig loved me. We had a baby, did you know that? But he died and Craig—Craig never forgives."

"Mrs. Zarath, if you're unhappy maybe you should go away."

"Where would I go?"

"Mexico. Hawaii. Float around the world. Get back your health." Forget Craig Zarath, I wanted to add.

"I can't do that. I won't make it easy for him. I'm not going to give him up."

"What if he makes the break himself?" I asked bluntly.

"Craig will never leave me."

"Won't he?"

She shook her head stubbornly. "He wouldn't. He can't. Go 'way now, leave me alone. I want to—go sleep . . ."

With her words feeding my apprehension, I left her and went downstairs to call Rita. She said she thought she knew somebody—which didn't surprise me. Rita has more sources of information than the CIA—I can depend on her.

She called back an hour later. "When Zarath Construction incorporated, Craig and Margaret kept the majority of the stock in equal amounts. The rest was sold publicly to various investors."

"So Craig Zarath has the controlling interest as long as he votes his wife's share."

"Yep. It was Margaret's money originally, it seems. One interesting fact, Delilah. Somebody's buying up stock. I don't know who, just that it isn't your boy. Help any?"

"Yeah, Rita, thanks."

It didn't though. It explained why Zarath put up with a wife who lived like a zombie—he couldn't risk a divorce—but it didn't explain his concern over her survival. The fact was, he'd be better off with his wife dead.

I slept in snatches until Zarath slunk in about one A.M. The rest of the night I prowled the hall, stopped again and again to listen to Margaret's ragged breathing, and knew my vigil wasn't to protect Margaret from herself.

When sunrise clotted the fog and chased it out to sea, the primitive sense of danger quieted, I relaxed. It's instinctive to lower your guard once the terrors of night are over.

That's my excuse, but it doesn't help much. Warm, sunny mornings will haunt me for a long time.

The day began with Margaret stumbling down to make breakfast. Her hands shook, and her eyes were hollow and sick. I drank coffee, chewed toast, and studied Zarath. He ate, as he did everything, with controlled savagery. There was tension too; a pulse jumped in his temple and he kept looking at his watch. Still, when he caught my interest, his eyes gleamed with a speculation that made my skin crawl. I got up abruptly and began clearing the table before Margaret noticed.

"I didn't hear you come in last night, Craig." Her tentative words were soft. I wanted to shout: Speak up, woman!

"The meeting ran late," Zarath said.

"Could we have a talk this morning? Please?"

"It will have to wait, darling. I'm meeting somebody. I have a few things to go over with Mrs. West and then I'll be off." With a sudden show of tenderness he cupped Margaret's chin and kissed her. I felt cold. "Leave all this stuff for the maid, Maggie; go up and sit in the sun. It's a lovely day."

Her face lit and she nodded blindly. "Will you be home for dinner, Craig?" she asked hopefully.

He smiled, promising.

As soon as she went upstairs he motioned me into the den. "Watch her, Delilah." His face was grim. "The accident happened two years ago today."

"She seemed happy this morning."

"Perhaps. I hope you're right." He shuffled papers and stuffed some into his briefcase. Over his shoulder, the lion devoured his kill. "I'll come home as soon as I can. Stick close to her." He slapped his coat in annoyance. "I left my pen someplace. No, don't bother, I'll find it."

He was back quickly with Margaret's sunglasses in his hand. "She left these in the kitchen. Take them up, will you?"

He sounded almost as though he loved his wife, unless you remembered the sound of love in a man's voice. I remembered.

I decided to have another talk with Margaret. On the deck, she relaxed on a redwood chaise. Mexican pots of yellow daisies splashed sun colors even in the shade.

"Did Craig go? My sunglasses, I wonder where—"

"You left them in the kitchen." Absently she put them across her hair like a bandeau. "I brought coffee for us. Do you mind?" It seemed like a good excuse.

"Oh, thanks. I'd like that." The glow was still on her face; all it had taken was a few kind words from Zarath. His return to cold indifference would quickly snuff it out.

As I picked up the coffeepot, the telephone rang distantly.

"It's Craig's business line downstairs," Margaret said. "You'd better answer it."

One of Zarath's secretaries had a long message full of figures. "Can't this wait?" I asked irritably. Although Margaret was in good spirits, I still felt uneasy. I cut off the girl's indignant reply and her voice buzzed on and on. Only part of me wrote down her words. Inside I waited, straining to hear something other than silence, and then Margaret screamed.

As I threw down the phone and raced upstairs, her scream choked off. I pounded across the empty deck to the railing just as Zarath ran from the parking area under the deck and slid down the slope yelling her name.

Doctor, ambulance—my mind offered the frantic hope, but I already knew it was too late. I knew it as I ran from the house and skittered toward the blue blotch in the ravine. She lay with her head at a horrible angle. Blood formed a pool under the broken glasses beside her face and sunlight glittered in a mixture of redness and glass shards. Zarath crouched over her body.

"Is she—" I couldn't bear to touch the skinny wrist.

"Dead. She's dead. I decided to check through my briefcase and I saw her—where the hell were you? I told you to stay close."

"There was a phone call. She seemed all right."

"Seemed." He swore and started to pick her up.

"You'd better leave her there, Mr. Zarath." Despite my numbness, training clicked off a prescribed routine. "I'll call the police."

After that I lost track of time. Official cars arrived. Zarath answered questions; I corroborated his answers. Yes, Mrs. Zarath was despondent. She drank too much. I knew she'd attempted suicide before. Zarath carefully made no remark about my dereliction of duty. Margaret's body was taken away and the police left with words of condolence to Craig Zarath.

He waited only long enough to speak to me. "I apologize for the things I said, Delilah. The shock, I suppose. I really shouldn't blame you. Margaret had made up her mind, so . . ." He got into his car and started the engine. "I'll send you a check for the balance of your fee."

I must have nodded. He drove away and left me standing there with all that blasted sunlight pouring over the golden hills. Averting my eyes from the ravine where Margaret's blood was soaking into the rocky earth, I headed for the bar in Zarath's den, gulped down brandy, and stared at the pictures lining the walls.

For the first time I truly understood Margaret's aversion to the photographs. I looked at the lion ravaging the broken body of the gazelle and recognition raised an icy braille of hackles on my neck. Out there in the ravine when Zarath lifted his head—for a split second that same feral victory blazed in his eyes.

He killed her.

I stood there, with his presence filling the room like animal scent, and knew it. What's more, he used me. Brought me here and lied to me and set me up as a witness. He killed her, and he was going to get away with it unless I stopped him.

Gut-deep anger burned away the sickness that had paralyzed my judgment ever since I'd heard Margaret Zarath's dying scream. Zarath didn't know it but sometime during the night I'd stopped working for him and taken his wife for my client.

I poured more brandy and thought about Zarath's actions just before Margaret's death. He'd been in a hurry to leave but once outside he'd dithered around checking papers in his briefcase. So—why? If he'd heard the telephone and knew I was busy in the den, did he slip back inside and push his wife off the deck?

Well, he hadn't come in the front door—I had a view of it from the den—and even if he entered through the kitchen I was out of this room as soon as Margaret screamed. Which put him on the deck with only seconds to get down to the parking area.

I knew it was impossible, but I went up to the deck anyway. Given time and a rope he could have gone down the concrete pillars, I suppose. I'd bet money he hadn't. So, figure he was down there beneath the deck. After that touching moment at breakfast, if he'd called to her she'd have rushed over to the railing. I gripped the solid barrier and looked down—as Margaret must have looked. If he called from the shadows beneath the deck, she'd lean over, far over. My hands grew slimy with sweat as I tried to crawl back in time. Had he counted on her simply falling?

Would a lion expect the gazelle to trip and break its neck? Neither would Zarath. A weapon, then. Not a gun meant to kill; this was to be suicide. A tranquilizer gun.

It fit.

A gun like that makes a minimum of noise. At any rate, the only thing I'd heard was Margaret's scream. I'd never forget it. I remembered exactly: it was not drawn out, not wavering and falling in the peculiar echo of a cry going away down through space, but choking off. In the silence there were other sounds: a sliding hiss of fabric over wood and the final thump of a body striking rock. The pattern made sense if she'd been unconscious when she fell.

If Zarath planned a hiding place for the gun close by, he could figure on getting to the body and removing the dart before I saw it. His car was the logical place; but by now the gun, along with dart, would be somewhere below salt water.

It made sense except for one thing. Why did Zarath take it for granted that Margaret would freeze and give him a clear shot? If she'd seen him standing there aiming a gun at her, wouldn't she jump back instinctively? If she'd seen him. That was the question.

For the second time that day I ran out of the house and down the slope. The sunglasses marked the spot where Margaret had fallen. Both lenses were cracked. One was intact; the other partially knocked out. I remembered Zarath handing them to me to take to her and Margaret absently slipping them across her hair. When Zarath called, she would have slid them down on her nose. I'd seen her do it yesterday.

My hands shook as I picked them up. The cracked lens stayed in place. My stomach lurched as my beautiful theory fell to pieces like the shards of glass littering the ground.

I felt like banging my head against the rock with frustration. Would the autopsy turn up the drug? Instinctively, I knew he'd plan for that and use something untraceable. There would be a mark where the dart entered her body. Enough evidence . . . maybe. But Zarath had laid his groundwork carefully. I could hear his attorney asking: "Why would Margaret Zarath stand there and let her husband shoot her?" The whole thing was sufficiently bizarre to plant doubt in a jury's mind.

Although I was stymied, I went inside for an envelope and picked up the pieces of glass with their rusty coating of dried blood. In the den I spread them out on Zarath's desk like a dark jigsaw puzzle.

The answer was there as I suspected.

I made two phone calls. One confirmed the only thing left to nag me. My voice still retained enough official bluster to find out that Zarath's secretary had been instructed to call at precisely ten o'clock.

Drained, I stood up to go pack my bag, but outside wheels crunched on gravel. I sat back down and waited for Zarath.

He must have read my face but he chose to bluff it out and contemptuously ignored the litter of glass.

"I thought you'd gone, Delilah. Margaret's dead. You lost your job when you let her jump and break her neck."

"I'm not buying it anymore. I know you killed her."

He came across the room, catlike, and leaned over me. "Be very careful, Delilah. The police don't want guesses. They want proof."

"It was clever," I admitted, "and all carefully timed. That phone call, for instance. It kept me far enough away so I couldn't be sure of what I heard. The only variable was the weather. I suppose you'd simply have postponed things if it hadn't been sunny enough for her to be on the deck. But she was and—tell me, Mr. Zarath, was she really dead when you got to her or did you have to finish the job?"

"She was dead all right; you saw for yourself."

"I imagine it simplified things for you. As it was you were very busy. You had to hide the gun, get to her before I did and remove the tranquilizer dart. And then there were the glasses."

"You really are reaching, Delilah."

"Margaret was nearsighted, but vain enough to wear

only prescription sunglasses. I should have realized yesterday, when she thought I was somebody else. You switched the glasses. When she looked down at you from the deck, you were a myopic blur. She didn't know you had a gun in your hands. After she fell, you simply switched them back with a quick crack against a rock to make the prescription pair look realistic. I admit it threw me off—until I realized there were too many pieces of glass. The other pair shattered badly in the fall, didn't they? You put the frames in your pocket, but you couldn't hide the broken glass just then; it was a bloody mess. I suspect you'd have gone down later to tidy up."

He moved fast, slid open the right-hand drawer of the desk and came up with a gun, not a tranquilizer gun but a very efficient-looking revolver.

"It sounds weak, Delilah. Very weak. But I can't take the chance of your babbling it, can I?"

"Oh, don't be an ass," I said wearily. "I've already called the police."

I'd talked long enough. We both heard the car outside and the authoritative knocking. I stood up deliberately and walked to the door. My insides quivered but when I turned he stood there with the gun dangling uselessly. Behind him, the lion stared at me with arrogant fierceness.

The cat didn't remind me of Craig Zarath anymore.

CHEE'S WITCH

A Jim Chee story

Tony Hillerman

FIRST APPEARANCE: *The Blessing Way,* 1970

Tony Hillerman found the right formula for hitting the bestseller list when he combined his two series characters, Joe Leaphorn and Jim Chee, into one series. Since *A Thief of Time* (1989), every one of his books has made the bestseller lists. He has won a Spur Award from the Western Writers of America and an Edgar Award from the Mystery Writers of America. He was also named a Grand Master by MWA, in 1991.

This story, which features Jim Chee, first appeared in the pages of *New Mystery.*

Snow is so important to the Eskimos they have nine nouns to describe its variations. Corporal Jimmy Chee of the Navajo Tribal Police had heard that as an anthropology student at the University of New Mexico. He remembered it now because he was thinking of all the words you need in Navajo to account for the many forms of witchcraft. The word Old Woman Tso had used was "anti'l," which is the ultimate sort, the absolute worst. And so, in fact, was the deed which seemed to have been done. Murder, apparently. Mutilation, certainly, if Old Woman Tso had her facts right. And then, if one believed all the mythology of witchery told among the fifty clans who comprised The People, there must also be cannibalism, incest, even necrophilia.

On the radio in Chee's pickup truck, the voice of the young Navajo reading a Gallup used-car commercial was replaced by Willie Nelson singing of trouble and a worried mind. The ballad fit Chee's mood. He was tired. He was thirsty. He was sticky with sweat. He was worried. His pickup jolted along the ruts in a windless heat, leaving a white fog of dust to mark its winding passage across the Rainbow Plateau. The truck was gray with it. So was Jimmy Chee. Since sunrise he had covered maybe two hundred miles of half-graded gravel and unmarked wagon tracks of the Arizona–Utah–New Mexico border country. Routine at first—a check into a witch story at the Tsossie hogan north of Teec Nos Pos to stop trouble before it started. Routine and logical. A bitter winter, a sand storm spring, a summer of rainless, desiccating heat. Hopes dying, things going wrong, anger growing, and then the witch gossip. The logical. A bitter winter, a sand storm spring, a summer awry. The trouble at the summer hogan of the Tsossies was a sick child and a water well that had turned alkaline—nothing unexpected. But you didn't expect such a specific witch. The skinwalker, the Tsossies agreed, was the City Navajo, the man who had come to live in one of the government houses at Kayenta. Why the City Navajo? Because everybody knew he was a witch. Where had they heard that, the first time? The People who came to the trading post at Mexican Water said it. And so Chee had driven westward over Tohache Wash, past Red Mesa and Rabbit Ears to Mexican Water. He had spent hours on the shady porch giving those who came to buy, and to fill their water barrels, and to visit, a chance to know who he was until finally they might risk talking about witchcraft to a stranger. They were Mud Clan, and Many Goats People, and Standing

Rock Clan—foreign to Chee's own Slow Talking People—but finally some of them talked a little.

A witch was at work on the Rainbow Plateau. Adeline Etcitty's mare had foaled a two-headed colt. Hosteen Musket had seen the witch. He'd seen a man walk into a grove of cottonwoods, but when he got there an owl flew away. Rudolph Bisti's boys lost three rams while driving their flocks up into the Chuska high pastures, and when they found the bodies, the huge tracks of a werewolf were all around them. The daughter of Rosemary Nashibitti had seen a big dog bothering her horses and had shot at it with her .22 and the dog had turned into a man wearing a wolfskin and had fled, half running, half flying. The old man they called Afraid of His Horses had heard the sound of the witch on the roof of his winter hogan, and saw the dirt falling through the smoke hole as the skinwalker tried to throw in his corpse powder. The next morning the old man had followed the tracks of the Navajo Wolf for a mile, hoping to kill him. But the tracks had faded away. There was nothing very unusual in the stories, except their number and the recurring hints that the City Navajo was the witch. But then came what Chee hadn't expected. The witch had killed a man.

The police dispatcher at Window Rock had been interrupting Willie Nelson with an occasional blurted message. Now she spoke directly to Chee. He acknowledged. She asked his location.

"About fifteen miles south of Dennehotso," Chee said. "Homeward bound for Tuba City. Dirty, thirsty, hungry, and tired."

"I have a message."

"Tuba City," Chee repeated, "which I hope to

reach in about two hours, just in time to avoid running up a lot of overtime for which I never get paid."

"The message is FBI Agent Wells needs to contact you. Can you make a meeting at Kayenta Holiday Inn at eight P.M.?"

"What's it about?" Chee asked. The dispatcher's name was Virgie Endecheenie, and she had a very pretty voice and the first time Chee had met her at the Window Rock headquarters of the Navajo Tribal Police he had been instantly smitten. Unfortunately, Virgie was a born-into Salt Cedar Clan, which was the clan of Chee's father, which put an instant end to that. Even thinking about it would violate the complex incest taboo of the Navajos.

"Nothing on what it's about," Virgie said, her voice strictly business. "It just says confirm meeting time and place with Chee or obtain alternate time."

"Any first name on Wells?" Chee asked. The only FBI Wells he knew was Jake Wells. He hoped it wouldn't be Jake.

"Negative on the first name," Virgie said.

"All right," Chee said, "I'll be there."

The road tilted downward now into the vast barrens of erosion which the Navajos call Beautiful Valley. Far to the west, the edge of the sun dipped behind a cloud—one of the line of thunderheads forming in the evening heat over the San Francisco Peaks and the Cococino Rim. The Hopis had been holding their Niman Kachina dances, calling the clouds to come and bless them.

Chee reached Kayenta just a little late. It was early twilight and the clouds had risen black against the sunset. The breeze brought the faint smells that rising humidity carries across desert country—the perfume of sage, creosote brush, and dust. The desk clerk said that Wells was in room 284 and the first name was Jake. Chee no longer cared. Jake Wells was abrasive but he was also smart. He had the best record in the special FBI Academy class Chee had attended, a quick, tough intelligence. Chee could tolerate the man's personality for a while to learn what Wells could make of his witchcraft puzzle.

"It's unlocked," Wells said. "Come on in." He was propped against the padded headboard of the bed, shirt off, shoes on, glass in hand. He glanced at Chee and then back at the television set. He was as tall as Chee remembered, and the eyes were just as blue. He waved the glass at Chee without looking away from the set. "Mix yourself one," he said, nodding toward a bottle beside the sink in the dressing alcove.

"How you doing, Jake?" Chee asked.

Now the blue eyes reexamined Chee. The question in them abruptly went away. "Yeah," Wells said. "You were the one at the Academy." He eased himself on his left elbow and extended a hand. "Jake Wells," he said.

Chee shook the hand. "Chee," he said.

Wells shifted his weight again and handed Chee his glass. "Pour me a little more while you're at it," he said, "and turn down the sound."

Chee turned down the sound.

"About thirty percent booze," Wells demonstrated the proportion with his hands. "This is your district then. You're in charge around Kayenta? Window Rock said I should talk to you. They said you were out chasing around in the desert today. What are you working on?"

"Nothing much," Chee said. He ran a glass of water, drinking it thirstily. His face in the mirror was dirty—the lines around mouth and eyes whitish with dust.

The sticker on the glass reminded guests that the laws of the Navajo Tribal Council prohibited possession of alcoholic beverages on the reservation. He refilled his own glass with water and mixed Wells's drink. "As a matter of fact, I'm working on a witchcraft case."

"Witchcraft?" Wells laughed. "Really?" He took the drink from Chee and examined it. "How does it work? Spells and like that?"

"Not exactly," Chee said. "It depends. A few years ago a little girl got sick down near Burnt Water. Her dad killed three people with a shotgun. He said they blew corpse powder on his daughter and made her sick."

Wells was watching him. "The kind of crime where you have the insanity plea."

"Sometimes," Chee said. "Whatever you have, witch talk makes you nervous. It happens more when you have a bad year like this. You hear it and you try to find out what's starting it before things get worse."

"So you're not really expecting to find a witch?"

"Usually not," Chee said.

"Usually?"

"Judge for yourself," Chee said. "I'll tell you what I've picked up today. You tell me what to make of it. Have time?"

Wells shrugged. "What I really want to talk about is a guy named Simon Begay." He looked quizzically at Chee. "You heard the name?"

"Yes," Chee said.

"Well, shit," Wells said. "You shouldn't have. What do you know about him?"

"Showed up maybe three months ago. Moved into one of those U.S. Public Health Service houses over by the Kayenta clinic. Stranger. Keeps to himself.

From off the reservation somewhere. I figured you federals put him here to keep him out of sight."

Wells frowned. "How long you known about him?"

"Quite a while," Chee said. He'd known about Begay within a week after his arrival.

"He's a witness," Wells said. "They broke a car-theft operation in Los Angeles. Big deal. National connections. One of those where they have hired hands picking up expensive models and they drive 'em right on the ship and off-load in South America. This Begay is one of the hired hands. Nobody much. Criminal record going all the way back to juvenile, but all nickel-and-dime stuff. I gather he saw some things that help tie some big boys into the crime, so Justice made a deal with him."

"And they hide him out here until the trial?"

Something apparently showed in the tone of the question. "If you want to hide an apple, you drop it in with the other apples," Wells said. "What better place?"

Chee had been looking at Wells's shoes, which were glossy with polish. Now he examined his own boots, which were not. But he was thinking of Justice Department stupidity. The appearance of any new human in a country as empty as the Navajo Reservation provoked instant interest. If the stranger was a Navajo, there were instant questions. What was his clan? Who was his mother? What was his father's clan? Who were his relatives? The City Navajo had no answers to any of these crucial questions. He was (as Chee had been repeatedly told) unfriendly. It was quickly guessed that he was a "relocation Navajo," born to one of those hundreds of Navajo families which the federal government had tried to reestablish forty years ago in Chicago, Los Angeles, and other urban centers.

He was a stranger. In a year of witches, he would certainly be suspected. Chee sat looking at his boots, wondering if that was the only basis for the charge that City Navajo was a skinwalker. Or had someone seen something? Had someone seen the murder?

"The thing about apples is they don't gossip," Chee said.

"You hear gossip about Begay?" Wells was sitting up now, his feet on the floor.

"Sure," Chee said. "I hear he's a witch."

Wells produced a pro-forma chuckle. "Tell me about it," he said.

Chee knew exactly how he wanted to tell it. Wells would have to wait awhile before he came to the part about Begay. "The Eskimos have nine nouns for snow," Chee began. He told Wells about the variety of witchcraft on the reservation and its environs: about frenzy witchcraft, used for sexual conquests, of witchery distortions, of curing ceremonials, of the exotic two-heart witchcraft of the Hopi Fog Clan, of the Zuni Sorcery Fraternity, of the Navajo "chindi," which is more like a ghost than a witch, and finally of the Navajo Wolf, the anti'l witchcraft, the werewolves who pervert every taboo of the Navajo Way and use corpse powder to kill their victims.

Wells rattled the ice in his glass and glanced at his watch.

"To get to the part about your Begay," Chee said, "about two months ago we started picking up witch gossip. Nothing much, and you expect it during a drought. Lately it got to be more than usual." He described some of the tales and how uneasiness and dread had spread across the plateau. He described what he had learned today, the Tsossie's naming City

Navajo as the witch, his trip to Mexican Water, of learning there that the witch had killed a man.

"They said it happened in the spring—couple of months ago. They told me the ones who knew about it were the Tso outfit." The talk of murder, Chee noticed, had revived Wells's interest. "I went up there," he continued, "and found the old woman who runs the outfit. Emma Tso. She told me her son-in-law had been looking for some sheep, and smelled something, and found the body under some chamiso brush in a dry wash. A witch had killed him."

"How—"

Chee cut off the question. "I asked her how he knew it was a witch killing. She said the hands were stretched out like this." Chee extended his hands, palms up. "They were flayed. The skin was cut off the palms and fingers."

Wells raised his eyebrows.

"That's what the witch uses to make corpse powder," Chee explained. "They take the skin that has the whorls and ridges of the individual personality— the skin from the palms and the finger pads, and the soles of the feet. They take that, and the skin from the glans of the penis, and the small bones where the neck joins the skull, and they dry it, and pulverize it, and use it as poison."

"You're going to get to Begay any minute now," Wells said. "That right?"

"We got to him," Chee said. "He's the one they think is the witch. He's the City Navajo."

"I thought you were going to say that," Wells said. He rubbed the back of his hand across one blue eye. "City Navajo. Is it that obvious?"

"Yes," Chee said. "And then he's a stranger. People suspect strangers."

"Were they coming around him? Accusing him? Any threats? Anything like that, you think?"

"It wouldn't work that way—not unless somebody had someone in their family killed. The way you deal with a witch is hire a singer and hold a special kind of curing ceremony. That turns the witchcraft around and kills the witch."

Wells made an impatient gesture. "Whatever," he said. "I think something has made this Begay spooky." He stared into his glass, communing with the bourbon. "I don't know."

"Something unusual about the way he's acting?"

"Hell of it is I don't know how he usually acts. This wasn't my case. The agent who worked him retired or some damn thing, so I got stuck with being the delivery man." He shifted his eyes from glass to Chee. "But if it was me, and I was holed up here waiting, and the guy came along who was going to take me home again, then I'd be glad to see him. Happy to have it over with. All that."

"He wasn't?"

Wells shook his head. "Seemed edgy. Maybe that's natural, though. He's going to make trouble for some hard people."

"I'd be nervous," Chee said.

"I guess it doesn't matter much anyway," Wells said. "He's small potatoes. The guy who's handling it now in the U.S. Attorney's Office said it must have been a toss-up whether to fool with him at all. He said the assistant who handled it decided to hide him out just to be on the safe side."

"Begay doesn't know much?"

"I guess not. That, and they've got better witnesses."

"So why worry?"

Wells laughed. "I bring this sucker back and they put him on the witness stand and he answers all the questions with I don't know and it makes the USDA look like a horse's ass. When a U.S. Attorney looks like that, he finds an FBI agent to blame it on." He yawned. "Therefore," he said through the yawn, "I want to ask you what you think. This is your territory. You are the officer in charge. Is it your opinion that someone got to my witness?"

Chee let the question hang. He spent a fraction of a second reaching the answer, which was they could have if they wanted to try. Then he thought about the real reason Wells had kept him working late without a meal or a shower. Two sentences in Wells's report. One would note that the possibility the witness had been approached had been checked with local Navajo Police. The next would report whatever Chee said next. Wells would have followed Federal Rule One—Protect Your Ass.

Chee shrugged. "You want to hear the rest of my witchcraft business?"

Wells put his drink on the lamp table and untied his shoe. "Does it bear on this?"

"Who knows? Anyway there's not much left. I'll let you decide. The point is we had already picked up this corpse Emma Tso's son-in-law found. Somebody had reported it weeks ago. It had been collected, and taken in for an autopsy. The word we got on the body was Navajo male in his thirties probably. No identification on him."

"How was this bird killed?"

"No sign of foul play," Chee said. "By the time the body was brought in, decay and the scavengers hadn't left a lot. Mostly bone and gristle, I guess. This was a long time after Emma Tso's son-in-law saw him."

"So why do they think Begay killed him?" Wells removed his second shoe and headed for the bathroom.

Chee picked up the telephone and dialed the Kayenta clinic. He got the night supervisor and waited while the supervisor dug out the file. Wells came out of the bathroom with his toothbrush. Chee covered the mouthpiece. "I'm having them read me the autopsy report," Chee explained. Wells began brushing his teeth at the sink in the dressing alcove. The voice of the night supervisor droned into Chee's ear.

"That all?" Chee asked. "Nothing added on? No identity yet? Still no cause?"

"That's him," the voice said.

"How about shoes?" Chee asked. "He have shoes on?"

"Just a sec," the voice said. "Yep. Size ten D. And a hat, and . . ."

"No mention of the neck or skull, right? I didn't miss that? No bones missing?"

Silence. "Nothing about neck or skull bones."

"Ah," Chee said. "Fine. I thank you." He felt great. He felt wonderful. Finally things had clicked into place. The witch was exorcised. "Jake," he said. "Let me tell you a little more about my witch case."

Wells was rinsing his mouth. He spit out the water and looked at Chee, amused. "I didn't think of this before," Wells said, "but you really don't have a witch problem. If you leave that corpse a death by natural causes, there's no case to work. If you decide it's a homicide, you don't have jurisdiction anyway. Homicide on an Indian reservation, FBI has jurisdiction." Wells grinned. "We'll come in and find your witch for you."

Chee looked at his boots, which were still dusty.

His appetite had left him, as it usually did an hour or so after he missed a meal. He still hungered for a bath. He picked up his hat and pushed himself to his feet.

"I'll go home now," he said. "The only thing you don't know about the witch case is what I just got from the autopsy report. The corpse had his shoes on and no bones were missing from the base of the skull."

Chee opened the door and stood in it, looking back. Wells was taking his pajamas out of his suitcase. "So what advice do you have for me? What can you tell me about my witch case?"

"To tell the absolute truth, Chee, I'm not into witches," Wells said. "Haven't been since I was a boy."

"But we don't really have a witch case now," Chee said. He spoke earnestly. "The shoes were still on, so the skin wasn't taken from the soles of his feet. No bones missing from the neck. You need those to make corpse powder."

Wells was pulling his undershirt over his head. Chee hurried.

"What we have now is another little puzzle," Chee said. "If you're not collecting stuff for corpse powder, why cut the skin off this guy's hands?"

"I'm going to take a shower," Wells said. "Got to get my Begay back to L.A. tomorrow."

Outside the temperature had dropped. The air moved softly from the west, carrying the smell of rain. Over the Utah border, over the Coconino Rim, over the Rainbow Plateau, lightning flickered and glowed. The storm had formed. The storm was moving. The sky was black with it. Chee stood in the darkness, listening to the mutter of thunder, inhaling the perfume, exulting in it.

He climbed into the truck and started it. How had

they set it up, and why? Perhaps the FBI agent who
knew Begay had been ready to retire. Perhaps an accident had been arranged. Getting rid of the assistant
prosecutor who knew the witness would have been
even simpler—a matter of hiring him away from the
government job. That left no one who knew this minor
witness was not Simon Begay. And who was he? Probably they had other Navajos from the Los Angeles
community stealing cars for them. Perhaps that's what
had suggested the scheme. To most white men all Navajos looked pretty much alike, just as in his first years
at college all Chee had seen in white men was pink
skin, freckles, and light-colored eyes. And what would
the imposter say? Chee grinned. He'd say whatever
was necessary to cast doubt on the prosecution, to cast
the fatal "reasonable doubt," to make—as Wells had
put it—the U.S. District Attorney look like a horse's
ass.

Chee drove into the rain twenty miles west of Kayenta. Huge, cold drops drummed on the pickup roof
and turned the highway into a ribbon of water. Tomorrow the backcountry roads would be impassable.
As soon as they dried and the washouts had been
repaired, he'd go back to the Tsossie hogan, and the
Tso place, and to all the other places from which the
word would quickly spread. He'd tell the people that
the witch was in custody of the FBI and was gone
forever from the Rainbow Plateau.

DEATH OF THE
MALLORY QUEEN

A Chip Harrison story

Lawrence Block

FIRST APPEARANCE: *Make Out with Murder*, 1974

Does anyone have as many continuing series characters as Lawrence Block does? In addition to his long-running Matt Scudder and Bernie Rhodenbarr series, Mr. Block has revived both Chip Harrison and Evan Tanner in recent years. We reprinted the first Bernie story in *First Cases*, and then the first Scudder in *First Cases 2*. Here we present the very first Chip Harrison story, which is actually the first Chip Harrison/Leo Haig story. This means we probably still have fodder for future first-case appearances from Mr. Block, for Evan Tanner and possibly his attorney character Ehrengraf.

After Chip appeared in two coming-of-age non-mystery novels Block introduced the character of Leo Haig into the mix, and had for himself one of the more successful Nero Wolfe takeoffs, with Chip in the role of Archie Goodwin.

This story was written specifically for one of Mr. Block's single author collections, *Like a Lamb to Slaughter*, in 1984.

"I am going to be murdered," Mavis Mallory said, "and I want you to do something about it."

Haig did something, all right. He spun around in his swivel chair and stared into the fish tank. There's a whole roomful of tanks on the top floor, and other aquariums, which he wishes I would call aquaria, scattered throughout the house.

(Well, not the whole house. The whole house is a carriage house on West Twentieth Street, and on the top two floors live Leo Haig and Wong Fat and more tropical fish than you could shake a jar of tubifex worms at, but the lower two floors are still occupied by Madam Juana and her girls. How do you say *filles de joie* in Spanish, anyway? Never mind. If all of this sounds a little like a cut-rate, low-rent version of Nero Wolfe's establishment on West Thirty-fifth Street, the similarity is not accidental. Haig, you see, was a life-long reader of detective fiction, and a penny-ante breeder of tropical fish until a legacy made him financially independent. And he was a special fan of the Wolfe canon, and he thinks that Wolfe really exists, and that if he, Leo Haig, does a good enough job with the cases that come his way, sooner or later he might get invited to dine at the master's table.)

"Mr. Haig—"

"*Huff,*" Haig said.

Except that he didn't exactly *say* huff. He *went* huff. He's been reading books lately by Sondra Ray and Leonard Orr and Phil Laut, books on rebirthing and physical immortality, and the gist of it seems to be that if you do enough deep circular breathing and clear out your limiting deathist thoughts, you can live forever. I don't know how he's doing with his deathist thoughts, but he's been breathing up a storm lately, as if air were going to be rationed any moment and he wants to get the jump on it.

He huffed again and studied the rasboras, which were the fish that were two-and-froing it in the ten-gallon tank behind his desk. Their little gills never stopped working, so I figured they'd live forever, too, unless their deathist thoughts were lurking to do them in. Haig gave another huff and turned around to look at our client.

She was worth looking at. Tall, willowy, richly curved, with a mane of incredible red hair. Last August I went up to Vermont, toward the end of the month, and all the trees were green except here and there you'd see one in the midst of all that green that had been touched by an early frost and turned an absolutely flaming scarlet, and that was the color of Mavis Mallory's hair. Haig's been quoting a lot of lines lately about the rich abundance of the universe we live in, especially when I suggest he's spending too much on fish and equipment, and looking at our client I had to agree with him. We live in an abundant world, all right.

"Murdered," he said.

She nodded.

"By whom?"

"I don't know."

"For what reason?"

"I don't know."

"And you want me to prevent it."

"No."

His eyes widened. "I beg your pardon?"

"How could you prevent it?" She wrinkled her nose at him. "I understand you're a genius, but what defense could you provide against a determined killer? You're not exactly the physical type."

Haig, who has been described as looking like a basketball with an Afro, huffed in reply. "My own efforts are largely in the cerebral sphere," he admitted. "But my associate, Mr. Harrison, is physically resourceful as well, and"—he made a tent of his fingertips—"still, your point is well taken. Neither Mr. Harrison nor I are bodyguards. If you wish a bodyguard, there are larger agencies which—"

But she was shaking her head. "A waste of time," she said. "The whole Secret Service can't protect a president from a lone deranged assassin. If I'm destined to be murdered, I'm willing to accede to my destiny."

"Huff," Haig huffed.

"What I want you to do," she said, "and Mr. Harrison, of course, except that he's so young I feel odd calling him by his last name." She smiled winningly at me. "Unless you object to the familiarity?"

"Call me Chip," I said.

"I'm delighted. And you must call me Mavis."

"Huff."

"Who wants to murder you?" I asked.

"Oh, dear," she said. "It sometimes seems to me that everyone does. It's been four years since I took over as publisher of *Mallory's Mystery Magazine* upon my father's death, and you'd be amazed how many enemies you can make in a business like this."

Haig asked if she could name some of them.

"Well, there's Abner Jenks. He'd been editor for years and thought he'd have a freer hand with my father out of the picture. When I reshuffled the corporate structure and created Mavis Publications, Inc., I found out he'd been taking kickbacks from authors and agents in return for buying their stories. I got rid of him and took over the editorial duties myself."

"And what became of Jenks?"

"I pay him fifty cents a manuscript to read slush pile submissions. And he picks up some freelance work for other magazines as well, and he has plenty of time to work on his own historical novel about the Venerable

Bede. Actually," she said, "he ought to be grateful to me."

"Indeed," Haig said.

"And there's Darrell Crenna. He's the owner of Mysterious Ink, the mystery bookshop on upper Madison Avenue. He wanted Dorothea Trill, the Englishwoman who writes those marvelous gardening mysteries, to do a signing at his store. In fact he'd advertised the appearance, and I had to remind him that Miss Trill's contract with Mavis Publications forbids her from making any appearances in the States without our authorization."

"Which you refused to give."

"I felt it would cheapen the value of Dorothea's personal appearances to have her make too many of them. After all, Crenna talked an author out of giving a story to *Mallory's* on the same grounds, so you could say he was merely hoist with his own petard. Or strangled by his own clematis vine, like the woman in Dorothea's latest." Her face clouded. "I hope I haven't spoiled the ending for you?"

"I've already read it," Haig said.

"I'm glad of that. Or I should have to add you to the list of persons with a motive for murdering me, shouldn't I? Let me see now. Lotte Benzler belongs on the list. You must know her shop. The Murder Store?"

Haig knew it well, and said so. "And I trust you've supplied Ms. Benzler with an equally strong motive? Kept an author from her door? Refused her permission to reprint a story from *Mallory's* in one of the anthologies she edits?"

"Actually," our client said, "I fear I did something rather more dramatic than that. You know Bart Halloran?"

"The creator of Rocky Sledge, who's so hard-boiled he makes Mike Hammer seem poached? I've read him, of course, but I don't know him."

"Poor Lotte came to know him very well," Mavis Mallory purred, "and then I met dear Bart, and then it was I who came to know him very well." She sighed. "I don't think Lotte has ever forgiven me. All's fair in love and publishing, but some people don't seem to realize it."

"So there are three people with a motive for murdering you."

"Oh, I'm sure there are more than three. Let's not forget Bart, shall we? He was able to shrug it off when I dropped him, but he took it harder when his latest got a bad review in *Mallory's*. But I thought *Kiss My Gat* was a bad book, and why should I say otherwise?" She sighed again. "Poor Bart," she said. "I understand his sales are slipping. Still, he's still a name, isn't he? And he'll be there Friday night."

"Indeed?" Haig raised his eyebrows. He's been practicing in front of the mirror, trying to raise just one eyebrow, but so far he hasn't got the knack of it. "And just where will Mr. Halloran be Friday night?"

"Where they'll all be," Mavis Mallory said. "At Town Hall, for the panel discussion and reception to celebrate the twenty-fifth anniversary of *Mallory's Mystery Magazine*. Do you know, I believe everyone with a motive to murder me will be gathered together in one room?" She shivered happily. "What more could a mystery fan ask for?"

"Don't attend," Haig said.

"Don't be ridiculous," she told him. "I'm Mavis Mallory of Mavis Publications. I *am Mallory's*—in fact I've been called the Mallory Queen. I'll be chairing the panel discussion and hosting the celebration. How could I possibly fail to be present?"

"Then get bodyguards."

"They'd put such a damper on the festivities. And I already told you they'd be powerless against a determined killer."

"Miss Mallory—"

"And please don't tell me to wear a bulletproof vest. They haven't yet designed one that flatters the full-figured woman."

I swallowed, reminded again that we live in an abundant universe. "You'll be killed," Haig said flatly.

"Yes," said our client, "I rather suspect I shall. I'm paying you a five-thousand-dollar retainer now, in cash, because you might have a problem cashing a check if I were killed before it cleared. And I've added a codicil to my will calling for payment to you of an additional twenty thousand dollars upon your solving the circumstances of my death. And I do trust you and Chip will attend the reception Friday night? Even if I'm not killed, it should be an interesting evening."

"I have read of a tribe of Africans," Haig said dreamily, "who know for certain that gunshot wounds are fatal. When one of their number is wounded by gunfire, he falls immediately to the ground and lies still, waiting for death. He does this even if he's only been nicked in the finger, and, by the following morning, death will have inevitably claimed him."

"That's interesting," I said. "Has it got anything to do with the Mallory Queen?"

"It has everything to do with her. The woman"—he huffed again, and I don't think it had much to do with circular breathing—"the damnable woman is convinced she will be murdered. It would profoundly disappoint her to be proved wrong. She *wants* to be murdered, Chip, and her thoughts are creative, even as yours and mine. In all likelihood she will die on Friday night. She would have it no other way."

"If she stayed home," I said. "If she hired body-guards—"

"She will do neither. But it would not matter if she did. The woman is entirely under the influence of her own death urge. Her death urge is stronger than her life urge. How could she live in such circumstances?"

"If that's how you feel, why did you take her money?"

"Because all abundance is a gift from the universe," he said loftily. "Further, she engaged us not to protect her but to avenge her, to solve her murder. I am per-fectly willing to undertake to do that." *Huff.* "You'll attend the reception Friday night, of course."

"To watch our client get the ax?"

"Or the dart from the blowpipe, or the poisoned cocktail, or the bullet, or the bite from the coral snake, or what you will. Perhaps you'll see something that will enable us to solve her murder on the spot and earn the balance of our fee."

"Won't you be there? I thought you'd planned to go."

"I had," he said. "But that was before Miss Mallory transformed the occasion from pleasure to business. Nero Wolfe never leaves his house on business, and I think the practice a sound one. You will attend in my stead, Chip. You will be my eyes and my legs. *Huff.*"

I was still saying things like *Yes, but* when he swept out of the room and left for an appointment with his rebirther. Once a week he goes all the way up to Washington Heights, where a woman named Lori Schneiderman gets sixty dollars for letting him stretch out on her floor and watching him breathe. It seems to me that for that kind of money he could do his huffing in a bed at the Plaza Hotel, but what do I know?

He'd left a page full of scribbling on his desk and I cleared it off to keep any future clients from spotting it. *I, Leo, am safe and immortal right now,* he'd written five times. *You, Leo, are safe and immortal right now,* he'd written another five times. *Leo is safe and immortal right now,* he'd written a final five times. This was how he was working through his unconscious death urge and strengthening his life urge. I tell you, a person has to go through a lot of crap if he wants to live forever.

Friday night found me at Town Hall, predictably enough. I wore my suit for the occasion and got there early enough to snag a seat down front, where I could keep a private eye on things.

There were plenty of things to keep an eye on. The audience swarmed with readers and writers of mystery and detective fiction, and if you want an idea of who was in the house, just write out a list of your twenty-five favorite authors and be sure that seventeen or eighteen of them were in the house. I saw some familiar faces, a woman who'd had a long run as the imperiled heroine of a Broadway suspense melodrama, a man who'd played a police detective for three years on network television, and others whom I recognized from films or television but couldn't place out of context.

On stage, our client Mavis Mallory occupied the moderator's chair. She was wearing a strapless and backless floor-length black dress, and in combination with her creamy skin and fiery hair, its effect was dramatic. If I could have changed one thing it would have been the color of the dress. I suppose Haig would have said it was the color of her unconscious death urge.

Her panelists were arranged in a semicircle around her. I recognized some but not others, but before I could extend my knowledge through subtle investigative technique, the entire panel was introduced. The members included Darrell Crenna of Mysterious Ink and Lotte Benzler of The Murder Store. The two sat on either side of our client, and I just hoped she'd be safe from the daggers they were looking at each other.

Rocky Sledge's creator, dressed in his standard outfit of chinos and a T-shirt with the sleeve rolled to contain a pack of unfiltered Camels, was introduced as Bartholomew Halloran. "Make that Bart," he snapped. *If you know what's good for you,* he might have added.

Halloran was sitting at Mavis Mallory's left. A tall and very slender woman with elaborately coiffed hair and a lorgnette sat between him and Darrell Crenna. She turned out to be Dorothea Trill, the Englishwoman who wrote gardening mysteries. I always figured the chief gardening mystery was what to do with all the zucchini. Miss Trill seemed a little looped, but maybe it was the lorgnette.

On our client's other side, next to Lotte Benzler, sat a man named Austin Porterfield. He was a Distinguished Professor of English Literature at New York University, and he'd recently published a rather learned obituary of the mystery story in the *New York Review of Books*. According to him, mystery fiction had drawn its strength over the years from the broad base of its popular appeal. Now other genres had more readers, and thus mystery writers were missing the mark. If they wanted to be artistically important, he advised them, then get busy producing Harlequin romances and books about nurses and stewardesses.

On Mr. Porterfield's other side was Janice Cowan, perhaps the most prominent book editor in the mystery field. For years she had moved from one important publishing house to another, and at each of them she had her own private imprint. "A Jan Cowan Novel of Suspense" was a good guarantee of literary excellence, whoever happened to be Miss Cowan's employer that year.

After the last of the panelists had been introduced, a thin, weedy man in a dark suit passed quickly among the group with a beverage tray, then scurried off the stage. Mavis Mallory took a sip of her drink, something colorless in a stemmed glass, and leaned toward the microphone. "What Happens Next?" she intoned. "That's the title of our little discussion tonight, and it's a suitable title for a discussion on this occasion. A credo of *Mallory's Mystery Magazine* has always been that our sort of fiction is only effective insofar as the reader cares deeply what happens next, what takes place on the page he or she has yet to read. Tonight, though, we are here to discuss what happens next in mystery and suspense fiction. What trends have reached their peaks, and what trends are swelling just beyond the horizon."

She cleared her throat, took another sip of her drink. "Has the tough private eye passed his prime? Is the lineal descendant of Sam Spade and Philip Marlowe just a tedious outmoded macho sap?" She paused to smile pleasantly at Bart Halloran, who glowered back at her. "Conversely, has the American reader lost interest forever in the mannered English mystery? Are we ready to bid adieu to the body in the library, or"—she paused for an amiable nod at the slightly cockeyed Miss Trill—"the corpse in the formal gardens?

"Is the mystery, if you'll pardon the expression, *dead* as a literary genre? One of our number"—and a cheerless smile for Professor Porterfield—"would have us all turn to writing *Love's Saccharine Savagery* and *Penny Wyse, Stockyard Nurse.* Is the mystery bookshop, a store specializing in our brand of fiction, an idea whose time has come—and gone? And what do book publishers have to say on this subject? One of our number has worked for so many of them; she should be unusually qualified to comment."

Mavis certainly had the full attention of her fellow panelists. Now, to make sure she held the attention of the audience as well, she leaned forward, a particularly arresting move given the nature of the strapless, backless black number she was more or less wearing. Her hands tightened on the microphone.

"Please help me give our panel members full attention," she said, "as we turn the page to find out"— she paused dramatically—"What Happens Next!"

What happened next was that the lights went out. All of them, all at once, with a great crackling noise of electrical failure. Somebody screamed, and then so did somebody else, and then screaming became kind of popular. A shot rang out. There were more screams, and then another shot, and then everybody was shouting at once, and then some lights came on.

Guess who was dead.

That was Friday night. Tuesday afternoon, Haig was sitting back in his chair on his side of our huge old partners' desk. He didn't have his feet up—I'd broken him of that habit—but I could see he wanted to. In-

stead he contented himself with taking a pipe apart
and putting it back together again. He had tried smoking pipes, thinking it a good mannerism for a detective, but it never took, so now he fiddles with them.
It looks pretty dumb, but it's better than putting his
feet up on the desk.

"I don't suppose you're wondering why I summoned you all here," he said.

They weren't wondering. They all knew, all of the
panelists from the other night, plus two old friends of
ours, a cop named Gregorio who wears clothes that
could never be purchased on a policeman's salary, and
another cop named Seidenwall, who wears clothes that
could. They knew they'd been gathered together to
watch Leo Haig pull a rabbit out of a hat, and it was
going to be a neat trick because it looked as though
he didn't even have the hat.

"We're here to clear up the mysterious circumstances of the death of Mavis Mallory. All of you assembled here, except for the two gentlemen of the
law, had a motive for her murder. All of you had the
opportunity. All of you thus exist under a cloud of
suspicion. As a result, you should all be happy to learn
that you have nothing to fear from my investigation.
Mavis Mallory committed suicide."

"Suicide!" Gregorio exploded. "I've heard you
make some ridiculous statements in your time, but
that one grabs the gateau. You have the nerve to sit
there like a toad on a lily pad and tell me the red-
headed dame killed herself?"

"Nerve?" Haig mused. "Is nerve ever required to
tell the truth?"

"Truth? You wouldn't recognize the truth if it dove
into one of your fish tanks and swam around eating
up all the brine shrimp. The Mallory woman got hit

by everything short of tactical nuclear weapons. There were two bullets in her from different guns. She had a wavy-bladed knife stuck in her back and a short dagger in her chest, or maybe it was the other way around. The back of her skull was dented by a blow from a blunt instrument. There was enough rat poison in her system to put the Pied Piper out of business, and there were traces of curare, a South American arrow poison, in her martini glass. Did I leave something out?"

"Her heart had stopped beating," Haig said.

"Is that a fact? If you ask me, it had its reasons. And you sit there and call it suicide. That's some suicide."

Haig sat there and breathed, in and out, in and out, in the relaxed, connected breathing rhythm that Lori Schneiderman had taught him. Meanwhile they all watched him, and I in turn watched them. We had them arranged just the way they'd been on the panel, with Detective Vincent Gregorio sitting in the middle where Mavis Mallory had been. Reading left to right, I was looking at Bart Halloran, Dorothea Trill, Darrell Crenna, Gregorio, Lotte Benzler, Austin Porterfield and Janice Cowan. Detective Wallace Seidenwall sat behind the others, sort of off to the side and next to the wall. If this were novel length I'd say what each of them was wearing and who scowled and who looked interested, but Haig says there's not enough plot here for a novel and that you have to be more concise in short stories, so just figure they were all feeling about the way you'd feel if you were sitting around watching a fat little detective practice rhythmic breathing.

"Some suicide," Haig said. "Indeed. Some years ago a reporter went to a remote county in Texas to investigate the death of a man who'd been trying to expose irregularities in election procedures. The coroner had recorded the death as suicide, and the reporter checked the autopsy and discovered that the deceased had been shot six times in the back with a high-powered rifle. He confronted the coroner with this fact and demanded to know how the man had dared call the death suicide.

" 'Yep,' drawled the coroner. 'Worst case of suicide I ever saw in my life.' "

Gregorio just stared at him.

"So it is with Miss Mallory," Haig continued. "Hers is the worst case of suicide in my experience. Miss Mallory was helplessly under the influence of her own unconscious death urge. She came to me, knowing that she was being drawn toward death, and yet she had not the slightest impulse to gain protection. She wished only that I contract to investigate her demise and see to its resolution. She deliberately assembled seven persons who had reason to rejoice in her death, and enacted a little drama in front of an audience. She—"

"Six persons," Gregorio said, gesturing to the three on either side of him. "Unless you're counting her, or unless all of a sudden I got to be a suspect."

Haig rang a little bell on his desk top, and that was Wong Fat's cue to usher in a skinny guy in a dark suit. "Mr. Abner Jenks," Haig announced. "Former editor of *Mallory's Mystery Magazine*, demoted to slush reader and part-time assistant."

"He passed the drinks," Dorothea Trill remembered. "So that's how she got the rat poison."

"I certainly didn't poison her," Jenks whined. "Nor did I shoot her or stab her or hit her over the head or—"

Haig held up a hand. There was a pipe stem in it,

but it still silenced everybody. "You all had motives,"
he said. "None of you intended to act on them. None
of you planned to make an attempt on Miss Mallory's
life. Yet thought is creative and Mavis Mallory's
thoughts were powerful. Some people attract money
to them, or love, or fame. Miss Mallory attracted violent death."

"You're making a big deal out of nothing," Gregorio said. "You're saying she wanted to die, and
that's fine, but it's still a crime to give her a hand with
it, and that's what every single one of them did.
What's that movie, something about the Orient Ex-
press, and they all stab the guy? That's what we got
here, and I think what I gotta do is book 'em all on
a conspiracy charge."

"That would be the act of a witling," Haig said.
"First of all, there was no conspiracy. Perhaps more
important, there was no murder."

"Just a suicide."

"Precisely," said Haig. *Huff.* "In a real sense, all
death is suicide. As long as a man's life urge is
stronger than his death urge, he is immortal and invul-
nerable. Once the balance shifts, he has an unbreak-
able appointment in Samarra. But Miss Mallory's
death is suicide in a much stricter sense of the word.
No one else tried to kill her, and no one else succeeded. She unquestionably created her own death."

"And shot herself?" Gregorio demanded. "And
stuck knives in herself, and bopped herself over the
head? And—"

"No," Haig said. *Huff.* "I could tell you that she
drew the bullets and knives to herself by the force of
her thoughts, but I would be wasting my—" *huff!*
"—breath. The point is metaphysical, and in the present context immaterial. The bullets were not aimed at

her, nor did they kill her. Neither did the stabbings, the blow to the head, the poison."

"Then what did?"

"The stopping of her heart."

"Well, that's what kills everyone," Gregorio said, as if explaining something to a child. "That's how you know someone's dead. The heart stops."

Haig sighed heavily, and I don't know if it was circular breathing or resignation. Then he started telling them how it happened.

"Miss Mallory's death urge created a powerful impulse toward violence," he said. "All seven of you, the six panelists and Mr. Jenks, had motives for killing the woman. But you are not murderous people, and you had no intention of committing acts of violence. Quite without conscious intent, you found yourselves bringing weapons to the Town Hall event. Perhaps you thought to display them to an audience of mystery fans. Perhaps you felt a need for a self-defense capability. It hardly matters what went through your minds.

"All of you, as I said, had reason to hate Miss Mallory. In addition, each of you had reason to hate one or more of your fellow panel members. Miss Benzler and Mr. Crenna are rival booksellers; their cordial loathing for one another is legendary. Mr. Halloran was romantically involved with the panel's female members, while Mr. Porterfield and Mr. Jenks were briefly, uh, closeted together in friendship. Miss Trill had been very harshly dealt with in some writings of Mr. Porterfield. Miss Cowan had bought books by Mr. Halloran and Miss Trill, then left the books stranded when she moved on to another employer. I could go on, but what's the point? Each and every one of you may be said to have had a sound desire to murder each and every one of your fellows, but in the ordinary course of things nothing would have come of any of these desires. We all commit dozens of mental murders a day, yet few of us ever dream of acting on any of them."

"I'm sure there's a point to this," Austin Porterfield said.

"Indeed there is, sir, and I am fast approaching it. Miss Mallory leaned forward, grasping her microphone, pausing for full dramatic value, and the lights went out. And it was then that knives and guns and blunt instruments and poison came into play."

The office lights dimmed as Wong Fat operated a wall switch. There was a sharp intake of breath, although the room didn't get all that dark, and there was a balancing *huff* from Haig. "The room went dark," he said. "That was Miss Mallory's doing. She chose the moment, not just unconsciously, but with knowing purpose. She wanted to make a dramatic point, and she succeeded beyond her wildest dreams.

"As soon as those lights went out, everyone's murderous impulses, already stirred up by Mavis Mallory's death urge, were immeasurably augmented. Mr. Crenna drew a Malayan kris and moved to stab it into the heart of his competitor, Miss Benzler. At the same time, Miss Benzler drew a poniard of her own and circled around to direct it at Mr. Crenna's back. Neither could see. Neither was well oriented. And Mavis Mallory's unconscious death urge drew both blades to her own body, even as it drew the bullet Mr. Porterfield meant for Mr. Jenks, the deadly blow Mr. Halloran meant for Miss Cowan, the bullet Miss Cowan intended for Miss Trill, and the curare Miss Trill had meant to place in Mr. Halloran's glass.

"Curare, incidentally, works only if introduced into

the bloodstream; it would have been quite ineffective if ingested. The rat poison Miss Mallory did ingest was warfarin, which would ultimately have caused her death by internal bleeding; it was in the glass when Abner Jenks served it to her."

"Then Jenks tried to kill her," Gregorio said.

Haig shook his head. "Jenks did not put the poison in the glass," he said. "Miss Lotte Benzler had placed the poison in the glass before Miss Mallory picked it up."

"Then Miss Benzler—"

"Was not trying to kill Miss Mallory either," Haig said, "because she placed the poison in the glass she intended to take for herself. She had previously ingested a massive dose of Vitamin K, a coagulant which is the standard antidote for warfarin, and intended to survive a phony murder attempt on stage, both to publicize The Murder Store and to discredit her competitor, Mr. Crenna. At the time, of course, she'd had no conscious intention of sticking a poniard into the same Mr. Crenna, the very poniard that wound up in Miss Mallory."

"You're saying they all tried to kill each other," Gregorio said. "And they all killed her instead."

"But they didn't succeed."

"They didn't? How do you figure that? She's dead as a bent doornail."

"She was already dead."

"How?"

"Dead of electrocution," Haig told him. "Mavis Mallory put out all the lights in Town Hall by short-circuiting the microphone. She got more than she bargained for, although in a sense it was precisely what she'd bargained for. In the course of shorting out the building's electrical system, she herself was subjected to an electrical charge that induced immediate and permanent cardiac arrest. The warfarin had not yet had time to begin inducing fatal internal bleeding. The knives and bullets pierced the skin of a woman who was already dead. The bludgeon crushed a dead woman's skull. Miss Mallory killed herself."

Wong Fat brought the lights up. Gregorio blinked at the brightness. "That's a pretty uncertain way to do yourself in," he said. "It's not like she had her foot in a pail of water. You don't necessarily get a shock shorting out a line that way, and the shock's not necessarily a fatal one."

"The woman did not consciously plan her own death," Haig told him. "An official verdict of suicide would be of dubious validity. Accidental death, I suppose, is what the certificate would properly read." He huffed mightily. "Accidental death! As that Texas coroner would say, it's quite the worst case of accidental death I've ever witnessed."

And that's what it went down as, accidental death. No charges were ever pressed against any of the seven, although it drove Gregorio crazy that they all walked out of there untouched. But what could you get them for? Mutilating a corpse? It would be hard to prove who did what, and it would be even harder to prove that they'd been trying to kill each other. As far as Haig was concerned, they were all acting under the influence of Mavis Mallory's death urge, and were only faintly responsible for their actions.

"The woman was ready to die, Chip," he said, "and die she did. She wanted me to solve her death and I've solved it, I trust to the satisfaction of the lawyers for her estate. And you've got a good case to write up. It won't make a novel, and there's not nearly enough sex in it to satisfy the book-buying public, but I shouldn't wonder that it will make a good short story. Perhaps for *Mallory's Mystery Magazine*, or a publication of equal stature."

He stood up. "I'm going uptown," he announced, "to get rebirthed. I suggest you come along. I think Wolfe must have been a devotee of rebirthing, and Archie as well."

I asked him how he figured that.

"Rebirthing reverses the aging process," he explained. "How else do you suppose the great detectives manage to endure for generations without getting a day older? Archie Goodwin was a brash young man in *Fer-de-lance* in nineteen thirty-four. He was still the same youthful wisenheimer forty years later. I told you once, Chip, that your association with me would make it possible for you to remain eighteen years old forever. Now it seems that I can lead you not only to the immortality of ink and paper but to genuine physical immortality. If you and I work to purge ourselves of the effects of birth trauma, and if we use our breath to cleanse our cells, and if we stamp out deathist thoughts once and forever—"

"Huh," I said. But wouldn't you know it? It came out *huff*.

SNOW

A Porfiry Rostnikov story

Stuart M. Kaminsky

FIRST APPEARANCE: *Death of a Dissident*, 1981

Stuart Kaminsky presently has four series running at the same time, perhaps the only writer in this collection who can rival Lawrence Block in that area. His longest-running series features 1940s Hollywood P.I. Toby Peters. He also writes about Chicago Detective Abe Lieberman and is the author of two original Rockford Files novels.

His greatest success, however, has come from his series featuring Inspector Porfiry Petrovich Rostnikov, set in Russia. In 1988 *A Cold Red Sunrise* won the Shamus Award for Best Mystery Novel of the Year. Among his other idiosyncrasies Rostnikov reads bootleg copies of Ed McBain's 87th Precinct books. These books, featuring Rostnikov and his colleagues, are in the best spirit of that long-running police procedural series.

"Snow" is the very first story to feature Inspector Rostnikov, written for this collection.

If there had been less blood, following the trail in the snow would have been quite difficult. For one thing, the sun was just beginning, slowly, lazily, to rise over Moscow. For another thing, the snow was still falling. Not as heavily as it had throughout the night but enough to quickly fill in footprints.

Porfiry Petrovich Rostnikov, though the temperature hovered in the 20s, was warm in the heavy wool coat of his uniform. And his cap? He perspired under it and would gladly have taken it off as he trudged forward if it were not for the watchful eye of the detective with whom he had been teamed on the call.

Rostnikov had been a policeman for less than a month. His training had been minimal and his apprenticeship to an indifferent veteran had been enough to make the young policeman briefly reconsider his choice of profession.

"This way," Rostnikov said over his shoulder.

Behind him Inspector Luminiov grunted and though Porfiry Petrovich did not turn his head, he could tell from the smell that the inspector had paused to light a cigarette.

The trail of blood went around a corner of the block of four-story concrete apartment buildings. Somewhere in the distance, Rostnikov heard the clang of a trolley.

Rostnikov wanted to run, to find the end of this stream of vermilion that rested atop the clean whiteness, but he could not. His left leg would not permit it. Rostnikov talked to his leg, muttered to his leg, sometimes within himself, sometimes aloud.

"Leg," he said now. "A child has been taken, a baby. The child is in the hands of a man who has killed, a man who may well be mad."

Although his leg did not use words, the answer was clear to the burly young policeman with a broad face that could only be Russian.

"When that German tank came, you could have pulled me out of its path," said his leg.

"We've been through this," said Rostnikov dragging his reluctant, crippled leg behind him. "I was a boy soldier, a little boy in a large ragged uniform. I was trapped."

"That does me little good," said the leg.

"Then," said Rostnikov, "we must simply learn to live together, to cooperate."

"I have no desire to cooperate," his leg responded.

"Then," said Rostnikov, "I shall have to resign myself to making the best of things."

"What? What did you say?" asked Luminiov, moving to Rostnikov's side.

"Talking to myself," said Rostnikov. "That way."

He pointed across the street. There was no traffic. In this forgotten neighborhood of crumpling ill-built tenements, there were no cars but those belonging to the police and no State-paid old women with brooms to tirelessly clear the sidewalks and streets.

The trail of blood led across the street toward the doorway of a building that looked like all the buildings that faced and surrounded it. Four-foot-high drifts of snow sloped up the side of the building, covering all but the very tips of the barred ground floor windows.

Luminiov let out a sigh of boredom, took a deep drag of his cigarette, and looked at the dark doorway. Luminiov was a lean man of about forty with white hair who looked as if he were half-asleep. Rostnikov knew his superior had been drinking heavily the night before, possibly even into the early hours of the morning. Vodka left no smell, but Rostnikov knew well the signs. They were with him every day on the streets of Moscow. Dostoyevsky had written about those signs and the dazed dangers of vodka a century ago.

Luminiov wore a black overcoat. He unbuttoned it and removed his pistol from a holster that was badly in need of polishing.

"Follow the trail," said Luminiov. "I'll stay out here in case he tries to escape this way."

Rostnikov nodded. He had no choice. Had he been given the choice he would have left Luminiov outside in any case. If the man were in the building, he was probably carrying the child. Rostnikov had no doubt that the Inspector at his side would fire at man and child if there were even the slightest chance that the man might be carrying a weapon.

Porfiry Petrovich Rostnikov had no desire to die. He had a wife. She was pregnant with their first child. He had much to live for, but the murderer who had entered the building had taken a baby.

Rostnikov limped toward the entryway of the apartment building. As he moved, he looked up at the falling snow. Looking up saved his life. The block of concrete was coming straight at him. Rostnikov rolled to his right as the jagged missile crashed through the snow a few feet away.

"Are you all right?" Luminiov called with a vague interest rather than real concern.

"I am alive. I appear to be uninjured," said Rostnikov, rolling over awkwardly and looking up to be prepared for any other rocks amid the snow.

"Good," said Luminiov.

Through the thin flurry of white flakes, Rostnikov could see a figure at the edge of the roof.

"Go away!" shouted the man. He had something in his arms. It wasn't a block of concrete. It was a baby. The baby was crying.

Rostnikov looked at Luminiov, who was drawing his gun, and shouted up at the man on the roof,

"Step back. I'm coming up."

"No."

Rostnikov rose awkwardly.

Though the distance was not great, the weather was a problem. Luminiov's shot struck the edge of the roof with an echoing RRRING.

"Don't!" shouted Rostnikov both at Luminiov and the man on the roof.

The man hesitated and raised the infant over his head.

"He won't shoot again," Rostnikov shouted to the man on the roof.

Luminiov was aiming more carefully now. Rostnikov turned to his superior and said loud enough for the man on the roof to hear, "If you are responsible for that baby's death, I will kill you."

"You will kill me?" said Luminiov, turning his weapon on the young officer.

"Yes," said Rostnikov calmly.

He had seen babies die in the war, had witnessed the bodies of many, but the babies, the dead babies had wounded him more than any wounds inflicted on him by the Nazis.

Luminiov put his gun hand to his side and said with a shrug, "We'll talk about this later. We will talk. Be sure of that."

Rostnikov knew that Luminiov had few choices. If he shot Rostnikov, not only would he have to explain why he had done so, he would also have to cope with the madman on the roof.

"Go," said Luminiov.

"I'm coming up," called Rostnikov. "Have you got a blanket, sweater, something up there?"

"Blanket? No."

"The baby must be very cold. Take off your coat or something."

The man on the roof stepped back. His uniform now wet with snow, Porfiry Petrovich Rostnikov moved into the entryway, which smelled of the thousands of cigarettes smoked by the out-of-work residents who gathered each day with nothing to do but argue and complain.

The door was not locked. None of the doors to these concrete tributes to Stalin were ever locked. There was no point to a lock. Any nine-year-old could get through with a piece of wire and a laugh.

The inner lobby was dark, cold, unheated. Since every building was heated by the central gas system, usually buildings like this were too hot or too cold. This one on this day was too cold.

There was a concrete stairway with a rusting metal railing. He went to it and began moving slowly upward, coaxing his complaining left leg, promising it rest later.

The climb was slow though Rostnikov wanted to move quickly. He encountered no one coming down. It was still too early and the gunfire may well have convinced those few who had reason to arise early that they had better reason to stay locked in their apartments a bit longer.

Luminiov had taken the call only an hour earlier. Rostnikov had been the only uniformed officer available in the district station. Luminiov had simply pointed to him and said, "You," not even asking the young uniformed officer his name. Rostnikov had been waiting for his partner, his senior partner who was, once again, late for their shift.

Rostnikov had followed the Inspector. They had said little on the way to the scene.

Rostnikov knew Luminiov by sight. Luminiov was vaguely aware of the short, burly policeman only because the man had sad eyes and a crippled leg. Luminiov, had he been able to stir enough interest within himself, might have asked how a cripple could become a policeman. Had he asked Rostnikov would have told him that he had drifted through jobs in a factory, as a trolley conductor until, at the age of thirty-three, he had decided to become a policeman. His war record had been enough to get him the job and, until now, a series of crimes no greater than rousting drunks. Most of his brief career as a policeman had involved following his partner, who made the rounds of blackmarketers who doled out bribe money which Rostnikov refused to take a share of. His refusal, rather than making his partner suspicious, had pleased the veteran, who did not have to share his take.

This moment, however, this very moment was the height of his brief career as a policeman. He did not think of that now. He would later, but not at this moment. He had glimpsed the baby on the roof and that sight now drove him. As he moved forward, he remembered the apartment where minutes ago they had discovered what remained of the dead woman.

There had been a tiny, single room large enough for a bed, a makeshift crib, a torn sofa, a wooden table with a piece of wood under one of the four legs to keep it from toppling over, and three unmatched chairs. There was a very small alcove which had been turned into a kitchen area. There was also the dead woman in the middle of the room.

She was very thin, and still wore a sweater she no longer needed to help ward off the cold. She no longer had a face.

The reason for her lost identity was a bloody block of wood near the door, a block of wood like so many in Moscow apartments, a block of wood to jam against the door to keep out intruders who ignored locks.

Luminiov had stepped back into the second floor

hallway and caught an old woman peeking out of her door.

"You," he called sternly. "Out here. We are the police."

The old woman reluctantly came into the hallway and down to the small apartment where Rostnikov was examining but not touching the body.

"Where is the baby?" Rostnikov asked before Luminiov could ask a question.

"Is she, yes, she is dead," said the old woman.

"The baby," Rostnikov repeated gently. "The crib is still warm, damp. The baby has a fever. Where is the baby?"

Luminiov had leaned back against the wall, lit a cigarette, and watched with a hint of amusement. This was routine. The husband or boyfriend had done this. Cramped in a little hole. No job. Too cold to walk off anger. Perhaps drunk. The baby crying. Regimes had changed but in more than 500 years, Russians had not. The baby was probably dead somewhere nearby. No one would miss it. And if it lived who would take care of it?

The sun was definitely out now though it was visible only as a vague sullen glow through the still falling snow. Now, people began to slowly emerge from the apartment buildings, bundled, trudging, glancing at Luminiov, who knew that he was supposed to secure the scene, keep people away. A falling child or, worse, a falling stubborn young policeman with a bad leg could hit one of them.

Luminiov looked up and saw nothing at the edge of the building. He stepped back a dozen paces into the doorway of a boarded-up apartment building.

Rostnikov climbed the last narrow stairway to the door to the roof. If it was locked or barricaded, he would have to decide on whether he would go back or attempt to break through. A breakthrough might panic the bleeding man.

The door was not locked but the wind made it difficult to push open. When he did, he looked around for the man and baby. The snow was swirling harder atop the roof than on the street below, but it was not a terrible snowstorm.

Even without the trail of blood on the rooftop snow and the deep footprints, he would have quickly found the man who made no attempt to hide or respond. The baby, wrapped in a thin sheet, was cradled in the man's right arm. The left arm hung at the man's side. He wore a flannel shirt, which was not tucked in, and blood dripped from his dangling fingers.

The man himself was big, overweight, thin hair, about forty years old, and filled with panic.

"You shoot me and I throw him over the edge. I swear. And I'll jump too. If you don't care, shoot me. You know what? I don't care. What is there for me? I'll go to jail, execution. Better to die now."

Below, on the street, a young woman urged on by her friends approached the policeman smoking in the doorway of the boarded-up building. Her mission was to find out what was happening. Her sister lived in the building the policeman was looking at.

She started to speak but Luminiov waved her away and looked up at the roof across the street. Loud voices were coming from up there and if there was silence Luminiov could just make out what was being said.

"What's the baby's name?" asked Rostnikov, moving forward a step.

"Alexander," the man said, looking at the baby.

"He is yours?"

"I think so. Who knows? She was no beauty. I mean . . . but there are men. And I'm not much . . . What difference does it make now?"

"Can you hold Alexander up so I can see his face?" asked Rostnikov as he limped another step forward.

"Stop!" shouted the man.

Rostnikov stopped.

"You mind if I sit over there? On the vent?"

"You'll be cold. You'll have to sit in the snow," the man said.

Rostnikov shrugged.

"Better a wet bottom than an angry leg."

"Sit, but I'm getting weak," said the man. "I'm going to throw him over the edge and then follow him."

Rostnikov moved to the vent and sat. It was cold. He looked around. The snow was now coming down harder.

"We're in for three feet at least," said Rostnikov, rubbing his left leg with his gloved hands.

"Is someone coming behind you? Are you planning to trick me? If someone comes through that door—"

"No one but me is coming," said Rostnikov. "You're cold. The baby's not wrapped warmly enough. Will you accept my coat? You can tuck the baby under it."

"Alexander," said the man.

"Yes, Alexander," repeated Rostnikov. "And you are?"

"A dead man."

"Yes, but does the dead man have a name?"

"Ivan," he said. And then he laughed. "Millions of Ivans. One more will die. Millions of Alexanders. Dead people don't need coats. When we were alive we could have used your coat but . . . dead people don't . . ."

". . . need coats," Rostnikov said, shifting his wet behind.

"Yes."

"What do you know about plumbing, Ivan?" asked Rostnikov.

"Plumbing. Nothing. I am . . . was a painter."

"Apartments?"

"Yes."

Rostnikov nodded solemnly.

"Are you a good painter?"

"When I have enough time, good brushes, good paint but I haven't had work for . . . I don't know."

Ivan tried to lift his dangling arm to put around the baby. The arm resisted and then slowly moved as Ivan bit his lower lip. When he did get his injured arm around the baby, the thin sheet was covered instantly in blood.

"Plumbing," Rostnikov said.

"I don't care about plumbing," said Ivan, tears welling in his eyes.

"Intricate," said Rostnikov. "Intricate but logical if done right like the inside of a body. You know, veins, arteries, intestines."

"I'm not interested," said Ivan.

Something stirred to Rostnikov's left. A man in an overcoat wearing a cap and carrying something in his right hand stomped up the stairs from below and onto the roof. Ivan moved to the edge of the roof, stumbling, bleeding.

Rostnikov forced himself up and called, "No, he is not a policeman."

The baby began to whimper, too cold to really cry.

Ivan looked back at the bewildered man, who carried a shovel.

"What?" asked the man, looking at the policeman and the bleeding Ivan.

"Who are you?" Rostnikov asked.

"Who am I?"

"Yes, that is the question," said Rostnikov. "The prize for the correct answer may be the saving of a life, maybe two lives."

"I . . . I am Julian Korianovich. When it snows, I shovel the roof so it doesn't collapse the way it did in . . . I don't know, a year, two years after it was built."

"You get paid for this?" asked Rostnikov, turning his back to Ivan and the whimpering child.

Julian Korianovich looked at the baby and bleeding man. Julian Korianovich touched his full mustache with his gloved hand.

"Paid? Something, a little, not much. I have a room, my wife and I. We don't . . . What is happening?"

"Snow," said Rostnikov, looking up. "We are talking and watching the snow fall."

"Stop!" shouted Ivan.

Rostnikov turned to the man.

"Why did you kill her?"

"She . . . No room. She complained, complained, complained. She drove me mad. I didn't think. I just wanted her to unfold her arms and stop looking at me like that, stop playing with the buttons on that damned sweater."

"How did you get injured?"

Ivan looked down at his arm. His face had turned nearly white from the loss of blood.

"She shot me," he said. "She had a gun. I didn't know she had a gun. We could have sold it. Instead she shot me. I had just hit her once. She said she had decided to shoot me the next time I hit her. She shot me and then . . . Where did she get money to buy a gun?"

"Where is the gun?" asked Rostnikov.

"I don't know. In the room."

"No," said Rostnikov.

The baby continued to whimper.

"Then," said Ivan, trying to think, "it is in my pocket."

With that he attempted to move his injured arm to the pocket of his pants, but the arm would not obey. He could not shift the baby.

"It is in my pocket," he said. "If I could get it out, I would shoot myself. Maybe I would shoot you and the shoveler too. Why should you live if my baby and I are dead? You don't believe me, do you?"

"I believe you," said Rostnikov.

"I believe you too," said Julian the roof shoveler.

"Now, it is time," said Ivan sadly, looking down at the baby.

Rostnikov began moving toward the man and the whimpering infant, circling to the left. Ivan moved back.

"I'm enjoying our talk," Rostnikov said.

"I am too weak to talk," said Ivan. "Too weak. And there is nothing to talk about."

"Did you know that the American president was murdered?" asked Rostnikov, moving slowly forward.

"Kennyadi is dead? You lie."

"Why would I lie? Would you like to know how he died? Where? It was in Texas."

"A cowboy shot him," said Julian the shoveler.

"Don't run at me," said Ivan, who had backed up to the very edge of the roof.

"With this leg? I can do many things, but running is not one of them. The snow is stopping. It is time to end this. Hand me the baby."

"No," said Ivan, crying. He bent his head, kissed the child, and with what little remained of his strength he dropped the baby off the roof.

Julian screamed in sudden fury and ran at Ivan, shovel held high. Rostnikov stepped between the two men and put his arms around the screaming attacker. The man found himself lifted into the air.

"Stop," Rostnikov said gently. "I have work to do."

He dropped the man gently in the snow and Julian began to weep.

"I just came up to shovel the snow," he said.

Ivan was tottering on the edge of the roof. With his free hand he fumbled at the pocket where the gun was awkwardly tucked. Rostnikov tried to move forward quickly but he was unable to reach Ivan before he pulled out the weapon.

Instead of aiming it at his own head, the pale bleeding man pointed it weakly in the general direction of Porfiry Petrovich Rostnikov.

The shot crackled in the cool morning air.

Ivan let out a small sigh, crumpled, and tumbled backward off the roof. Rostnikov moved as quickly as he could to the place where Ivan had fallen. Below him, the dead Ivan lay sprawled, a snow angel, and Inspector Luminiov stood with his gun in his hand and a whimpering baby in his arms.

"The baby," cried a thoroughly confused Julian, tugging at his mustache. "The baby."

"The baby is alive," Rostnikov said, limping to the open door.

When he got to the street, Luminiov stood alone next to the body in the snow. People were watching from a distance, uncertain about what they had seen beyond a baby being thrown from a roof and a man being shot by the police.

Luminiov handed the child to Rostnikov and took off his coat to wrap the baby in.

"You are a man to be watched," Luminiov said, putting his weapon back in the now exposed holster.

"Watched?" asked Rostnikov, touching the baby's cheek. It was cool but not cold and the baby was crying. A good sign. Rostnikov wrapped Alexander in Inspector Luminiov's coat, removed the glove on his right hand, and put his small finger into the infant's mouth. The baby began to suck. Another good sign.

"You maneuvered him to the edge of the roof," said Luminiov, lighting a cigarette. "I heard. You maneuvered him over the deepest drift of snow. You kept him talking while he grew weaker so he couldn't throw the baby, only drop it. And when it was clear the snow was about to stop and the drift wouldn't get any deeper . . . Confirm my observation, Officer."

Rostnikov was looking at the baby.

"I am not that smart, Inspector."

"Oh, but you are. You are a man to watch, Officer—?"

"Rostnikov, Porfiry Petrovich Rostnikov."

"I've had someone call an ambulance," said Luminiov. "Let's get out of the cold. When they take the baby and the body, I'll let you buy me a drink."

"I would like to go to the hospital with Alexander," said Rostnikov.

"Alexander?"

"The baby."

"Yes, Alexander. Sentiment can ruin a promising career," said Luminiov with a smile.

Rostnikov said nothing. The snow had completely stopped. Moscow was covered in white. It was winter, the favorite season of Russians.

SOMEONE ELSE

A Fred Carver story

John Lutz

FIRST APPEARANCE: *Tropical Heat*, 1986

John Lutz has two continuing P.I. series, the comic Alo
Nudger series set in his hometown of St. Louis and the
more serious Fred Carver series set in his adopted
home, Florida. The first Nudger story appeared in *First
Cases*, the first book in this series. This story first appeared in one of my PWA anthologies, *Justice for Hire*,
1990, and I'm pleased to present it to you for a second
time. Mr. Lutz has won two Shamus Awards—for a
Nudger short story, "Ride the Lightning," and for a
Carver book, *Kiss*—and the Life Achievement Award
from PWA, and has served as president of both PWA
and MWA.

This Wayne Garnett was Carver's first client in the
new office on Magellan Avenue in downtown Del
Moray, Florida, or maybe the whole mess wouldn't
have happened.

Carver had decided to separate his business from
Edwina as much as possible; some hairy situations had
evolved that hadn't needed to include her. So Carver
had stopped working out of her house by the sea,
where he lived with her. Edwina told him it wasn't
necessary, that she didn't mind him using the house
for an office. But she was in real estate, and when
Carver insisted, she got him a deal on a year's lease
on the office on Magellan, in a fairly new cream-stucco

building that also housed an insurance brokerage and a car rental agency and was across the street from the Art Deco courthouse and jail.

So there Carver found himself, sitting behind his gleaming new executive desk and staring at his new beige filing cabinets, and in walked Garnett out of the glaring afternoon heat and said, "The lettering on the door says this is a detective agency. You follow wayward wives?"

"I have," Carver said.

Which opened up a lot of possible clever remarks by Garnett, only he was a serious type and sat down and let out a long breath and didn't smile.

"Your wife?" Carver asked, meeting serious with serious.

Garnett nodded. He was a big man, about six feet tall and going to fat in a hurry. Maybe forty-five, fifty years old. He was wearing tan dress slacks, gray suede shoes, and a white polo shirt that had brown horizontal stripes that accentuated his paunch. He'd been handsome, but now his regular-featured face was fleshy and blotched, and his straight dark hair was thinning. Another five years and he'd be as bald on top as Carver. "Gloria's her name. Gloria Garnett. I'm Wayne Garnett. I own a car dealership over on West Palm Drive. Maybe you've seen it. Maybe you've seen our television commercial, where I show how you can afford payments on a new Volkswagen just by cutting back on smoking and junk food."

Enough about you, Carver thought. He said, "Tell me about Gloria."

And without asking about Carver's rates, Garnett began describing his problems with his wife. That should have been a warning to Carver, but he was the new boy on the block and eager to make good, and right now any client looked like luck.

"Gloria's younger than me," Garnett said. "Only twenty-eight years old." He fished his wallet from a hip pocket and drew out a color snapshot, which he tossed on the desk.

Carver bent forward and saw an attractive, dark-haired woman with dramatic Latin features. She was smiling into the camera, squinting a little in bright sunlight, and there was a teasing kind of fire in her dark eyes. A vivacious woman even in two dimensions. The word "spitfire" came to mind.

"Nice-looking," Carver said. "Why do you want her followed?"

"The reason you might guess. I think she's secretly seeing someone else. Things have changed between us—she's gotten colder toward me. I phone her from the office and she's hardly ever home. Her car's logging a lot of mileage she can't explain. Thing is, Carver, she's hiding something from me—I can tell! That gnaws on me, goddammit! I gotta know what it is! *Who* it is!"

"What if you don't like what I find out?"

"That won't concern you. I'll pay you in advance." He tilted sideways in his chair to raise one wide buttock and got out his wallet again. Pulled a wad of bills from it and peeled off ten hundreds and fanned them out on Carver's bare new desk. "Refund what you don't use, and tell me if and when you need more."

Carver got up and limped with his cane over to the shiny file cabinets. Garnett noticed the stiff left knee and the cane and looked for a moment as if he might have some misgivings, as if he doubted Carver could keep up with the wayward Gloria. Then he seemed to consider that the sign on the door had said Private

Investigator and that meant Carver could do the job, otherwise he'd be in some other line of work.

"I'll type up a standard contract for you to sign," Carver said, pulling open the top drawer on its smooth nylon casters.

"I don't wanna sign anything," Garnett said. "That's why I'm paying in cash. I don't want Gloria to ever be able to say I hired somebody to follow her, that I didn't trust her or I harassed her."

Carver figured that Garnett was already thinking ahead to possible divorce proceedings, as if his wife's infidelity could be taken for granted.

"If you're looking for absolute proof of adultery—" Carver began.

Garnett interrupted him. "I don't need absolute *proof*, Carver—I just wanna know! You understand?"

Carver understood enough to take the job. Wished later that he'd understood enough to turn it down.

The Garnetts lived on Verde Avenue, a palm tree–lined street in an old but fashionable part of town. Theirs was one of the few newer homes, an expensive brick ranch house set well back from the street and surrounded by a jungle of lush foliage.

Carver parked his ancient and rusting Oldsmobile convertible down the street where he could see the Garnetts' driveway. The car's canvas top was up to shade the interior from the fierce Florida sun, though it was only eight A.M., ten minutes before Wayne Garnett was due to leave for work at his car dealership.

Right on time, Garnett pulled out of the driveway in a black Volkswagen GT with tinted windows. He turned left, away from Carver, and the little car putt-putted smoothly around a gentle curve in the sun-dappled street and disappeared.

Gloria wasted little time. Carver had drunk only half the coffee he'd stopped to get at a McDonald's drive-through when a white VW convertible bounced out of the Garnett driveway. The little car's top was down and it passed Carver going fast and still accelerating. The pretty dark-haired woman in the photograph was driving.

Carver started the Olds and drove around the block in a hurry so he could catch up.

Gloria Garnett headed east, then turned north on Beachside Drive. She was driving slower now. Carver, in the Olds, hung far back. He could afford the distance between them; Beachside was wide and straight here, bordering the whitecaps rolling in on the pale stretch of sand. The fetid, rotting scent of the sea was pushed ashore by a soft breeze off the ocean. A low-flying gull with flashing white swings kept pace with the car for a while, then screamed as if in alarm and arced seaward, soaring on the breeze. Gloria drove as if she knew where she was going, her long black hair whipping in the whirl of wind in the little convertible.

She surprised Carver. Suddenly the car slowed, then made a right turn onto a deserted parking lot that overlooked a stretch of public beach.

Gloria stopped the convertible with its snub nose pointing toward the sea. Carver drove past the gravel lot and parked on the road shoulder where he could see what went on in the lot without being obvious.

He watched Gloria get out of her car and stride toward a wooden bench that was facing the ocean. She was wearing a loose-fitting blue blouse and a darker blue long skirt that billowed in the wind and occasionally afforded a glimpse of tanned, shapely legs. There was the same snap in her walk that he'd noticed in her eyes. When she reached the beach her sandals began flapping and tossing sand up behind her heels. She was carrying a book in one hand, a large straw purse in the other.

Carver drove onto the lot and parked at the other end, away from the VW convertible. He got out of the Olds and limped to an iron rail, the tip of his cane dragging in the gravel. He leaned casually on the warm rail and gazed at the sun-hazed horizon, as if studying the undulating, sparkling ocean.

The bench was at the edge of a concrete walkway that ran parallel with the sea. A few people were walking the beach barefoot, either in swimming trunks or suits or with their cuffs rolled up. Now and then someone fully dressed strolled past on the sidewalk that led to a cluster of condominiums farther down the beach. Gloria didn't seem to notice anyone. She'd sat down on the bench, put on a pair of sunglasses, and, facing the ocean, was engrossed in reading her book.

Gloria didn't glance up at the people who infrequently walked past the bench. After about half an hour, a blond woman in a white uniform—maybe a nurse's uniform—who was pushing an elderly white-haired man in a wheelchair, stopped near the bench. Carver figured they'd come from the condos up the beach. The old guy was hunched forward and had a blanket or shawl over him despite the warm morning. Probably a private nurse with her patient.

The woman sat down next to Gloria on the bench, and Gloria's head jerked up and back as if she hadn't been reading at all but had been dozing and was suddenly awakened. Then she sat with her head bowed, maybe reading again. The nurse said something to her, smiled, and got up and pushed the old man in the wheelchair back toward the condominium towers glimmering in the sun.

Gloria sat reading a while longer, not even glancing up when some teenage boys ran past yelling at each other. A few other passersby glanced over at her, then continued on their way.

After about twenty minutes, it struck Carver that she hadn't moved. Hadn't turned a page or looked up at a low-flying pelican flapping past. Asleep again?

Feeling uneasy, he took the three wooden steps to the beach, set his cane tentatively in the soft sand, and limped toward the bench.

When he was twenty feet away he noticed the dark stains spotting the sand beneath the bench. When he was ten feet away he knew the stains were blood.

When he limped around in front of the bench he saw that there were dark stains on the open book in Gloria Garnett's lap, that she was dead.

Lieutenant William McGregor was seated at his desk and adding powdered cream to his coffee. He stirred. Sipped. Smiled. He hadn't offered Carver any coffee.

McGregor was a towering blond man who looked more Swedish than Scottish. He had narrow shoulders and a lanky, loose-jointed frame, an obscene smile, and a wide gap between his front teeth that he often prodded with the pink tip of his tongue. He also had the most sour breath ever aimed at Carver. One of McGregor's friends might have told him about the breath, only McGregor had no friends and didn't deserve any. He liked it that way.

His office in Del Moray police headquarters was spacious and modern and had a window with a peek-a-boo view of the ocean several blocks away. He'd recently been promoted to Homicide, which was why he was interested in Gloria Garnett's death.

He picked up the packet he'd torn open and whose contents he'd sprinkled in his coffee and said, "They call this stuff nondairy whitener. Know why? 'Cause if you read the label close you find out there ain't a drop of cream or milk in it." He tossed the crumpled packet aside. "Kinda shit oughta be against the law."

"You called me here to talk about Gloria Garnett," Carver said. "Her murder *is* against the law."

"The M.E.'s still working on her," McGregor said, "but she was killed by a .38 bullet through the heart. That much we do know. What we don't know is what you were doing at the scene."

Carver told him. Everything. This was a homicide and nothing to get cute over.

McGregor leaned back and laced his fingers behind his long neck. He studied Carver with his creepy little close-set eyes. He said, "So you figure this nurse pushing the old fucker in the wheelchair did this Gloria with a silencer, hey?"

"I didn't say that."

"You implied it."

"I told you her head snapped back and then forward when the nurse sat down next to her on the bench. I thought then maybe she'd been dozing and had awakened suddenly. Now I'm telling you that might be when she was shot."

"By the nurse?"

"More likely by the old guy in the wheelchair. Had a gun with a silencer concealed beneath his shawl. The nurse probably sat down to prop up Gloria in case she started to fall and draw attention to what had happened."

"Don't make sense. Sounds about as real as the cream in this coffee."

"Find the nurse and the old guy, maybe it will make sense."

"There is no nurse and old guy. Not so far."

"What about Garnett? You talked to him yet?"

"Told him his wife was dead. He acted upset. Who wouldn't be? She was a fine-looking piece. Great bazooms. Younger than him, too, by about fifteen years."

Carver had forgotten how much he disliked McGregor, now it was coming back. "Why don't you get your sick mind working on finding out if he has any idea about who might have killed her?"

"He might have killed her himself," McGregor said. "In fact, he probably did. He's being questioned now."

Carver didn't understand this. "You can't have enough on him for a murder charge. You must know that."

"So right you are. We'll eventually have to let him walk." McGregor leaned back in his chair, gazed down his nose at Carver. "Something *you* oughta know. Garnett owns this car dealership out on West Palm, sells a couple of foreign makes. Maybe you seen him on TV lying his ass off about how you can give up cigarettes and Twinkies and afford a new car. Anyway, Narcotics got tipped a while back that he was also into the drug game in a big way. Know who tipped the narcs? Mrs. Garnett."

"She informed on her husband?" Carver didn't like where McGregor might be going with this. "Why would she do that?"

"Good question. But, hey, I got a good answer. Garnett was seeing a woman on the side, according to Gloria. He'd deny it whenever she'd ask him about it, and they'd have a big brawl. The neighbors could tell you all about it. Hubby beat her up about a month ago. She says he tried to choke her with her gold neck chain. The Garnetts didn't get along, it seems."

"Guess not."

"Interesting thing is," McGregor said, "she was having second thoughts about testifying against him. She really loved him, for all the twisted reasons women love scumbags like Garnett. When it came right down to it, I don't think she'd really have given us anything on him in court."

"Something we'll never find out," Carver said.

"That was the object of her murder," McGregor said. "Though if Garnett hadn't killed her, one of his associates would have eventually done it. The drug business is nasty. She was probably dead the moment she talked to us. Only so many ways to protect a witness, and none of 'em perfect."

Carver knew that was true.

"But we come now to a little lesson in international trade," McGregor said, "so listen close. Volkswagens are built in Mexico, some of them, and some of those are shipped to Garnett's dealership. In certain cars, somebody at the other end of the supply line in Mexico would replace the insulation above the headliners with cocaine, which Garnett would remove and wholesale here in the States. Gloria knew about it, had some trouble with hubby, and came to us. She was scared of him as well as in love with him, mixed-up cunt that she was. And she was supposed to give us her deposition against him after his arrest, which was going to take place when the next coke shipment arrived at his dealership. But without the wife's testimony, Narcotics has got no case. Nothing. They're over at the car dealership now searching for evidence, but they won't find any. It's all been removed."

"So Garnett found out his wife was going to rat on him and had her killed."

McGregor sat forward and said, "Almost right, Carver. He's got an airtight alibi for the time of her death—says he was with some friends. They'll swear to it. Drug buddies. They're lying, all of them. Know why?"

Carver knew why.

"That's right," McGregor said. "Garnett was the man in the wheelchair, the old guy with the gray wig and the shawl. And the gun equipped with a silencer."

Carver felt a seething rage boil up in his stomach, move through his body. He was squeezing the crook of his walnut cane so hard his knuckles were bloodless and ached. "And the nurse pushing him was his other woman."

"Hey, that's awful astute of you," McGregor said, "but too late. Gloria was in the habit of driving to the beach every morning and reading, and Garnett took advantage of that. And of you. Don't you get it, shit-for-brains? Garnett hired you so you could witness Gloria's murder by an old man in a wheelchair. So you could tell us it wasn't Garnett who killed his wife."

"But we know damned well it *was* him!"

McGregor's eyes got tiny and cold. "Do we? Does a judge? A jury? You saw a nurse and an old man in a wheelchair near Gloria . . . *maybe* at the time she was shot. Ever heard of reasonable doubt?"

Carver planted the tip of his cane and levered himself to his feet. If he hadn't had the bad leg he would have paced angrily, maybe punched a wall.

McGregor gave him a mean smile. "You're the reason for the reasonable doubt."

*   *   *

Carver didn't at all like furnishing a killer with an alibi. Bad for business. Bad for the soul.

Garnett would be occupied at police headquarters for a while longer. Carver figured if he was going to be an accessory to a perfect murder, a little breaking and entering was nothing to cause concern. Maybe there'd be something in Garnett's house on Verde Avenue that would provide a way to nail him for murdering his wife.

After parking down the block, Carver limped to Garnett's address and up the long and winding concrete driveway. Palm trees and azalea bushes lined the drive, making most of it, and the house, invisible from the street. A million cicadas ratcheted noisily in the bushes, but that was the only sound. A guy like Garnett, with a lot to hide, must like it here.

Carver rang the bell and waited a long time to make sure no one was home. Then he tried the knob. The front door was locked, but it had a window in it and he didn't see any alarm wiring on the glass.

After a glance around, he used his cane to break out the glass, then he reached in and released a deadbolt lock. He tried the door again, and it opened.

The inside of the house was cool and more luxurious than he'd expected. Modern furniture, all smoked glass and sharp angles. Peach-colored carpet and drapes. He could see through the kitchen and out sliding glass doors to a screened-in pool behind the house. The water in the pool was rippling gently, holding captive the sunlight that had filtered through the screen.

He roamed about, saw a desk in Garnett's office. The drawers yielded nothing other than the usual household correspondence and a few innocuous business letters. The bookshelf behind the desk contained automotive manuals and a stack of paperback western novels. On the desk's corner was a small empty brass picture frame; probably it had contained the photo of Gloria Garnett that her husband had shown to Carver when he'd hired him and made him an unwitting accomplice in murder.

The master bedroom was vast. It smelled strongly of rose-scented perfume, as if some had been spilled and would pervade the room forever. One wall was entirely mirror, and the bed was round and covered with a blue quilted spread. Carver set the tip of his cane in the soft carpet and limped over to one of the dressers.

It was Gloria's. The drawers contained expensive lingerie, sweaters, and blouses, yet they were only half full. The top drawer held a jewelry box, empty.

Garnett's dresser revealed that he wore silk underwear. Carver wasn't surprised. He opened other drawers and searched through socks and neatly folded sportshirts and denims. All expensive labels. In the bottom drawer, beneath some folded beachwear, lay half a dozen empty picture frames of various sizes.

Carver walked over to the closet and rolled open the tall sliding doors. There were a few dresses on one side of the closet, and the other side was stuffed with men's clothing. He looked at the empty wire hangers dangling between the dresses, wondering what it all meant.

He limped out of the bedroom and into the kitchen. The refrigerator was well stocked. There was a bottle of red wine chilling in a special temperature-controlled compartment. On top of the refrigerator was a wooden wine rack that held half a dozen more bottles, tilted forward so their contents would keep the corks from drying out.

A door from the kitchen led to the garage. Carver stood on the single step and looked at a silver-blue Mercedes convertible, the only vehicle in the three-car garage other than a ten-speed Schwinn bike and a red riding mower that looked like an expensive kid's toy. Somewhere in the garage a wasp droned like a miniature and continuous alarm buzzer. There was something about the way the Mercedes was parked, with its sleek nose almost touching the front wall of the garage, as if to leave maximum room behind the car.

Carver stood thinking about the empty picture frames, the depleted dresser drawers and closet in the master bedroom. He went back into Garnett's office and searched through some keys he'd noticed in one of the drawers.

It took him only a few seconds to find the spare keys to the Mercedes. He limped back out into the garage and opened the car's trunk.

It held three suitcases and a garment bag. He unzipped the bag partway and saw a silky dress. Worked the latches on one of the suitcases and opened it far enough to reveal a gauzy nightgown, a travel clock, and a small electric hair-dryer. The smallest suitcase, a blue nylon carry-on, contained stacks of ten- and twenty-dollar bills, fastened neatly with rubber bands. Hell of a lot of money.

Carver closed the trunk lid and leaned on it. The garage was warmer than the rest of the house and he was perspiring, but he hardly noticed. Gloria had been having second thoughts about testifying against her husband, McGregor had said. Maybe Wayne Garnett had also had second thoughts about his future.

Hot as it was in the garage, Carver felt ice on the back of his neck.

He was about to limp into the kitchen when he heard a car stop outside in the driveway. Quickly he made his way to the garage's overhead door and peered through one of its narrow dusty windows.

A cab had stopped in the driveway, far enough up so that whoever got out wouldn't be visible from the street.

Carver watched the cab back out and drive away, its exhaust fumes wavering in the heat. Watched the woman who had climbed out stride in her high heels up the sun-bleached driveway toward the house.

He reached over and punched the button that started the electric garage door opener.

The opener growled to life. The wide door jerked, then laboriously and noisily began to roll itself up section-by-section to flatten out again along the garage ceiling.

The woman standing surprised in the driveway wore a terrified expression. She was dainty and attractive, with strong Latin features and long dark hair too thick and wavy to tame. Her skin-tight blue skirt was short; so were her legs, but they were shapely and she had nice knees and ankles and could get by with any skirt she wanted to wear.

Carver could understand why, when she'd had second thoughts, so had Wayne Garnett. Why they'd chosen the ugly but only way out for both of them. She looked something like the woman in the photograph Garnett had shown Carver in the office. Put a blond wig on her and she'd look more like the nurse pushing the wheelchair on the beach—the one who'd watched while the woman Wayne Garnett had hired to carry a purse and a book, and drive to a bench by the sea and read—and whose corpse he'd later identified as that of his wife—died of a bullet to the heart.

Who had the victim been? One of life's untraceables, no doubt, without friends or relatives. Probably an illegal alien, or maybe a prostitute up from Miami. She'd been someone who didn't matter to Wayne Garnett. Or to his wayward wife.

Carver limped out onto the sun-washed driveway toward the woman. The cicadas were ratcheting again. Screaming their timeless, desperate mating call. Love making the world go round.

He said, "Hello, Gloria."

She backed a wobbly step and started to shake her pretty head in denial.

Then she shrugged, smiled sadly, and said hello back. Said it a certain way.

God, she was beautiful!

But not worth it.

POLO AT THE RITZ
A Nick Polo story
Jerry Kennealy

FIRST APPEARANCE: *Polo Solo*, 1987

Jerry Kennealy is not only a P.I. writer, but has been a
P.I. in San Francisco for many years. A former vice
president of the Private Eye Writers of America, he has
now gone on to write three successful suspense novels
in addition to his popular *Polo* books. This story first
appeared in the pages of *New Mystery*.

The Ritz. The words immediately bring visions of
high frescoed-ceiling lobbies with polished marble
walls, tuxedoed desk clerks and bellboys wearing styl-
ish red velvet jackets and fez hats. Couples looking
like young Freds and Gingers skipping lightly across
the parqueted dance floor. Starched waiters perfectly
balancing long-stemmed cocktail glasses on silver
trays. And that may be how it is even today at The
Ritz. The ones in Paris, London or New York. In San
Francisco you better tell the cab driver to take you to
the Ritz-Carlton, or you're in for a big surprise, because the just plain old Ritz is the pits. Or that other
rhyming word that may come to mind.

Our Ritz sits smack in the middle of The Tenderloin
District, an area given over to porno bookstores,
sleazy bars catering to hookers and dope dealers. The
prospective buyer has a wide variety to choose from:
heroin, cocaine, crack, ice, LSD, speedballs. Marijuana
is not considered dope in the Tenderloin. Too tradi-

tional. Too yuppy. The dealers are on every corner, young men with soft smiles and hard eyes, dressed in oversized topcoats with more inner pockets than the ones that Harpo Marx used to pull out all those rubber chickens and bicycle horns. Standing close to the dealer will be his batman, so called not because of the comic strip but because of the aluminum baseball bat swinging slowly from one hand to another. Baseball bats that will never see a playground, or a baseball for that matter. It's the new rage in urban weaponry. "I didn't mean to hit that man, Officer. I was just practicing my swing and his head got in the way."

The whores can be even deadlier than the dope dealers. Siliconed transvestites and transsexuals, faces splattered with makeup to keep the twelve o'clock shadow away. The more bizarre they are, the more money they make. A pimp would give away his last Cadillac El Dorado for a former basketball star that had gone through a sex change operation and had told the world about it on the Phil Donahue show. He'd throw in his Porsche if he–she had done a short stint as a priest or nun. For the old-fashioned shopper there are even mini-skirted girls that actually are girls.

The drug dealers give the hookers the prime spots on the street to peddle their wares, relying on the trickle-down economy of the Tenderloin. Eventually the money the whores get will find its way back to the dealers. A vice squad officer once described a Tenderloin hooker this way: "If she had as many needles sticking out of her as she had stuck into her, she'd look like a porcupine."

My appearance on the street turned the multitude into politicians at a no host bar. Business ceased. I had plainclothes cop written all over me. Anyone in clean clothes and wearing a tie in the Tenderloin had to be a cop. I used a quarter to tap on the grimy glass front door of the Ritz. A burned-out case, mid-fifties, thin hair the color of fireplace ash with a two days' growth of stubble on his face and red-rimmed eyes turned the lock and waved me in.

"Can I help you, Officer?" he asked.

I reached in my pocket and handed him a five-dollar bill.

"You ain't no policeman," he said in a two-pack a day hacker's voice, turning the bill over in his hand and examining it closely.

"Private," I said. "You in charge of security?"

"Day shift. But I just stay by the door. Don't let nobody in that can't show a room key or who ain't got legitimate business."

I tried to hazard a guess as to just what would be considered legitimate business. Probably anything except assembling nuclear weapons.

He blinked his rheumy eyes and ran the sleeve of a battered tan herringbone sports coat under his nose. "What I gotta do to keep this here piece of paper?" he asked, waving the five-dollar bill at me, then jamming it quickly in his coat pocket.

I took out a business card and wrote down the name Bill Casserly on the back of it. "Go to Mr. Casserly's room. Tell him I'd like to meet with him. It's about the murder of Wayne Salkind."

Someone banging on the door interrupted his train of thought for a moment. He let in a redhead in a tight green dress made of nylon meant to look like silk. The redhead had long, curvy legs covered with black fishnet stockings that had holes big enough to let a trout wiggle through. The red wig was slightly askew and a beard was showing through the rouge. It was either time for a shave or to call it a night.

I got a quick once-over, an obvious no-sale sign rang up and high heels clattered over to the elevator.

I turned my attention back to the doorman.

"What's your name?"

For the time it took him to reply you would have thought I was Alex Trebeck asking a Double Jeopardy question.

"Dick," he finally said, giving his nose another sleeve wipe.

"Well, Dick. Go get Mr. Casserly for me or I'll have to take that five spot back."

Poor old Dick took that as a real threat. Had it been a thousand-dollar bill, I'd have been reluctant to reach into his grimy coat pocket.

He turned around and slowly made his way to the elevator.

The lobby crowd, frail-looking elderly men and women bundled up to the chins, stared back at me from faded couches and cracked-vinyl lounge chairs, going back to their newspapers or just gazing out the window when they got tired of the sight of me.

I moved around the cracked-tile floor, my rubber soles making sickly, sticking sounds, and waited for Mr. Casserly.

I could have saved myself, or rather the insurance company, the five-dollar tip I'd given poor old Dick, and just gone and knocked on Casserly's door myself, but Dick certainly looked like he could use the money, and it kept me from seeing what the rest of the Ritz looked like.

I had a good idea. My client was an insurance company that insured a neighboring hotel, the Wilson, less than a block away. The Wilson was no better, and

maybe worse than the Ritz itself. Eleven months ago
a long-time tenant at the Wilson, Wayne Salkind, had
been murdered. Beaten and robbed, dying two days
later in San Francisco General Hospital as a result of
the beating. The police had never arrested the killer,
who was described by Bill Casserly, then the night
security man at the Wilson Hotel, as a young black
male in his mid-twenties.

Wayne Salkind was close to seventy, a retired mer-
chant seaman, like many of the Wilson's tenants. Judg-
ing from the police reports, Salkind didn't have much:
some battered luggage, a dark blue suit tailored for
him in Hong Kong that they buried him in, some casual clothes, shoes, underwear. Nothing worth stealing,
so whoever had killed him had got nothing much but
what was in the poor man's pockets.

Salkind had a small pension and a monthly social
security check. He also had a daughter in Des Moines,
Iowa, who hadn't seen her father in forty years. She
came to San Francisco for the funeral. She saw his
casket. She saw the police reports. She saw an attorney, who saw that for all its shabby appearance the
Wilson was a prosperous operation owned by a
wealthy gentleman who operated a dozen similar hotels in the city and who paid his insurance premiums
on time.

Bingo. While the police department was not able to
supply justice by catching the murderer, Mr. Salkind's
daughter, with the help of her attorney, would see
that civil justice prevailed. The Wilson Hotel's security
system should have prevented the terrible tragedy
from happening in the first place. Money would never
bring back her father, the tearful daughter said, but a
million dollars would teach the hotel owners a lesson

and spare other grieving children from suffering a similar loss.

I had a friend on the police department run the Wilson Hotel's address through the computer. In the year prior to the murder, there had been forty-six calls for police assistance. Calls ranging from burglaries to assaults and rapes. The last two assaults were by a suspect whose description matched that of the man who had allegedly beaten Salkind to death. Not a pretty picture, unless you were the attorney representing Salkind's daughter.

The Wilson Hotel's security system consisted of Bill Casserly sitting in a lobby couch and supposedly wandering the hallways from eight in the evening until four in the morning. In exchange for his services, Casserly was given a break on his rent.

Since Mr. Salkind's death the hotel had installed a TV monitor and an around-the-clock shift of uniformed security guards. A classic case of closing the barn door much too late.

The case was getting ready to go to trial. My job was to locate Casserly before Wayne Salkind's daughter's attorney did. Evaluate Casserly and see just how much he would either help or hurt the insurance company's case.

Casserly had left for parts unknown shortly after Salkind's death. I traced him back to New York where he'd disappeared. I ran credit checks on him with all the major agencies, but people who end up living in places like the Ritz and the Wilson don't have much to do with credit cards. If Casserly hadn't been arrested for being drunk and disorderly just three days ago, I probably never would have developed his current address.

Dick came shuffling back to the lobby a few minutes

later. He held up his hands in a display of defeat.
"Not there," he said. "I think I might have seen him
leave earlier this morning."

"Where would he go?" I asked, already reaching
for my money clip.

Dick frowned and looked at his palm as if trying to
read his own fortune. "Hard to say, mister."

I dropped another five-dollar bill in his hand.
"Think hard."

"Probably the Fireball, down the street. They serve
pretty good food and the drinks are cheap."

"Let's go take a look," I suggested.

He screwed up his face and shook his head. "I can't
leave here, mister. I'm working."

I dropped another five-dollar bill into his palm.
"Find someone to take your place for a few minutes."

The Fireball had a neon sign out front showing an
orange flame dropping into a dark blue sea. The orange was faded and the neon tubes circling the ball
were broken in spots and filled with rusty-looking
water.

The inside smelled like all down-and-out bars do;
the thick odors from years of spilled booze and emp-
tied bladders, the walls impregnated with cigarette and
cigar smoke, the floor black from ground-out butts.
Two battered pinball machines stood against one wall.
A large-screen TV on the end of the bar was showing
a billiard match.

On a scale between dirty and filthy, the needle was
closer to filthy, still there were at least twenty people
inside, a half dozen sitting at the bar, the others scattered around scarred wooden tables set in front of an
open kitchen in the back of the room.

A Chinese chef was busy scooping up rice and

something green onto oatmeal-colored plates. A hand-printed sign showed that the special of the day was chow mein.

Old Dick nudged me with an elbow, unfortunately from the same sleeve he used as a handkerchief. "That's him over at the bar," he said. "Guy with the raincoat."

Casserly was easy to spot. It hadn't rained in six months. I thanked Dick and left him holding his empty paw out in expectation of more money.

I slid onto the stool next to Casserly. He was somewhere in his sixties, a long, drawn face. He was bald, with untidy wisps of gray hair settling about his ears.

The bartender, a six footer with a big belly, hustled over as soon as he saw me.

"Bud light," I said, wanting to order something I could drink directly from the bottle, "and give this gentleman whatever he's having."

Casserly moved his head slowly, as if it weighed. He had sad, bloodhound eyes. His face was grainy white and puffy like boiled rice. He reached for his glass and drained it. I could hear the ice hitting his teeth.

"Who're you?" he asked in a slurred voice.

"I want to talk to you about Wayne Salkind's murder."

The bartender put my beer down in front of me, along with a glass and a paper napkin covered with drawings of racehorses. He filled Casserly's glass half-way up with a bottle of the house bourbon.

I dropped some money on the counter, but the bartender waved it away. "No charge, Officer," he said, trying to make his voice sound sincere. Looking like a policeman does have its perks sometimes.

Casserly snorted. "Cop, huh. I knew it. I knew it. It's all gone, anyway. I got just one left."

"Just one, huh?" I said, trying not to sound too confused.

"Shit. You'd think they'd last longer, wouldn't you? All that shit going on? You think the prices would go up. Damn Arabs. That's what it is. The Arabs and the Russians. Damn Russians need the money, so they're dumping all their gold on the market. Keeps the price down. Dirty bastards."

I was sorry I hadn't taken a better look at the label on the house bourbon. Whatever Casserly was drinking, it was powerful stuff.

"Just one," he murmured into his glass. "Hell, I knew you'd find me."

"You did, huh?" When they're talking like that you don't want to interrupt them. Keep them talking is the name of the game, even though you don't know what the hell it is they're talking about.

"Should have stayed back east," Casserly continued in a voice heavy with regret. "But, man, it's expensive back there." His eyes roamed around the dingy bar. "Worse than here."

He stayed silent for a full minute.

"Where is the one you have left?" I prodded him.

He took a swig of his drink, rolling the bourbon around in his mouth as if it were a fine wine before swallowing it. "Guess it don't matter much now, anyway, does it?"

"Guess not," I agreed, but to what I didn't know.

He put his drink down, leaned back on his stool, dug his right hand into his pants pocket and slowly pulled it out, dropping a yellow coin on the bar. "Krugerrand," he said. "Funny about that. They got the same amount of gold as them Canadian coins or the

American Eagle, but they're worth less. Why the hell is that?"

I picked up the coin. It was wrapped in a piece of Saran wrap–type plastic.

"I never should have come back, huh?" Casserly said.

"Would you have got me if I stayed back east?"

"I doubt it," I said, the dim lightbulb in my brain finally stammering to life. "How many coins did Salkind have?"

"Don't you now?"

"We just had a rough idea."

He shook his glass, the ice cubes rattling around like dice. "One hundred of them. Kept them in a leather case. Beautiful damn things."

I hadn't paid much attention to the price of gold, but I didn't think it had gotten over the $350 an ounce price in the last year. "How did you know Salkind had them?"

Casserly tapped his glass on the warped mahogany bar. "Damn fool told me. Right in here. Drunk as a skunk. Didn't usually drink that much. Retired sailor. Been all around the world. Bored the shit out of you with his stories. That night he was really drunk. Pissed off at them damn Ruskies for dumping all their gold on the market. He worried about them damn coins all the time. Kept them in a locker sometimes, sometimes in his room. I told him I was interested in buying a couple."

"So you saw your chance and killed Salkind."

Casserly's eyes turned inward and his forehead corduroyed in thought. "Damn it, man. I was going to buy one. Thought it might be a good investment. Then I saw the case with all that gold. Went kind of crazy I guess. Never saw that much money at one time before.

Salkind was right though. The Arabs and the Russians. They fucked up the market."

I waved the bartender over and pointed at Casserly's glass. "Give him a double. It may be a long time between drinks."

THE PIG MAN

A Saxon story

Les Roberts

FIRST APPEARANCE: *An Infinite Number of Monkeys,* 1987

Les Roberts was the first winner of the PWA/St. Martin's Press Best First Private Eye Novel contest. The book introduced his L.A. P.I. Saxon, and was nominated for a Shamus. Since then he has gone on to create his most popular protagonist, Cleveland P.I. Milan Jacovich. Of all the winners of the contest Mr. Roberts seems to have taken the ball and run the farthest with it. He has written fifteen novels, and went on to become president of PWA. This story first appeared in *Deadly Allies II* in 1994.

I make half my living involved with people you'd never ask to dinner. Punks, wise guys, skels, grifters, junkies, hookers, and the bigger, dirtier fish who feed off them. It can get sticky sometimes. Nevertheless, I don't consider myself a violent person. I cross the streets to avoid confrontation, and when I do find myself hip-deep in hard guys and loaded guns, I keep kicking myself for not paying more attention to my second career, which is acting. It's why I came to Los Angeles in the first place, and while no one in their right mind would call show business a kindlier, gentler profession than being a private investigator, it's considerably less dangerous.

My agent had packed me off to Minnesota for a

picture, which sounded okay until they had an early snow and fell behind schedule, and I wound up doing seven weeks in a town so bereft of anything to do that the locals think it's big time when they drive over to Duluth on a Saturday night and have supper at Denny's. Tends to lull one into a feeling of safety and security to spend so much time in a place where the most heinous crime they've ever heard of is crossing against the municipality's single red light.

So when I came home to Los Angeles I was ready for some excitement. I wasn't prepared for terror and sudden death.

Since my plane arrived in L.A. at nearly midnight on a Sunday, I hired a limo to ferry me from the airport to my rented house on one of the canals in Venice. Anyone who thinks you can't drive from LAX to Venice must be thinking of the city in Italy; we have one in Los Angeles, too, just a few blocks from the ocean, built as a tourist attraction near the turn of the century and now home to a colorful collection of yuppies, druggies, elderly home owners who've been there thirty years, and a counter-culture stunning in its infinite variety. If you don't believe me, check out Ocean Front Walk some Sunday afternoon, where third runners-up in a Michael Jackson look-alike contest and turbaned evangelists and one-man bands on roller skates zoom past Small World Books and the endless line of stalls and shops selling sunglasses and T-shirts.

The limo was an indulgence I couldn't afford but felt I'd earned. The backseat, the well-stocked bar, and the wraparound sound system made me feel like a Sybarite. I like that word—like a warring tribe of ancient Judea. "And Samson rose up and slew the Sybarites. . . ." Of course, Samson had not slain the

Sybarites at all; they'd simply moved to Los Angeles, bought a BMW, and subscribed to *Daily Variety*.

I had invited my adopted son, Marvel, to join me in the wilds of Minnesota, but he'd turned his big brown eyes on me and said, "You got to be kidding!" So he went to stay with my best friend and my assistant, Jo Zeidler, and her husband Marsh. Jo spoils him and Marsh talks basketball to him more intelligently than I can, so Marvel didn't complain about the living arrangements.

I paid off the limo driver after we'd struggled into the bungalow together with seven weeks' worth of luggage, tipping him less lavishly than I'd planned when he observed that I must be carrying the baggage for the entire Yugoslavian army. Nobody likes a smartass.

It was good to get home after so long, to be surrounded by my own books and paintings and furniture. And my plants. Since my lifestyle doesn't allow for pets, I'm a plant freak. I have more than fifty in varicolored pots all over the living room and about eight in my bedroom, including a ficus I'd nursed back from near-extinction and moved from my last residence in Pacific Palisades. My house sometimes resembles the set of a Tarzan movie. My next-door neighbor, Stewart Channock, had graciously consented to come in and care for the greenery while I was gone, as well as pick up and forward my mail and start my car every few days so the battery wouldn't expire.

I refuse to eat airplane food, so after dumping my bags I checked the refrigerator. Not much after seven weeks of absence—a bottle of Chardonnay, a six-pack of Guinness Stout with one missing, and a forgotten wedge of cheese that had outlived its usefulness. Nothing you could make a meal out of. What I really wanted was the kind of fancy omelette Spenser always cooks before he makes love to Susan Silverman on the living room floor—but I was out of both eggs and Susan.

Sighing, I changed into a sweatshirt and jeans and went out to my car, which by prearrangement I park across the street in the lot of an apartment building. My destination was an all-night market four blocks away. Even in the dark I could see that someone had scrawled WASH ME in the dust on the trunk, a not unreasonable request after the car had sat out in the elements for seven weeks.

I was pleased that the engine started and made a mental note to buy Stewart a bottle of scotch for his trouble. I switched on the headlights. The windshield was smeared with an overlay of greasy California grit, in which someone had written with a wet finger: CIA. Damn kids, I thought as I Windexed the glass with a paper towel. It's not a bad area I live in, it just ain't a great one, but then unless you're in Beverly Hills or Bel Air, there are no great neighborhoods in Los Angeles.

The next morning I called my various children, friends, and lovers to announce my return, made plans to pick up Marvel that evening, walked to the corner for a *Times*, and read it out on my balcony with a mug of coffee at my side. Los Angeles doesn't have much going for it anymore except its weather; being able to read the paper outside in October is one of the few pleasures we have left.

I went into the small den I'd constructed from a storage room on the second floor of the house and booted up my computer. I'd ascertained from Jo that there was nothing pressing at the office and had decided to take a day for myself before getting back into the swing of things. I sat there reading the scrolling screen. Travel fatigue made it tough, trying to get my head back into reviewing some of my old cases, including a few that I hadn't yet closed, but it beat hell out of wearing a tie, fighting the freeways, punching a time clock, and putting up with crap from a boss. We self-employed people have the best life imaginable—if we can make a living.

By three o'clock I was in high gear. Overdue bills were paid, overdue letters written, and I was feeling almost back to normal. Until something hit my window with a thump.

I work beside a sliding glass door with a peaceful view of the canal, replete with noisy ducks, an occasional rowboat or paddleboat, and every so often an empty Slurpee cup or a used condom floating by. The window overlooking the street is across the room, and when the sound made me glance over there, something wet was running down the glass. I heard a voice, raspy with hatred, scream, "CIA *pig!*"

I ran to the window in time to see a battered brown Dodge van roaring around the corner as if the hounds of Hell were snapping at its tailpipe. On the sidewalk just below my window a can of Budweiser beer was still rolling.

I remembered the writing on my windshield I'd dismissed as a kid's prank, and a strange burning started in my stomach like yesterday's bratwurst sandwich. I didn't realize it then, but it was the icy heat of fear.

At six o'clock I went over to the cinder-block house next door with which mine shared a common front yard. Stewart Channock answered my knock holding a drink, wearing the dress shirt and tie in which he worked all day as a financial consultant, whatever that was. I didn't really know Stewart well; we were more neighbors than friends. We said hello in the parking lot, shared a gardener, and he'd kindly offered to water my plants while I was gone.

"Welcome home," he said. "When'd you get back?"

"Last night, late."

"Come on in. Drink?"

"I need one," I said.

He went into the kitchen and poured me more than a jigger of scotch. I swallowed it down as though I was thirsty.

"Hope I didn't kill your plants—I even talked to them. About football."

"You did a great job, Stewart. I appreciate it. Uh— when was the last time you started my car?"

He frowned, thinking. "Wednesday, I guess. Did the battery die?"

"No, no. Was anything—written on the windshield?"

"Written on the . . .? No, why?"

I told him what I'd found and about the beer can incident that afternoon and the brown Dodge van.

He laughed.

"It's not funny," I said.

"Sure it is. Listen, the people walking the streets in this town are Looney Tunes. You start letting them get to you, you might as well go back to Wisconsin to stay."

"Minnesota. But what if this guy thinks I really am with the CIA and wants to kill me?"

"Then he would have done it, and not left his calling card. Come on, this isn't one of your movies."

Right there you could tell Stewart wasn't in show business. Actors call them pictures, directors call them films, and distributors and theater owners call them shows. No one in the business ever uses the word "movie."

"So you think I should ignore it?"

"What's your other option? Go tell the cops some-one threw a beer can at you and wrote on your car, but you don't know who he is? What do you think, they're going to stake out the street and wait for him to do it again?"

I nibbled at my drink, feeling more than a little foolish. He was right, of course; I was overreacting. Seven weeks in the North Woods with nothing to do but watch haircuts, eating the Velveeta cheese which was a small town hotel's idea of gourmet food, and living out of a suitcase takes its toll, and I was un-doubtedly stretched thin.

"All right, Stewart, I'll forget it," I said, getting up. "And thanks again for the caretaking."

I went back to my own house, picking up the beer can and putting it in the big bag I take to a recycling center every few weeks. At least I'd made two and a half cents on the deal.

Jo and Marsh had invited me for dinner, and it was good to see them again. It was even better seeing Marvel. In the four years he'd been living with me I'd watched him grow from a scared, skinny adolescent who could barely read and write into a handsome, athletic, and witty young man who was beginning his senior year in high school. Considering the adoption had been unplanned and almost out of necessity rather than any desire on my part to share my life with a strange black kid, it had worked out well. He'd be-come part of who I am, a part I hadn't known existed, and I'd evidently done a damn good job raising him, because he was turning into a real champ.

I spent the evening recounting war stories from the

trenches in Duluth, and we didn't get back home until nearly eleven, late for a school night. Marvel went to sleep and I sat up and watched Johnny and then Dave, a habit I'd fallen into on location when there wasn't anything else to do.

The next morning I was refreshed and raring to go, but my feeling of well-being evaporated like a raindrop in Death Valley when I went out to get my car and drive it to my office in Hollywood and saw someone had spray-painted CIA in red letters on the sidewalk, with an arrow pointing to my door.

I've lived in big cities all my life, Chicago before L.A., and I've steadfastly refused to become one of those urban paranoiacs who triple-lock their doors, scan the street for possible muggers, and sleep with a .44 Magnum under their pillows which will undoubtedly discharge someday and blow off an ear. But this CIA business had me worried.

Trying to keep my mind on my work at the office was a bear. I kept worrying what might be happening at the house while I wasn't there. I decided to go home early.

I'd stopped at the store on my way home and picked up the very basics a gourmet cook like me needs to simply survive a few days—butter, garlic, tomato sauce and tomato paste, several different wedges of cheese that were not Velveeta, and milk. After changing into comfortable sweats and a pair of deck shoes with too many holes in them to wear outside, I went up to my den and sat down at my desk, reading while I ate the linguine with the sauce I'd made from scratch.

Then I heard the raspy shout from the street again. "CIA *pig!*"

This time I got to the window in time to see him. The Pig Man. He was over six feet tall, in his early forties with a droopy mustache, slim and ropy with a slight potbelly, long dirty-blond hair flowing almost to his shoulders from a balding crown, in blue jeans and a turquoise muscle shirt, and just climbing into the Dodge van parked halfway down the street. The set of his shoulders was tense and rigid. As far as I knew, I'd never set eyes on him before.

He sat in the van for a moment. From my vantage point I could only see him from the neck down, his fists clenched on the steering wheel. Finally he banged them on the dashboard before starting the motor and peeling away from the curb, leaving a strip of rubber. It was profoundly disturbing. God knows there are enough people ticked off at me for good reason without having to worry about some deluded stranger.

I dumped the remainder of my lunch into the garbage disposal and poured myself a Laphroaig, neat. I never drink during the day, but I was wound as tight as a three-dollar watch. Anybody bizarre enough to throw a beer can at my window and spray-paint my sidewalk was capable of worse.

Just past three the phone rang. My agent, asking me how it had gone in Minnesota and was I interested in reading for a new series on the Fox network. I was and I wasn't; getting tied down to a six-days-a-week job didn't appeal to me, but the kind of money they pay you for a series did. I was standing in the middle of the room with the phone cradled against my shoulder, pulling yellow leaves off my schefflera plant, when I glanced out the window and saw the brown van come around the corner again and park across the street.

"I'll call you back," I said. I hung up and went to the window, being careful to stay well out of sight. The Pig Man got out, cast a look of loathing toward

my house, and went into the building across the street.
I waited for about two minutes, then grabbed a pencil
and notepad and went downstairs to copy the number
on his license plate.

I peered into the front seat of the paneled van, half
expecting to see a claymore mine or a flamethrower
or a box of hand grenades. All that was in evidence,
however, was a crumpled Styrofoam box from Burger
King and a few cans of Budweiser, one empty. That
was hardly damning evidence; there must be at least a
million people in greater Los Angeles who drink Bud.

I came back inside, half expecting a bullet to smash
into my back. There were twelve apartments in the
building across the street, and I wondered which one
he was visiting, whether its window faced mine. I usually leave my drapes open all the time so the plants
can get light, but now I pulled them shut. I was as
safe in my own home as I was ever going to be, and
the security felt woefully inadequate.

Marvel came home and we chatted for a few minutes—it was World Series time and to my horror he
was rooting for Oakland. But he had homework to do
and repaired to his room, his stereo making the whole
house tremble. I tried to read, but I couldn't concentrate. Instead I paced and chain-smoked, every so
often sneaking a peek through the closed drapes to
see if the Dodge van was still there.

It was.

Somewhere around dinnertime I heard Stewart
Channock going into his house. Some human compan-
ionship would have been welcome, and I had the urge
to walk next door and have a drink with him, but he
would have thought it peculiar; we didn't have that
close a relationship. We had nothing in common. I
don't understand people who move numbers around

all day long, and I was sure he was equally mystified
by those who chase around after insurance cheats, em-
bezzlers, skips, children kidnapped by divorced parents, and occasionally, people who kill.

I decided I didn't want to be in the house anymore
that evening. My paranoia was going to turn me into
a candidate for the rubber room if I stayed there much
longer. I waited for Marvel to finish his studying and
we went out to a Japanese restaurant for sushi and
saki. As usual, Marvel talked up a storm, and it took
my mind off my troubles.

We got home at ten o'clock, and I noted with relief
that the brown van was gone. But in the living room
the drapes across the window were blowing. Marvel
went over to investigate, and his shoes crunched on
long, wicked shards of broken glass that hadn't been
there when we left.

"Marvel, stay back!" I said.

He froze, looking at me with eyes that were just
this side of frightened. I went past him and pulled the
drapes aside.

The window had been shattered, and lying on the
carpet amid the debris was a big rock. If I had been
sitting by the window with the drapes open, reading,
I would have been decapitated. The skin on the back
of my neck tingled unpleasantly.

Enough was enough.

The next morning, slightly cranky from a hangover
and from the onerous task of cleaning up the glass
from my carpet, I was at the front desk of the Culver
City division of the Los Angeles Police Department,
talking to the desk officer, whose silver name tag said
he was L. Tedescu.

I put the rock on the desk in front of him. "My

name is Saxon," I said, and told him my address. "This came through my living room window last night."

He looked at it without emotion. "See who did it?"

"I wasn't home at the time."

L. Tedescu's eyebrows—or eyebrow, rather, he only had one that went clear across his forehead—lifted.

"I'm being harassed," I went on, and told him about the man in the brown Dodge van. "From his age and the way he looked, the way he was dressed, I'd guess he was probably a Vietnam veteran with a grudge against the CIA."

"*Are* you with the CIA, Mr. Saxon?"

A real rocket scientist, L. Tedescu. I felt the essence of a headache starting behind my eyes. If I didn't get at least three aspirin down my throat in the next few minutes it was going to be a bitch kitty. "First off, if I were with the CIA I wouldn't tell you. Secondly, I'd take care of it myself."

"Don't even think about taking the law into your own hands, sir," he said pompously. "You'll be the one in trouble."

"If I was going to do that I wouldn't have come here for help. I have the guy's license number." I pushed the number from my notepad across the glass-topped counter. L. Tedescu looked at it as if he could divine the mysteries of the ages from it. Then he handed it back to me. "There's not much we can do about this."

"Why not?"

"He hasn't committed any crime."

"Throwing a rock through a window isn't a crime?"

"You didn't see it. You don't know it's the same man."

"Who else could it be?"

He looked at me, his face a mask of apathy. "You'd know that better than I would, sir."

"Well, what about screaming outside my window? It scares the crap out of me."

"That may be, but it's not a crime."

"Disturbing the peace?"

He shook his head. "We'd have to arrest everyone who raised his voice. Now, if he calls you on the phone and makes threats, that's a crime. But if he does it in person it isn't, and we can't take any official action."

For a bit I was too stunned to reply. The best I could come up with was "That's the dumbest thing I ever heard."

L. Tedescu's eyes turned to slits. "It's the law."

The rock sat incongruously on the desk between us. "He spray-painted the sidewalk. He wrote CIA on the city sidewalk. Defacing public property?"

"Yes it is, and he probably did it. But you didn't see him." He put his hand on the rock and moved it a few inches toward me. "Look, Mr. Saxon—right now, not five hundred yards from where we're standing, someone's probably selling illegal drugs to eight-year-olds. Armed robberies happen at gas stations and convenience marts four or five times a night in this division. People getting behind the wheel of a two-thousand-pound car when they're too drunk or stoned even to walk, driving up on a sidewalk and killing a kid. Rape. Spouse abuse. Child abuse. And I won't even mention the hookers and drug dealers and the knife fights in the bars."

"I understand all that . . ."

"I'm glad you do. Los Angeles just doesn't have nearly enough cops—even if what you know this guy to be doing was illegal, it'd be pretty low on our priority scale." He ran his fingers through his mouse-brown hair. "If he does anything else, if you *catch* him at it, let us know, all right? Otherwise . . ." He turned both hands palms up to show me he was powerless. "I can't even write up a report."

I glared at him for a moment, clenching my teeth to bite back all the angry, frustrated things I wanted to scream. Then I spun on my heel and stalked toward the glass doors. My righteous indignation was like a steel rod up the middle of me.

"Mr. Saxon?"

I stopped and turned back eagerly, hoping he'd change his mind and write up a report, that the police, whose motto in Los Angeles is "To Protect and Serve," would hunt down the Pig Man in the brown van so I could go on with my life and my work and not be spooked by every zephyr that stirred a tree or every stray cat prowling in a Dumpster for its dinner. "Yes, Officer?"

He held his hand out to me, and it wasn't until I got all the way back to the desk that I saw what the offering was.

"Did you want your rock?"

It's only a short walk from the police station to the sheriff's office in the Culver City municipal center. Last year's tragic murder of a young actress has made it more difficult to get someone's name and address from their automobile license plate, but nothing's impossible if you have a friend in a high place. At least I hoped she was still a friend.

Female law enforcement officers don't often look like Angie Dickinson or Stepfanie Kramer, but Sergeant Sharyl Capps came pretty close, with a headful of honey-blonde hair, green eyes, and an overbite that could drive a person crazy. We'd met when I was researching my first novel some years ago and had enjoyed a nine-week fling that ended, as most such relationships do, with a gradual distancing that eventually turned to nothing at all. She was almost as tall as I, with several medals and commendations in her service record. I wasn't sure how I would be received, but she smiled when I walked into her office—it wasn't the broadest, most welcoming smile I'd ever seen, but it was a smile nonetheless—and shook my hand in a manner that was a little too businesslike, considering.

"It's been a while," she said. The ironic lilt in her voice just made her more appealing.

"I guess it has. I've been busy."

"I know. I've seen some of your movies and TV stuff. I guess you're doing all right. Are you still a P.I. too?"

"Whenever anyone asks me. Sharyl, I've got a problem."

"I know." I suppose I deserved the dig. When I'd been with her I was commitment-phobic, and I guess she was still a little miffed. I winced. Then I told her about my adventures of the last few days. Her face remained passive but the amusement in her eyes annoyed hell out of me. "You're a big tough private eye," she said. "Why don't you take care of it yourself?"

"Take the needle out, Sharyl—this is serious."

"Well, the police told you right. There's not a damn thing they can do." She shrugged. "Nothing I can do, either."

I held out the paper with the license number. "You can run this for me."

She looked at it without touching it. "I'd get my butt in a sling," she said.

I thought about remarking that it would look good

even in a sling, but wisely desisted. "I'm not going gunning for him," I said. "Just on television."

"Then what's the point?"

"I'd like to know who my enemy is, at least."

She started to shake her head when I said, "Sharyl, you wouldn't want my murder on your conscience, would you?"

She regarded me narrowly. "Not unless I got to do it myself," she said. She took the paper from me, pointing to a chair opposite her desk. "Park it. I'll be back in a minute."

She left me sitting there with nothing to do. Unlike dentists and lawyers, deputy sheriffs don't have back-dated magazines in their offices to browse through while you wait. I did notice a framed photograph on her desk, a smiling Sharyl and a big beefy muscle-hunk, both on bicycles down by Venice Beach, looking the way Southern Californians in love are supposed to.

In twenty minutes she was back.

"Who's your friend?" I said, pointing at the photo.

"He's my partner. Name's Frank Trone."

"Was that taken one day out on bicycle patrol?"

"None of your business. Look, Saxon, I've already violated procedure here. You want this stuff or not?" She waved some computer printouts at me.

I sighed. Sometimes it seems as though life is one long series of what ifs and might have beens. "Sure," I said.

"The van is registered to one Harlan Panec," she said, handing me one of the printouts. Harlan Panec lived over in North Hollywood, in the San Fernando Valley. Not a high-rent district.

"I never heard of him."

"You sure?"

"Sharyl, if you'd ever met a guy named Harlan Panec, wouldn't you remember?"

"Just for the hell of it, I put him through the computer to see if he had a sheet," she said. "He's a naughty boy. Forty-three years old, dishonorable discharge from the army in '73, misdemeanor possession of marijuana, assault, drunk and disorderly, and several citations for speeding."

I jotted the address down in my notebook.

Sharyl frowned. "Stay away from this guy, Saxon."

I tried to be casual. "Why? He's not exactly a master criminal."

"Because." Her laser gaze reduced me to a small dust pyramid. "You're not nearly as tough as you think you are."

I called a glazier to fix the window, but of course he couldn't come for three days, so I made do with natural air-conditioning and prayed for no rain. The brown van didn't appear the rest of that day, or if it did, the Pig Man didn't indulge his penchant for screaming under windows like Brando in *A Streetcar Named Desire*, but the curiosity that was eating a hole in my gut, the twin of the one caused by fear, got to me by the next morning.

I had to see Harlan Panec, tell him he was mistaken, that he had me mixed up with somebody else, so I could get on with my life without waiting for another rock to come through my window—or worse.

The street address Sharyl Capps had given me was just off Lankershim Boulevard near Vanowen Street, a neighborhood of small industrial buildings and a few houses that were tiny, old, and dilapidated. Not many of the residents spoke English as their first language, and when I pulled my car around the corner at about

eleven o'clock they were all out on the street in the
sunshine, watching the black-and-white squad cars and
the city ambulance, talking in Spanish or Korean or
Farsi in the hushed tones reserved for the presence
of death.

I pulled over to the curb and watched with them.
There must have been twenty uniformed policemen
running around on the barren front lawn of the house
where Harlan Panec lived. The brown van was parked
in the weed-choked driveway, and behind it an ancient
Volkswagen Bug. On the sagging porch a woman of
about forty, in baggy jeans and a tie-dyed shirt that
was a holdover from the Woodstock years, was crying
and screaming while a policewoman who didn't look
like Angie Dickinson tried to talk to her. There were
reddish-brown stains on the hysterical woman's hands
and arms. It was hard to tell because emotion dis-
torted her features, but she looked vaguely familiar to
me. It took me a few minutes to remember where I'd
seen her—going in and out of the apartment building
across the street from me.

I got out of the car and stood near the curb as a
team of paramedics wheeled a gurney out of the house
and lifted it carefully down the steps. I couldn't iden-
tify its passenger because he was wrapped in a plastic
bag from top to toe, but I knew in my heart it was
the Pig Man I'd seen beneath my window.

"What happened?" I said to an Asian woman
nearby as they loaded the body into the ambulance.
She glanced at me fearfully and moved away. I wandered down the sidewalk and repeated my question
to a short, muscular black man in a tank top.

"The woman come over this morning," he said, "an'
found him." He rolled his eyes and drew his finger

across his throat, making a hideous sound with his mouth. "They got him in the bed."

I shoved my hands into my pockets. That way no one would see them shaking.

When I got home at about one in the afternoon I poured myself a Laphroaig and downed it in two swallows. It was too good—and expensive—to gulp down like that, but sometimes need overcomes nicety. Thus fortified, I crossed the front yard, nearly tripping over a duck, and rapped on Stewart Channock's door. I'd seen his car in its space across the street, so I knew he was home. I'd known he would be anyway.

"Yes?" he said, his voice muffled.

"It's me, Stewart. We have to talk."

"I'm a little busy right now." I heard him move away.

I banged on the door again, harder this time, with more authority.

"Not now," he said through the door.

"CIA pig!" I yelled. There was a pause—a loud one—and then he opened up.

We just looked at each other. Then he sighed and moved aside. "Come on in," he said.

There were two suitcases on the floor near the sofa. "Taking a trip, Stewart?"

"What do you want?"

"You know what I want. Except for a real dumb cop and a real smart lady sheriff, you were the only one who knew about the guy who was hassling me and throwing rocks through my window. Now he's dead."

"That's got nothing to do with me."

"It's everything to do with you," I said. "The guy saw you getting out of my car last week after you'd gone over to start it up for me, right? He recognized you. He must have known you from Vietnam. I happen to know he was in the army in 1973 so it figures. Then he saw you come in here to water the plants, and he thought this was your house."

He shrugged.

"What was it, drugs? You were involved in covert CIA drug-smuggling in Asia and poor old Harlan Panec—that was his name—was in the wrong place at the wrong time and saw you."

"You have a vivid imagination, Saxon."

"A lot of guys who never got over Nam have vivid imaginations," I went on. "They came back home in the early seventies to a country that didn't give a damn, and have been fighting the war in their heads ever since, probably because they realized they'd been over there fighting for a government no better than the sleaziest drug peddler. Panec looked like he was one of them; he had that half-crazy, stretched-too-tight look. When he saw you again after all these years, the poor bastard snapped like a frayed rubber band. But he was too dumb to do anything except throw rocks and yell."

"You're talking crap you don't know anything about."

"Then pay no attention, let me ramble. Maybe you're still with the Agency, maybe not. But whatever you are doing it's probably illegal, so when I told you about the writing on my car, the brown van, the spray painting under my window, you realized you'd been blown. You waited for the van to show up again and you followed it to Panec's place in North Hollywood and cut his throat. Probably not the first guy you ever killed."

"You'll never prove any of this, you know."

"Maybe not."

"But you're going to try?"

"I have to," I said.

He pushed himself away from the door where he'd been leaning casually. "Let's head into the bathroom, shall we?"

I shook my head. "I don't have to go."

"Move it," he said, and there was a gun in his hand. It was a small gun that fit in his palm, the kind women might carry in their purses. At close range it would kill as efficiently as a bazooka. I hesitated, and he said, "Don't be stupid. You know I'll use this if I have to."

"Those are noisy little devils," I said. "People will hear."

He moved toward me. "Do you want to take the chance?"

I didn't. I don't like having guns aimed at me. I should be used to it, but I'm not. On TV, of course, the private investigator would have slapped it out of his hand and overpowered him, but it had already been pointed out to me that I'm not as tough as I think I am.

I walked into the bedroom ahead of him. Another suitcase, half full, was open on the bed. He went over to the dresser, opened a drawer, and felt around inside. Then he pulled out a pair of silvery handcuffs.

"I never knew you were into kinky sex, Stewart."

"Shut up." He motioned with the gun and I went into the bathroom with him right behind me. He switched on the light, and the exhaust fan in the ceiling began humming noisily. There were cute little aqua and black mermaids on the shower curtain.

"Kneel down on the floor by the john. Do it!"

I did it. The porcelain tile was cold on my knees through my jeans. He took my hand and fastened one of the cuffs around my wrist. "Not too tight?" he said.

He put the chain around the thick pipe running from the toilet into the wall, then braceleted my other hand and snapped the cuffs shut so I was kneeling over the closed toilet as though at prayer.

"There's no window," he said, "and the fan will muffle the noise, so don't bother yelling. Besides, no one else in the neighborhood will be home until evening."

"And by that time you're in another city with a whole new identity. Stewart, you're a slime."

"There's things you don't understand, so don't be so damned judgmental. If I was such a slime you'd be dead by now."

"You aren't going to shoot me?"

He considered it for more than a moment. Then he shook his head. "Finally you have to say 'enough' to killing." He went to the door. "You okay?"

"I'm real comfy," I said bitterly.

He looked at me for a minute. I suppose he was trying to decide whether he'd made a mistake, whether he should just shoot me in the head and be done with it. But my luck held.

"Ciao," he said, and left me there.

I couldn't hear much through the closed door, but I did hear him leave the house. He was an invisible man, marching through life carrying out his own twisted agenda, and if some other poor fool like Harlan Panec got in his way, he'd take care of it the same way and disappear again, vanishing into the mist like Brigadoon. It takes a special mind-set, I imagine, to live rootless without family or friends, worrying that someone was always in the shadows, watching. Not for nothing were guys like Stewart Channock known as "spooks."

I shifted around on the tile floor, trying to get comfortable, and flexed the fingers of my imprisoned hands. Between the toilet and the cabinet that housed the sink was a wooden magazine rack. From my vantage point I saw two *Newsweek*s, a *Forbes*, yesterday's *Wall Street Journal*, a crossword puzzle magazine, and a couple of paperback books—but I wasn't much in the mood for reading.

I knew what would happen when he got to his car—my making a simple phone call had ensured it—but in the completely closed room I could barely hear the gunshots from the parking lot, and I had no way of knowing who shot whom until Sharyl Capps and her partner/lover from the sheriff's office kicked in the door and told me.

AND PRAY NOBODY SEES YOU

An Aaron Gunner story

Gar Anthony Haywood

FIRST APPEARANCE: *Fear of the Dark,* 1988

Gar Haywood was the second winner of The Private Eye Writers of America/St. Martin's Press Best First P.I. Novel contest. The book was *Fear of the Dark*, which went on to win the Shamus for Best First Novel of 1988. Those who read it for the contest agree that the first line in the book virtually sold it.

Since then, in addition to his Gunner books Mr. Haywood has begun chronicling the adventures of the Loudermilks, a middle-aged couple who travel around the country in a trailer, finding trouble along the way.

This story first appeared in the anthology *Spooks, Spies and Private Eyes* (1995) and went on to win the Shamus for Best P.I. short story. I am proud to present it here for your enjoyment.

It doesn't happen often, but every now and then a good story will buy you a free drink at the Deuce. Lilly has to be feeling charitable and business has to be slow, say, down to three lifeless regulars and maybe another new face, somebody who likes to treat a single shot of *Meyer's* like a lover they're afraid to part with. Lilly will get tired of watching Howard Gaines slide dominoes across her bar, or listening to Eggy Jones whine about the latest indignity he's suffered at the hands of his wife Camille, and will demand that somebody tell her a story entertaining enough to hold her interest. She calls herself asking, Lilly, but she's too big to ask for anything; everything she says sounds like a demand, whether it comes with a "please" or not.

She was in the mood for a story a couple of Tuesdays back, and as usual, looked to me first to do the honors. I don't always take the prize on these occasions, but I manage to get my share. Maybe it's the line of work I'm in.

This particular evening, I answered Lilly's call with the following.

And watched the Wild Turkey flow afterward.

It started with a U-turn.

Brother driving a blue Chrysler did a one-eighty in the middle of Wilmington Avenue, two o'clock on a Thursday afternoon, in broad daylight. Mickey Moore, Weldon Foley, and me were standing outside Mickey's barber shop when we saw him go by on the eastbound side of the street, stop, then yank the Chrysler around like he'd just seen somebody who owed him money. We would have all ducked for cover, smelling the week's latest drive-by in the making, except that the driver looked too old to be a gangbanger and the three of us were the only people on the street. That left us nothing else to believe but that we'd just seen the act of a fool, nothing more and nothing less.

"You see that? That nigger's crazy," Mickey said.

"Sure is," Foley agreed, nodding his hairless head. I sometimes suspect Mickey keeps him around precisely for that purpose; he sure as hell never has to take his clippers to him.

"And look: Not a goddamn cop in sight. Now, if that was me—"

"Or me," I said, thinking the same thing my landlord

was thinking. I'd never gotten away with a U-turn in my life.

The Chrysler was now headed back in our direction on the westbound side of the street, cruising in the right lane the way cars do when the people driving them are looking for a parking space. It was an old '71 Barracuda, a clean and chromed-out borderline classic with a throaty exhaust and tires you could hide a small country in. It was grumbling like a California earthquake when it finally pulled to a stop at the curb, directly in front of us.

The driver got out of the car and approached us, his left arm folded up in a white sling. We let him come without saying a word.

"One of you Aaron Gunner?" he asked. He was a wiry twenty-something, six-one or six-two, with razor lines cut all along the sides and back of his head, something I imagined he'd had done in hopes of drawing attention from his face. It was sad to say, but the boy looked like a black Mr. Potato Head with bad skin.

"That's me," I told him, before Weldon or Mickey could point me out. "What can I do for you?"

He openly examined the front of Mickey's shop, as if he were looking for the fine print on the sign above the door, and said, "This is your office, right?"

"That's right. I've got a room in the back."

He glanced at my companions briefly. "All right if we go back there to talk?"

I shrugged. "Sure. Come on in."

Mickey was insulted by the slight of not being introduced, but he didn't say anything.

I led my homely visitor past Mickey's three empty barber chairs, through the beaded curtains in the open doorway beyond, and into the near-vacant space that has passed for my office for the last four years. The lamp on my desk was already on, so all I had to do was sit down and wait for my friend to find the couch and do the same.

He never did.

He just stood in front of my desk and said, "You're a private detective."

"Yes. Can't you tell?"

"I want to hire you."

"To do what?"

"I want you to find a car for me."

"A car?"

"Yeah." He nodded. "Sixty-five Ford Mustang, tangerine orange. Two-plus-two fastback, fully restored and cherried out."

"A sixty-five?"

"Yeah. First year they were made. Probably ain't but fifty of 'em in the whole country still on the road."

"Two-eighty-nine, or six?"

"Come on. If it was the six, man, I'd let 'em have the damn car."

He had a point. A sixty-five Mustang two-plus-two without the V-8 under the hood might have been worth a few dollars to somebody, but any true collector would've considered it a stiff. Cherried out or no.

"It sounds nice," I told him.

"Man, fuck 'nice.' It's a classic. There ain't but fifty of 'em still in existence, like I said."

I nodded my head to show him I was finally paying attention. "And your name was . . . ?"

"Purdy. David Purdy. Look—"

"This car we're talking about, Mr. Purdy. I take it it belongs to you?"

"Does it belong to me? Hell, yes, it belongs to me. Why else would I be here talkin' to you?"

"I give up. Why *are* you here talking to me?"

"Because I got *jacked* last night, man. What else? Over on Imperial and Hoover, over by my girl's house. Little motherfucker shot me at the stoplight and took my goddamn car."

"You call the police?"

"The police? Of course. I told you, man, I got shot." He tried to gesture with his left arm, but just moving the sling an inch from his side seemed to bring tears to his eyes.

"So? What do you need with me?" I asked him.

Purdy answered the question with a crooked, toothy grin meant to convey incredulity. "Man, you're jokin', right? What do I need with *you*? I need you to get the goddamn car back for me. What do you think?"

He'd been looking for a foot in his ass since he'd stepped out of the Chrysler, and now he'd finally earned it. Still, I let the comment pass. I'd spent the retainers of rude jackasses before, and their money went just as far as anyone else's. Purdy's would be no different.

"You don't think the police can find the car?" I asked.

"Let's just say I'm not countin' on it," Purdy said. "Least, not until there ain't nothin' left of it but a goddamn frame."

"I take it you didn't have one of those electronic tracking devices on it—the kind the police can home in on?"

"No. I didn't."

"That's too bad."

"Yeah, it is. I fucked up. I put a lot of time and money in that car, then turned around and didn't protect it right. So it's gone. But that don't mean I gotta forget about it, like the cops said I should. Hell, no. I want that car back, Mr. Gunner, and I want it back *now,* 'fore some fuckin' chop shop can hack it all to pieces."

"If that's possible, you mean," I said.

"It's possible. It just ain't gonna be easy. I'd find the car myself if the shit was easy."

I fell silent, pretending to be mulling things over, when all I was really doing was deciding on a fee.

"Somebody said you were the man for the job, so I looked you up. But if you're not—"

"What do you figure the car's worth? Ten, fifteen grand?" I asked.

"Shit. Try twenty-five," Purdy said.

"Okay, twenty-five. Here's the deal. I locate the car within forty-eight hours, in its original condition, you owe me twenty-five hundred. Ten percent of its worth, cash on delivery. If I don't find it, or I do and it's already been chopped up, you only owe me for my time. Three hundred dollars a day, plus expenses, half of which you've got to pay me now, just to get me started."

"No problem," Purdy said. Nothing I'd said had made him so much as blink.

"No problem?"

"No, man, no problem. I told you: I want the car back, and you're supposed to be the man can get it for me." He was already peeling some bills off a wad of green he'd removed from his pocket.

"I'm gonna need a description of the carjacker and the license plate of the car. And a phone number where you can be reached at any time, day or night."

Purdy threw four hundred dollars on the desk in front of me and said, "You've got it."

I still had my reservations about the man, but now I was bought and paid for.

It was time to go to work.

The first thing I did was go see Mopar.

Mopar used to steal cars. Lots of them. It was what he did for fifteen years, from the time we were in high school together right up until his last bust, when a fight in the joint left him crippled for life and scared the thief right out of him, for good. His mother still called him Jerome, but he was Mopar to everyone else; back in high school, he could steal any car you cared to name, but he did all his racing in Chryslers.

Today, Mopar was in the body shop business.

He had his own place over on Florence Avenue, between Denker and La Salle. He'd started out working there, hammering dents out of Buicks and Oldsmobiles, then slowly bought into the business, buying bigger and bigger chunks as the years went by until finally, little over a year ago, he became the man holding all the paper. And all with only one good leg.

He was standing behind the counter in the office when I came in, just hanging up the phone. He was damn near as fat as Lilly these days, and only twice as jolly. The sight of my approach brought a broad grin to his face, same one he used to wear as a kid.

"Tail Gunner! What it be like?"

That was what he used to call me back in school, Tail Gunner. I can't tell you how glad I was that the nickname never caught on with anyone else.

"It's your world, Mopar," I said, burying my right hand deep in his. "I'm just livin' in it."

"Shit, you ain't livin' in *my* world. Otherwise, I'd see you more often 'round here."

I shrugged apologetically. "What can I say? I'm a busy man."

Mopar just laughed. "So what can I do you, man? This business, or pleasure?"

"Afraid it's business. I'm looking for somebody I think you might be able to help me find."

"Yeah? Who's that?"

"A 'jacker. Boy about fifteen to eighteen years old, five-seven, five-eight, a hundred and thirty pounds. Dark skin and dark eyes, with braces on his teeth. Likes to wear striped clothes and a San Antonio Spurs baseball cap turned sideways on his head, bill facing east. At least, that's how he was dressed last night."

"A 'jacker? Why you wanna ask me about a 'jacker?"

"Because you used to be one, Mopar. It hasn't been that long ago, man."

"Man, I wasn't never a 'jacker! I never pulled nobody out of a car in my life!"

"No, but—"

"These kids today, man, they're crazy! Shootin' people to steal a goddamn car. Man, I never even owned a gun till I got this place!"

"Okay, so you weren't a 'jacker. You're right, that was the wrong thing for me to say."

"Damn right it was."

"But your objective was still the same, right? To steal cars?"

Mopar didn't say anything.

"Look. I'm not saying you know the kid. I just thought you might, that's all. Because I know you've put a few of 'em to work for you in the past, tryin' to help 'em go straight like you did, and I thought, maybe this kid I'm lookin' for was one of 'em. Or maybe you've seen him hanging around somewhere, I don't know. It was just a thought."

Mopar just glared at me, his jovial mood a thing of the past. "You say this boy 'jacked a car last night?"

I nodded. "Orange sixty-five Mustang fastback, in primo condition. Owner says it happened over on Imperial and Hoover, a few minutes past midnight."

"Sixty-five fastback? You shittin' me?"

"Afraid not. Now you know why the man wants it found before somebody takes an air wrench to it."

"You mean the fool don't know they already did that eight hours ago?"

"I guess he's the optimistic type. I tried to tell him to save his money, but he's emotionally attached. So . . ."

I waited for the big man to make up his mind, but he seemed in no hurry to do so.

"Did I mention the fact that my client got shot? Clipped in the left wing, but it could've been worse. This kid who 'jacked him isn't just in it for the rides, Mopar. He likes to shoot people, too."

Still, Mopar offered me nothing but silence.

"Tell you what. Forget it," I said. "This was a bad idea, bothering you with this. Come by and see us at the Deuce sometime, huh?"

I turned and started out of the room.

"You say the kid wears braces?" Mopar asked.

I turned back around. "That's right."

He hesitated a moment longer, then said, "I can't give you a name. But I can tell you where to look."

I told him that would be fine.

Mopar said the kid liked to hang out in front of a liquor store on Western and 81st Street. Mopar remembered him because he'd had to chase him out of his shop once, when the kid had come around looking for one of Mopar's employees and had taken the news of the employee's recent dismissal badly. Every now and then since, Mopar'd see him at the liquor store, kicking it with his homies out on the sidewalk.

But he wasn't there Thursday night.

I know. I waited there six hours for him to show up. Three members of his crew were there—teenage boys dressed in oversized khaki pants and giant plaid jackets—but they were all the wrong size for the kid I was looking for, and none of them had braces on their teeth. I sat in my car across the street and thought about approaching them, but I knew all they'd do with my questions was tell me where I could stick them, so I decided to spare myself the aggravation and just stayed put.

When I'd inevitably given up watching the liquor store, I cruised the 'hood indiscriminately, hitting all the major intersections I could think of, but my results were the same. No kid with braces looking like a 'jacker on the prowl, no classic Mustangs in tangerine orange. I saw a howling parade of black-and-whites cut a swath through traffic on Normandie and Manchester, an old man roll off a bus bench into the gutter on Slauson and Vermont, and two hookers change a flat tire on a run-down convertible Pontiac on Prarie and One Hundred and Eighth—but I didn't see any carjackers anywhere.

So I went home.

The next morning, I called Matthew Poole with the L.A.P.D. and asked him if he knew anybody in Auto. Poole doesn't owe me any favors, but the homicide man helps me out when he can all the same, I don't really know why. Maybe it's because he thinks we're friends.

The man Poole eventually put me in touch with was a cop named Link, first name Sam. Over the phone, he sounded like one of those cops who came out of the womb flashing a badge and reading the obstetrician his rights; he was cordial enough, but you could tell he was of the opinion I was standing between him and his pension. I got right to the point and told him about Purdy, then asked him afterward if the story sounded familiar. The Mustang had been stolen only two nights before, I figured he ought to have heard something about the investigation, even if he himself hadn't been called out on it.

But Link said it was all news to him.

Nothing about the Mustang or Purdy struck him as familiar. And if a shooting had taken place during a 'jacking Wednesday night, he assured me he'd have known about it. In fact, he would have convinced me altogether that the whole of Purdy's story was a lie had my description of the kid I'd spent the previous night looking for not rung a bell with him.

"Striped clothes?" he asked me.

"Yeah."

"That could be Squealer. He's into stripes. You want to talk to him?"

He was offering to go pick him up for me.

"Yeah, but not formally. I need him conversant," I said, hoping he wouldn't be insulted by the insinuation the kid wouldn't talk downtown.

"You just want to know where to find him, then."

"If that wouldn't be too much trouble."

Link said it wouldn't be any trouble at all.

It took me all day to find him.

He wasn't at home and he wasn't at school. Link had given me a list of about a half-dozen places he liked to frequent, from the Baldwin Hills Crenshaw Plaza to the basketball courts at Jesse Owens Park, but he never appeared at any of them until a few minutes after seven P.M., when he showed up at a Baskin and Robbins ice cream parlor in a mini-mall on Budlong and Fifty-sixth Street, during my second visit to the site. His pants were black denim, no stripes, but his shirt was an oversized tee with alternating blue-and-green horizontal bands, and the cap turned sideways on his head was silver and black, the primary colors of the San Antonio Spurs. He had arrived on foot with two other kids who looked roughly the same age, a boy and a girl, and I had to watch the three of them eat ice cream and throw napkins at each other for well over an hour before he was ready to leave again.

I had hoped when the time came he'd leave alone, but I wasn't that lucky. He left the same way he came, with his two friends in tow. The trio walked northbound along Budlong and I trailed behind them in my car, keeping a good block, block-and-half between us at all times. I was prepared to go on like this all night if I had to, but I wasn't looking forward to it. Of the forty-eight hours I'd given myself to find Purdy's Mustang, more than thirty were already gone, and the clock was still running. I had to get the kid alone, or he had to lead me to the car, one or the other. And fast.

Things were looking dark when Squealer and his homies led me to a house on Fiftieth Street between Harvard and Denker, then disappeared inside. There was light in only one window, and the place was as quiet as an empty grave. The thought occurred to me they might have crashed there for the night, and an hour later, nothing had happened to rule that possibil-

ity out—until the porch light winked back on and
Squealer emerged from the house again.

Alone.

I got out of my car on the passenger side and
ducked low to hide behind it, waiting for the kid to
saunter past on the opposite side of the street. I was
going to make this quick. He'd already shot Purdy and
I had no reason to think he wouldn't shoot me, given
the chance, so getting the drop on him first seemed
to be the wise thing to do. He was stepping off the
curb to cross Harvard when I closed the distance between us and put him down, rapping the base of his
skull with the butt of my Ruger P-85. He fell like a
house of cards. I caught him on his way down, dragged
him over to my car, and tossed him in.

Then we went somewhere to talk.

There was nobody on the beach.

It was too cold for romance, and too dark for sight-
seeing. The moon was heavily shielded behind a thick
mask of cloud cover, and a mist hung over the water
like a frozen gray curse. The kid and I would not
be disturbed.

I had him trussed up like a calf at a rodeo. He was
bound, gagged, and blindfolded, stretched out flat
upon the wooden-plank walkway that ran beneath the
Santa Monica Pier. His gun was in my back pocket, a
small .22 I'd found shoved into the waistband of his
pants. Down here, the sound of the crashing waves
echoed between the pier's pylons like thunder in a
bottle, thoroughly directionless, and you could taste
the salt of the ocean spray with every intake of breath.

When I was certain he was awake, I knelt down
beside the kid and said, "I want my car."

He took that as a cue to start thrashing around, but

it didn't take him long to see the futility in it. He wasn't going anywhere.

"You haven't guessed by now, we're on the Santa Monica Pier," I said. "Down at the beach. Hear the waves down there? Care for a swim?"

I rolled him over a little.

He got the gist of my phony threat right away, and bought into it completely. I had to hold him down with both hands to keep him still.

"Okay. You get the picture. You don't tell me where my car is, I push you off this fucking pier and into the Pacific. Understand?"

He started to struggle again. I put my hand on his throat and asked him one more time: "Understand?"

Finally, he grew quiet, and slowly nodded his head.

"Very good. Car I'm looking for is a sixty-five Ford Mustang. Orange. You shot me in the arm and stole it from me Wednesday night, out on the corner of Imperial and Hoover. Remember?"

Squealer made no move to answer, so I rolled him over again, one full revolution.

"You're runnin' out of pier, homeboy," I said. Then, after a while, I asked him again: "Do you remember the car?"

This time, he nodded his head.

"Good. Now—I'm going to take your gag off, and you're going to tell me where I can find it. You're not going to scream, or cry, or call for your mama—you're just going to tell me where my car is. Otherwise . . ."

I let him think about that a moment, then peeled his gag away from his mouth.

"At the mall! At the mall, man!" he said, gasping to get the words out.

"What mall?"

"Fox Hills Mall, man! The Fox Hills Mall!"

"What, in the parking lot?"

"Yeah! In the parkin' lot! You know, the buildin'!"

"The building?" I had to think about that a moment. "You mean the parking structure?"

He nodded his head frantically. "Yeah, that's it! The parkin' structure!"

"What floor?"

"What floor? I don't know, man. Four, I think. Don't kill me, man, please!"

"Why'd you put it there?"

"Why? I don't—"

"Why didn't you take it in for chopping? Why'd you park it instead?"

"Shit, I wasn't gonna chop that ride, man! It was too sweet!"

"Too sweet?"

He nodded his head again.

"What were you going to do with it, you weren't going to chop it?" I asked him.

"I was gonna *keep* it. Just . . . let it chill at the mall for a while, then change it up. Get new papers on it, an' shit, so's it could be *my* ride."

I should have guessed.

I put the gag back in his mouth and stood up. Where this kid had found the courage to shoot a man, I couldn't begin to guess. He was scared shitless and seemingly willing to do whatever was asked of him to stay alive.

Odd.

I was going to leave him as he was, anticipating the worst, bouncing about on the wooden walkway floor like a beached whale waiting to die . . . and then I thought of one more question to ask him.

Kneeling beside him again, I said, "Tell me something, junebug: What'd you shoot me for?"

And then he told me exactly what I'd thought he might.

He said I'd made him do it.

The Mustang was on the *third* floor.

Parked in a distant corner all by itself and covered with a tarp. I peeled the tarp off to look it over carefully, but I knew it was the car I was after inside of ten seconds. Everything about it matched Purdy's description: model, color, license plate number. With one notable exception.

It was a 'sixty-six.

'Sixty-fives had a crosshairs grill; this one had the eggcrate grill of a 'sixty-six. Which made it a rarity, yes, but not a classic. A man who knew cars might conceivably spend a small fortune to recover a stolen 'sixty-five, but a 'sixty-six? I didn't think so. Any more than I thought a man would take a bullet fighting to hold onto a 'sixty-six, as Squealer the 'jacker had claimed Purdy had done Wednesday night.

Obviously, there was more to this car than met the eye.

When I finally found out what it was, a little over ninety minutes later, I called Purdy to tell him the good news.

"It's over there," I said, pointing. "Across the street."

Purdy turned and saw the Mustang parked on the other side of La Brea Avenue, directly opposite the Pink's hot dog stand in Hollywood where we were sitting. I'd used the keys I'd taken off Squealer to come here, and had been well into my second chili dog when Purdy showed up.

"I don't believe it," he said now, eyeing the car.

"We were lucky," I said, feigning weary humility.

"Where did you find it?"

I shrugged. "Does it matter?"

"No. Not really. I just thought—"

"You have my money, Mr. Purdy?"

"Of course." He took an envelope from his coat pocket and opened it so I could see the bills inside, but didn't hand it over. "You mind if I look the car over first?" he asked.

"Not at all," I said, wiping chili from the sides of my mouth. "I'll just hold onto the keys."

That wasn't what he'd had in mind, but he could see the point was nonnegotiable. Without saying another word, he left to inspect the car, then returned a few minutes later.

"Twenty-five hundred dollars," he said, handing me the envelope he'd shown me earlier. He seemed infinitely relieved.

I told him thanks and gave him his keys.

He stood there for a moment, wanting to say more, then just turned and went back to the car. He got in, started the engine, and pulled away from the curb.

Halfway down the block, he made a U-turn.

And then his rearview mirror turned red.

Some people would say I set him up, but I don't look at it that way.

Purdy had hidden a two-pound bag of crack cocaine behind the Mustang's driver's side door panel, and when I found it out at the Fox Hills Mall parking lot that night, I knew I owed him. He'd played me for a sucker. Fed me some line about his classic car getting 'jacked, just so I could run down the small fortune in rock he'd stashed inside it.

And yet . . .

Technically, no harm had been done. The man had hired me to do a job, and I'd done it. I'd found his car, delivered it on time, and been paid the agreed-upon fee. So what if the whole thing was a lie? I'd still held up my end of the bargain, and Purdy had held up his.

I owed him, and yet I didn't owe him.

So I let him go. Sort of.

I put a little of his stash in his glove compartment with his registration, then put the rest back where I'd found it. I parked the car on the same street, in the same place where, only six weeks before, I'd gotten my last ticket for making a U-turn, on La Brea Avenue near Pink's. And finally, I parked his car on the northbound side of the street, facing away from the Gardena address printed on the business card Purdy had given me.

A setup? Not hardly.

All Purdy would have had to do to get off that night was not make that U-turn.

See? He screwed himself.

All I did was watch.

Later, at the Deuce, Lilly nearly busted a gut laughing. In the proper frame of mind, the giant barkeep's as appreciative of my cleverness as I am myself. Sometimes even more so.

"Tell me one thing, Gunner," she said.

"Shoot."

"You made any U-turns yourself since then? Or you out of the habit for good?"

I grinned at her, winked, and downed the last of my free drink, though all it was by now was ice water. "Naw," I said.

"Naw, what?"

"Naw, I'm not out of the habit. I just know how to do 'em right now, that's all."

"Do 'em *right*? And what way is *that*?"

"That's where you turn the wheel," I said, demonstrating, "and pray nobody sees you."

I pushed myself away from the bar and called it a night.

NOOSES GIVE

A Kate Shugak story

Dana Stabenow

FIRST APPEARANCE: *A Cold Day for Murder*, 1992

Since 1992, Dana Stabenow and Kate Shugak have
made quite an impression on the mystery field. Nominated for many awards, the Shugak series is one of the
freshest in mystery fiction, boasting a clever, intelligent
female character who no one would dare refer to as
"spunky." Dana presently lives in Alaska, where the series is set, and wrote this story for the anthology *The
Mysterious West*.

The bodies had fallen around the table like three
cards from a spent deck. Jeremy Mike, the jack
of spades. Sally Jorgenson, queen of hearts. Ted Muktoyuk, the king of diamonds. The King of the Key,
they called him from the bleachers, at five feet ten
the tallest center Bernie Koslowski had ever had the
privilege of coaching.

Bernie's mouth was set in a grim line. "What
happened?"

Billy Mike had a mobile moon face, usually beaming
with good nature and content. This morning it was
grim and tired. The jack of spades had been a nephew,
his youngest sister's only child. She didn't know yet,
and he didn't know how he was going to tell her. He
told Bernie instead. "They were drunk. It's Jeremy's
pistol."

"How do you know?"

Billy's face twisted. "I gave it to him for Christmas." Bernie waited, patient, and Billy got himself under control. "He must have brought it from home. Sally's parents are in Ahtna for a corporation conference, so they came here to drink."

"And play Russian roulette."

Billy nodded. "Looks like Ted lost. He was left-handed—remember that hook shot?"

"Remember it? I taught it to him."

"Sally was on his right. She couldn't have shot him in the left side of his head from where she sat." He pointed at the pistol, lying on the table a few inches from Sally's hand. "You know Ted and Sally were going together?"

Bernie grunted. "You figure Sally blamed Jeremy? For bringing the gun?"

"Or the bottle, or both." The tribal chief's nod was weary. "Probably grabbed the gun and shot Jeremy, then herself." He stooped and picked up a plastic liquor bottle from the floor.

He held it out, and Bernie examined the label. "Windsor Canadian. The bootlegger's friend. Retail price in Anchorage, seven-fifty a bottle. Retail price in a dry village, a hundred bucks easy."

"Yeah." The bottle dropped to the table, next to the gun.

"You talk to him?"

"I tried. He shot out the headlights on my snow machine."

"Uh-huh."

"Town's tense. You know the DampAct passed by only five votes. There's plenty who think he's just doing business, that he's got every right to make a living, same as the rest of us."

"No," Bernie said, "not the same as the rest of us."

"No," Billy agreed. "Bernie. The trooper's chasing after some nut who shot up a bank in Valdez, and the tribal police . . . well, hell, the tribal policemen are okay at checking planes for booze and getting the drunks home safe from the Roadhouse. Like I said, the town's tense. Anything could happen." A pause. "We're not going to be able to handle this on our own."

"No." Bernie's eyes met Billy's. "But we know someone who can."

The tribal chief hesitated. "I don't know, Bernie. There's some history there."

Bernie gave the bodies a last look, a gaze equal parts sorrow and rage. "All the better."

The next morning Bernie bundled himself into a parka, gauntlets, and boots, kissed his wife and children goodbye, and got on his snow machine. There had been a record amount of snow that winter, drifting twenty feet deep in places. Moose were unable to get at the tree bark that was their primary food source and were starving to death all over the Park, but the snow machining had never been better. An hour and thirty-five miles later, his cheeks frostbitten and his hands and feet numb, he burst into a small clearing. He cut the engine and slid to a stop six feet from the log cabin.

It sat at the center of a half circle of small buildings, including a garage, a greenhouse, a cache, and an outhouse. Snow was piled high beneath the eaves of the cabin, and neat paths had been cut through it from door to door and to the woodpile between cabin and outhouse. Beyond the buildings were more trees and a creek. Beyond the creek the ground fell away into a long, broad valley that glittered hard and cold and white in what there was of the Arctic noon sun, a valley that rose again into the Teglliq foothills and the Quilak mountain range, a mighty upward thrust of earth's crust that gouged the sky with 18,000-foot spurs until it bled ice-blue glaze down their sharp flanks.

It was a sight to steal the heart. Bernie Koslowski would never have seen any of it if he hadn't dodged the draft all the way into British Columbia in 1970. From there it was but a step over the border into Alaska and some fine, rip-roaring years on the Trans-Alaska Pipeline. By the time the line was finished, he had enough of a stake to buy the Roadhouse, the only establishment legally licensed to sell liquor in the twenty-million-acre Park, and he settled down to marry a local girl and make babies and boilermakers for the rest of his life.

He sold liquor to make a living. He coached basketball for fun. He had so much fun at it that Niniltna High School's Kanuyaq Kings were headed for the Class C State Championship. Or they had been until Ted Muktoyuk's resignation from the team. Bernie's eyes dropped from the mountains to the clearing.

She hadn't been off the homestead in the last four feet of snow; he'd had to break trail with the machine a quarter of a mile through the woods. The thermometer mounted next to the door read six below. He knocked. No answer. Smoke was coming from both chimneys. He knocked again, harder.

This time the door opened. She stood five feet tall and small of frame, dwarfed by the wolf-husky hybrid standing at her side. The wolf's eyes were yellow, the woman's hazel, both wary and hostile. The woman said, "What?"

"What 'what'?" Bernie said. "What am I doing here? What do I want? Whatever happened to this thing called love?" He gave a hopeful smile. There was no response. "Come on, Kate. How about a chance to get in out of the cold?"

For a minute he thought she was going to shut the door in his face. Instead she stepped to one side. "In."

The dog curled a lip at him, and he took this as tacit permission to enter. The cabin was a twenty-five-foot square with a sleeping loft. Built-in bookshelves, built-in couch, table and chairs, and two stoves, one oil, one wood, took up the first floor. Gas lamps hissed gently from brackets in all four corners. She took his parka and hung it next to hers on the caribou rack mounted next to the door. "Sit."

He sat. She poured out two mugs of coffee and gave him one. He gulped gratefully and felt the hot liquid creep all the way down his legs and out into his fingertips, and as if she had only been waiting for that, she said, "Talk."

Her voice was a hoarse, croaking whisper, and irresistibly his eyes were drawn to the red, angry scar bisecting the smooth brown skin of her throat, literally from ear to ear. None of the Park rats knew the whole story, and none of them had had the guts to ask for it, but the scar marked her throat the way it had marked the end of her career seven months before as an investigator on the staff of the Anchorage district attorney's office. She had returned to her father's homestead sometime last summer. The first anyone knew about it was when her mail started being delivered to the Niniltna post office. Old Abel IntHout picked it up and presumably brought it out to her homestead, and the only time anyone else saw her was when she came into Niniltna for supplies in October, the big silver wolf-husky hybrid walking close by her side, warning off any and all advances with a hard yellow stare.

Her plaid shirt was open at the throat, her long black hair pulled back into a loose braid. She wasn't trying to hide the scar. Maybe it needed air to heal. Or maybe she was proud of it. Or maybe it was only that she wasn't ashamed of it, which wasn't quite the same thing. He looked up from the scar and met eyes beneath an epicanthic fold that gave her face an exotic, Eastern flavor. She was an Aleut icon stepped out of a gilt frame, dark and hard and stern. "I've got a problem," he said.

"So?"

"So I'm hoping you'll make it your problem, too." He drank more coffee, preparing for a tough sell. "You know about the DampAct?" She shook her head. "In November the village voted to go dry. You can bring in booze for your own consumption but not in amounts to sell." He added, "I'm okay because the Roadhouse is outside tribal boundaries." She didn't look as if she'd been worrying about him or his business. "Well, Kate, it ain't working out too good."

There was a brief pause. "Bootlegger," she said.

"Yeah."

She doubled her verbal output. "Tell me." He told her. It must have been hard to hear. She was shirttail cousin to all three of the teenagers. Hell, there weren't very many people in the village of Niniltna or the entire Park for that matter she couldn't call cousin, including himself, through his wife. It was the reason he was here. One of them.

"You know who?" she said.

He snorted into his coffee and put the mug down with a thump. "Of course I know who. Everybody knows who. He's been flying booze into remote villages, wet or dry, for thirty years. Wherever there isn't a bar—shit, wherever there is a bar and somebody'd rather buy their bottle out of the back of a plane anyway—there's Pete with his hand out. God knows it's better than working for a living."

Her face didn't change, but he had the sudden feeling that he had all her attention, and remembered Billy Mike's comment about history. "Pete Liverakos," she said. He gave a gloomy nod. "Stop him. The local option law says the state can seize any equipment used to make, transport, sell, or store liquor. Start confiscating."

This time a gloomy shake. "We don't know where to start."

A corner of her wide mouth turned down. "Gee, maybe you could try his plane. You can pack a lot of cases of booze into the back of a 180, especially if you pull all the seats except the pilot's."

"He's not using it," Bernie said. "Since the Damp-Act passed, the tribal council has been searching every plane that lands at gunpoint. Pete's been in and out in his Cessna all winter, Billy Mike says clean as a whistle every time."

"How often?"

"Once a week, sometimes twice." He added, "He's not even bringing in anything for personal use, which all by itself makes me suspicious, because Pete and Laura Anne are a couple what likes a little caribou with their cabernet."

"Get the trooper."

"Kate, you know and I know the trooper's based in Tok, and his jurisdiction is spread pretty thin even before he gets within flying distance of Niniltna. Besides, he's already in pursuit of some yo-yo who shot up a bank in Valdez and took off up Thompson Pass, on foot, no less. So much for state law. The Damp-Act—" He shrugged. "The DampAct is a local ordinance. Even if they catch him at it, all the council can do is fine him a thousand bucks. Like a speeding ticket. In any given year Pete spends more than that on olives for martinis."

"He got somebody flying it in from Anchorage?"

Bernie gave a bark of laughter. "Sure. MarkAir." At her look, he said, "Shit, Kate, MarkAir runs specials with the Brown Jug in town. Guy endorses his permanent dividend fund check over at the local MarkAir office, MarkAir carries it to Anchorage and expedites it to the Brown Jug warehouse, Brown Jug fills the order, MarkAir picks it up and takes it out to the airport and flies it to the village."

"Competition for you," she said.

He met her eyes levelly. "That isn't what this is about, and you know it. I serve drinks, not drunks, and I don't sell bottles."

She looked away. "Sorry."

He gave a curt nod.

There was a brief silence. She broke it. "What do you want me to do?"

He drained his mug and set it on the table with a decisive snap. "I got a state championship coming up. I need sober players who come to practice instead of out earning their next bottle running booze for that asshole. Preferably players who have not previously blown their brains out with their best friend's gun. I want you to find out how Pete's getting the booze in, and stop him."

The next morning she fired up the Polaris and followed Bernie's tracks up the trail to the road that connected Niniltna with Ahtna and the Richardson Highway. The Polaris was old and slow, and the twenty-five miles between her homestead and the village took the better part of an hour, including the ten-minute break to investigate the tracks she spotted four miles outside the village. A pack of five wolves, healthy, hungry, and hunting. The 30.06 was always with her, and there was always a round in the chamber, but she stopped and checked anyway. One wolf was an appetite with attitude. Five of them looked like patrons of a diner, with her as the blue-plate special.

The tracks were crusted hard, a day old at least. Mutt's sniff was interested but unalarmed, and Kate replaced the rifle and continued up the road. It wasn't a road, really; it was the remains of the gravel roadbed of the Kanuyaq and Northwestern Railroad, built in 1910 to carry copper from the mine outside Niniltna to freighters docked in Cordova. In 1936 the copper played out, the railroad shut down, and locals began ripping up rails to get to the ties. It was an easy load of firewood, a lot easier than logging out the same load by hand.

The rails and ties were all gone now, although in summertime you could still pick up the odd spike in your truck tires. Twice a year, once after breakup, again just before the termination dust started creeping down the mountains, the state ran a grader over the rough surface to smooth over the potholes and the washouts. For the rest of the time they left itself to itself, and to the hundreds of Park rats who used it as a secondary means of transportation and commerce.

In the Alaskan bush, the primary means was ever and always air, and it was to the village airstrip Kate went first, a 4,800-foot stretch of hard-packed snow, much better maintained than the road. A dozen planes were tied down next to a hangar. Across the strip was a large log cabin with the U.S. flag flying outside, which backed up the wind sock at the end of the runway. Both hung limp this morning, and smoke rose straight up into the Arctic air from a cluster of rooftops glimpsed over the tops of the trees.

Kate stopped the snow machine next to the hangar, killed the engine, and stripped off her fur gauntlets. The round white thermometer fixed to the wall read twelve below. Colder than yesterday. She worked her fingers. It felt like it. Mutt jumped down and went trotting inside. A moment later there was a yell. "God*damn*!" Kate followed the sound.

A tall man in a gray coverall leaned up against the side of a Cessna 206 that looked as if it had enough hours on the Hobbs to put it into lunar orbit. The cowling was peeled back from the engine, and there were parts laid out on a canvas tarp. Both man and parts were covered with black grease. He scowled at her. "The next time that goddamn dog sticks her nose in my crotch from behind, I'm going to pinch her head off!"

"Hi, George."

Mutt nudged his hand with her head. He muttered something, pulled a rag out of a hip pocket, wiped his hands, and crouched down to give her ears a thorough scratching. She stood stock-still with an expression of bliss on her face, her plume of a tail waving gently. She'd been in love with George Perry since she was a puppy, and George had flown Milk-Bones into the setnet site Kate fished during her summer vacations. Kate had been in love with George since he'd flown Nestlé's Semi-Sweet Morsels into that same site.

The bush pilot gave Mutt a last affectionate cuff and stood to look at Kate. "I heard you were back."

She nodded in answer to his question, without offering an explanation. He didn't ask for one. "Coffee?"

She nodded again, and he led the way into his office, a small rectangular corner walled off from the rest of the building, furnished with a desk, a chair, and a Naugahyde couch heavily patched with black electrician's tape. The walls were covered with yellowing, tattered maps mended with Scotch tape. George went into a tiny bathroom and came out with a coffeepot held together with three-inch duct tape. He started the coffee and sat down at the desk. "So—how the hell are you, Shugak? Long time no see." His eyes dropped briefly to the open collar of her shirt. "*Long* time. You okay?" She nodded. "Good. Glad you're back anyway. Missed you."

"Me too."

"And the monster." He rummaged through a drawer for Oreo cookies and tossed one to Mutt. The coffeemaker sucked up the last of the water, and he poured out. Handing her a mug, he said, "What brings you into town?"

She nodded at the wall. "Wanted to take a look at your maps."

His eyebrows rose. "Be my guest." Mug in hand, she rose to her feet and began examining the maps beneath his speculative gaze, until she found the right one. Pete Liverakos's homestead was on Beaver Creek, about a mile downstream from the village. She traced a forefinger down the Kanuyaq River until she found it. The map indicated the homestead had its own airstrip, but then what self-respecting Alaskan homestead didn't?

George's voice sounded over her shoulder. "What are you looking for?"

She dropped her hand. "Just wanted to check something, and my maps are all about fifty years out of date."

"So are mine." He paused. "Dan O'Brien's bunch just did a new survey of the Kanuyaq. Source to delta, Copper Glacier to Kolinhenik Bar. They did the whole thing this summer. I thought those fucking—excuse me, Mutt—those frigging choppers never would leave."

"Have they got the new maps yet?" Though her voice was still harsh and broken, and according to the doctors always would be, the more she talked, the less it hurt. The realization brought her no joy.

He shook his head. "They're printing 'em this winter. They'll be selling 'em in the spring." He paused. "Dan's probably got the originals at Park Headquarters."

She drained her mug and set it on the desk. "Can I bum a ride up to the Step?"

He set his mug next to hers. "Sure. The Cub's prepped and ready to fly."

George took off hot, as straight up as he could with only 150 horsepower under the hood. The sky was clear and the air was still and it was CAVU all the way from the Quilak Mountains to the Gulf of Alaska. He climbed to 2,000 feet and stayed there, the throttle all the way out, a typical taxi driver whose sole interest was in there and back again. All rubbernecking did was burn gas. Twenty minutes later they landed on a small plateau in almost the exact geographical center of the Park. The north end of the airstrip began at the base of a Quilak mountain; the south end fell off the tip of a Teglliq foothill into the long river valley below. The airstrip on the Step was approximately 3,800 feet shorter than the one in Niniltna, and

George stood on the pedals the instant the Super Cub touched down. They roared to a halt ten feet from the front door of the largest building in the group of prefabricated buildings huddled together at the side of the runway. They climbed out, and Mutt vanished into the trees. "I won't be long," Kate said.

George nodded. "I'll go down to the mess hall and scare up a free meal."

Dan O'Brien had dodged alligators in the Everglades and a'a in Kilauea with enough success to be transferred to the Park on December 3, 1980, the day after Jimmy Carter signed the d-2 lands bill, which added over a hundred million acres to already existing park lands in Alaska. Dan was fiercely protective of the region under his jurisdiction, and at the same time respectful of the rights of the people around whose homesteads and fish camps and mines and villages the Park had been created, which was why he was the only national park ranger in the history of the state never to get shot at, at least not while on park duties. Ranger by day, he was a notorious rounder by night. He'd known Kate since she was in college, and he'd been trying to lay her for at least that long.

The news of her return hadn't reached the Step, and he started around the desk with a big grin and open arms, only to skid to a halt as she unzipped her parka and he saw the scar. "Jesus Christ, Shugak," he said in a shaken voice, "what the hell did you do to your neck?"

She shrugged open the parka but kept it on. "George Perry tells me your boys have been making some new maps of the Kanuyaq."

Her harsh voice grated on his ears. He remembered the guitar, and thought of all the long winter evenings spent singing sea chanteys, and he turned his back on the subject and walked away. It might be the only thing he could do for an old friend, but he would by God do it and do it right. He did ask one question. "Mutt okay?"

"She's fine. She's chasing lunch down outside. About those maps."

"Maps?" he said brightly. "You bet we got maps. We got a map that shows every hump and bump from Eagle to Anchorage. We got a census map that shows the location of every moose bull, cow, and calf from here to the Kanuyaq River delta. We got maps that show where every miner with a pickax sunk a hole more than a foot deep anywhere within two hundred miles. We got maps that show the spread of spruce beetles north of Ikaluq. We got—"

"I need a map that shows me any airstrips there might be around Beaver Creek."

"Pete Liverakos's place? Sure, he's got a strip. About twelve hundred feet, I think. Plenty long enough for his Cessna, but he lands her at Niniltna." His brow puckered. "Been curious about that myself. Why walk a mile downriver in winter when you can land on your own front doorstep?"

She nodded, although she wasn't curious; she knew why. "Is there another airstrip farther up the creek, say halfway between his homestead and Ahtna?"

He thought. "Yeah, I think there's an old mine up there somewheres. Let's take a look." He led the way into a map room, a place of large tables and cabinets with long, wide, shallow drawers. He consulted a key, went to a drawer, and produced a map three feet square, laying it out on a table with a double-jointed lamp bolted to the side. He switched on the light, and they leaned over the map. A stubby forefinger found Niniltna and traced the river from the village to Bea-

ver Creek, and from there up the creek to the homestead. He tapped once. "Here's Pete's place. A twelve-
hundred-foot strip just sitting there going to waste.
And Ahtna's up this way, to the northwest, about a
hundred miles from Niniltna," adding apologetically,
"the scale's too large to show it on this map." He
marked the spot with an eraser and produced a yardstick, laying it on the map, one end pointing at Beaver
Creek, the other at the eraser. With his hand he traced
the length of the yardstick. "And presto chango, there
it is. Like I thought, it's an airstrip next to a gold
mine. Two thousand footer. Probably needed the extra
to land heavy equipment. Abandoned in . . . oh, hell,
'long about '78? Probably about the time Carter de-
clared most of the state an antiquity." He patted her
on the ass and leered when her head snapped up.
"Just think what you'd be missing if he hadn't."

"Just think," she agreed, moving the target out of
range. "Is the strip maintained?"

He made a face. "I doubt it. Never was much gold
there to begin with, and too fine to get out in commercial quantities anyway. Myself, I think the mine was
just an excuse to come in and poach moose."

Her finger came back down the yardstick. "Beaver
Creek runs right up to it."

"Uh-huh." Showing off, he produced another map,
with a flourish worthy of Mandrake the Magician.
"This shows the estimated animal population in the
same area." They studied it. "Neat, huh? A couple
moose moved in five years ago, been real good about
dropping a calf or two every spring. There's half a
dozen pairs of eagles. Beaver, mostly, on the creek."
He snapped his fingers. "Sure. I remember one time
I was at the Roadhouse and Pete brought in a beaver
hide. Said he was running a trapline up the creek."

His lip lifted in a sneer. "Said he'd cured it himself. Shape it was in, nobody doubted it for a minute."

He looked up from the map. The hazel eyes had an edge sharp enough to cut. He remembered a time when those eyes could laugh. "Hell of a trapper and hunter," he said, "that Pete. That is, if you don't count him joining in that wolf hunt the state had last year." He grinned. "Nobody else does."

"Why not?"

"He shot three inches off the prop of his plane, leaning out to draw a bead on a running female."

"He wreck the plane?" Dan shook his head. "Too bad. Okay, Dan. Thanks."

He followed her out of the room. " 'Okay'? 'Thanks'? Is that it? Is that all I get? Of all the ungrateful—"

The front door shut on the rest of it.

George flew back to Niniltna by way of a stop at Ahtna to pick up the mail, fresh off the daily MarkAir flight from Anchorage. Kate waited by the Cub, watching cargo unload from the 737. Ahtna, at the junction of the Park road with the Richardson Highway, was a wet town, with a population of a thousand and three flourishing bars. An entire pallet of Olympia beer was marked for the Polar Bar, a case of Jose Cuervo gold and another of assorted liqueurs for the Midnight Sun Lounge. The 737 took off, and a Northern Air Cargo DC-6 landed in its place, off-loading an igloo of building supplies from Spenard Lumber and a pallet of Rainier beer, this one marked for the Riverside Inn.

No Windsor Canadian in either cargo, but then she didn't see Pete or his 50 Papa around anywhere, either. Once a week, Bernie had said. This wasn't the day.

Ahtna, like Niniltna, was on the Kanuyaq. Down-river was Niniltna. Farther downriver was Prince William Sound. Upriver was a state highway maintenance camp. Last year during a spring storm a corner of the yard had crumbled into the river, taking a barrel of methanol with it. The barrel had floated downriver, to wash ashore outside Ahtna. Four high school kids, two sixteen, one fifteen, one fourteen, already drunk, had literally stumbled across it and instead of falling in the river and drowning tapped the barrel and died of poisoning.

George returned with the bag as the pallet of Rainier was loaded onto the back of a flatbed. He read her silence correctly and said, "They're a common carrier, Kate, just like me. We fly anything, anywhere, anytime, for cash money. That's how we make a living."

"You don't fly booze."

He shrugged. "Not up to me. The town voted to go dry."

"And if it hadn't?"

He shrugged again. A half hour later they were back in Niniltna.

The land, low and flat near the river, began to rise soon after she left it. Blueberry bushes, cottonwoods, and scrub spruce were left behind for currants, birches, and hemlocks. The snow was so deep and was packed down so well beneath its own weight that the Polaris skimmed over it, doing better than forty miles an hour. In spite of the wide swing to avoid the homestead, she reached the abandoned gold mine at four-thirty, with more than an hour of twilight left.

She ran the machine into some birches, the nose pointing downhill, and cut branches for camouflage and to sweep the snow free of tracks. Strapping on

the snowshoes that were part of the standard winter
survival kit she kept beneath the Polaris's seat, she
shouldered her pack, slung the 30.06, and hiked the
quarter of a mile to the mine entrance that gaped
blackly from halfway up the hill next to the creek. It
was dark inside until she got out the flashlight. The
snow in the entrance was solidly packed down, as if
something heavy had been stacked there.

Kate explored and found a branching tunnel, where
she pitched the tent and unrolled the sleeping bag.
Taking the ax and a collapsible bucket, she went down
to the creek and chopped a hole in the ice beneath
an overhanging bush. She filled the bucket with ice
and water. Back at the tent, she lit the Sterno stove.
The exertion and the cold had left her hungry, and
she ate two packages of Top Ramen noodles sitting
at the entrance to the mine, surveying the terrain in
the fading light.

The airstrip ran parallel to the creek, which ran
southeast-northwest around the hill of the mine. A
narrow footpath led from the mine to one end of the
airstrip. She squinted. A second, wider trail started at
the other end of the strip, going in the opposite direction. Birches and scrub spruce clustered thickly at the
edges of the strip and both trails. The creek was lined
with cottonwoods and diamond willow. Mutt visited
them all, sniffing, marking territory.

Kate went back for a Chunky and sat again at the
mine entrance, gnawing at the cold, hard chocolate as
she waited for the moon to come up. An hour later
it did, full and bright. By Agudar's light she walked
down the footpath. Mutt trotted out of the woods and
met her on the strip. It was as hard and smooth as
the strip at Niniltna. The second, wider trail was a
snow machine track. It followed the creek southeast,

dodging back and forth, taking the easiest way through the trees and undergrowth without coming too close to the bank.

The creek itself was frozen over. No snares. No holes cut into the ice in any of the likelier places Kate spotted for snares.

She went back up to the mine and crawled into her sleeping bag, Mutt next to her. Mutt didn't dream. Kate did, the same dream as always, children in pain. In the night she moved, restless, half waking, moaning a little. In the night Mutt moved closer to her, the animal's 140-pound weight warm and solid. Kate slept again.

The next morning the sun was up by nine, and Kate and Mutt were on the creek trail as the first rays hit and slid off the hard surface of the frozen landscape. Kate kept to the trail to minimize the track she left behind. She moved slowly, ears cocked for the sound of an airplane engine, eyes on the creek side of the trail. Again there were no holes, and no snares for holes. There was nothing more to see. Old habits are hard to break, especially the habit of verification instinctive in every good investigator. It had compelled her to give Pete the benefit of the doubt. Now there was none. She went back to the mine.

They waited, camping in the tunnel, carrying water from the creek, Mutt grazing the local rabbit population, for three days. Every morning she broke down the camp and packed it down the hill to the Polaris, and every evening she packed it back up again.

She'd had worse stakeouts. The first morning a pair of eagles cruised by overhead, flying low and slow, eyes alert for any movement on the ground. A gaunt and edgy moose cow and her two calves passed through the area on the second day, moving like they had a purpose. That night they heard the long-drawn-out howl of a wolf. Purpose enough. Down by the creek, a gnawed stand of diamond willow confirmed the presence of Dan's beavers, although the winter's heavy snowfall kept Kate from spotting the dam until the second day. The third afternoon a fat black raven croaked at them contemptuously on his way to make mischief elsewhere. That evening Kate ran out of Top Ramen and had to fall back on reconstituted freeze-dried spaghetti. Some prices are almost too high to pay.

Late on the afternoon of the fourth day, as she was thinking about fetching her camp up again from the Polaris, Mutt's ears went forward and she got to her feet and pointed her muzzle west. Kate faded back into the mine, one hand knotted in Mutt's ruff, the other gripping the handle of her ax, as the Cessna 180 with the tail numbers marking 50 PAPA came into view over the trees. It touched down and used up all of the strip on the runout, bright shiny new in its fresh-off-the-assembly-line coat of red and white. Only bootleggers could afford new planes in the Alaskan bush.

The pilot was tall and rangy and well-muscled, and the unloading was easy and practiced. All the seats save the pilot's had been removed and the remaining space filled up with case after case of Windsor Canadian whiskey, in the plastic bottles. Glass bottles weighed more and took more gas to get into the air. Glass bottles cut into the profit margin.

When he had all the boxes out on the ground, he tucked one box beneath each arm and started up the path toward the mine. Kate and Mutt retreated farther into the darkness.

He made the trip up and back six times, twelve

cases in all, stacking them inside the mouth of the mine where the snow was packed down all nice and hard, where he'd stacked different cases many times before. He whistled while he worked, and when he was done he paused in the mine entrance to remove his cap and wipe his forehead on his sleeve. In the thin sun of an Arctic afternoon, his fifty-year-old face was handsome, although his nose and chin were a little too sharp, like his smile.

He replaced his cap and started down the hill, whistling again. He wasn't halfway to the plane before he heard it, and the sound spun him around on his heels.

Kate stood in front of the stack of boxes, swinging from the hips. The blade of the ax bit deep. A dark-brown liquid spurted out when she pulled it free. The smell of alcohol cut through the air like a knife.

"Hey!" he yelled. "What the hell!" He started back up the slope.

Without a break in her swing, Kate said one word. "Mutt."

A gray blur streaked out of the mine to intercept him, and he skidded to a halt and almost fell. "Shit!"

The blade bit into another case. More whiskey gushed out.

"Goddamn it! Kate!"

"Hello, Pete," she said, and swung.

"Kate, for chrissake cut that out—that stuff's worth a hundred bucks a bottle to me!"

The ax struck again. He made as if to move, but Mutt stood between them, lips drawn back from her teeth, head held low, body quivering with the eagerness to attack.

"You fly to Ahtna and pick up your shipment," Kate said, torn voice harsh in the still afternoon air. The ax bit into the sixth case. "You drop it here and store it in the mine entrance. You fly back to Niniltna, landing at the village strip so the tribal policemen can see how squeaky clean you are. You hike back down to your homestead and spend the next week running your trapline. You were catching beavers, you told everybody at the Roadhouse one night. You even showed them a pelt."

Cardboard and plastic crunched. "Only you don't have a trapline. There isn't a hole in the ice between here and your homestead, or a single snare to drop down a hole. You're not trapping beaver—you're using your snow machine to bring the booze down a case at a time."

He shifted from one foot to the other and tried a disarming smile. "Well, shit, Kate. Guy's got to make a living. Listen, can we talk about this? Don't!" he shouted when she swung again. "Goddamn it, I'll just buy more!"

"No, you won't."

"You can't stop me!"

"No?" She swung. The ax chunked.

It took fifteen minutes in all. Kate had always been very good with an ax. He cursed her through every second of it, unable to walk away. When she was finished, she struck a wooden match on the thigh of her jeans and tossed it into the pile of broken boxes. There was a whoosh of air and a burst of flame. She shouldered the ax and walked down the hill. Mutt followed, keeping between Kate and Pete, hard, bright gaze watching him carefully.

When she approached the Cessna, Pete's voice rose to a scream. "You fucking bitch, you lay a hand on that plane and I'll—"

Mutt snarled. He shut up. Kate raised the ax and swung with all her strength. The blade bit deep into the airframe just above the gear where the controls were located. She pulled the blade free, raised the ax for another swing, and several things happened at once.

A bottle she'd missed exploded in the mine entrance and everybody jumped. Mutt barked, a single, sharp sound, and kept barking. There was a scrabble of feet behind Kate. The ax twisted out of her hands and thudded into the snow six feet away, and she whirled to face a blade that gleamed in the reflection of the whiskey fire. She halted in a half crouch, arms curved at her sides.

Where was Mutt? A bark answered the question somewhere off to her right. She couldn't look away from the blade to see what Mutt had found more important than guarding her back. They would discuss the matter, in detail. Later.

The bootlegger's grin taunted her, and he wasn't looking so handsome anymore. "Sorry, Kate." He gestured at her scar with the knife. "Guess I get to finish what one of your baby-rapers started. No offense," he added. "I'm just making me too much money to let you walk away from this one."

"No offense," she agreed, and as he took a step forward dropped to her hands, kicked out with her right foot, hooked his ankle, and yanked his feet out from under him. He landed hard on his back, hard enough to jolt the knife out of his grip. She snagged it out of the air and in one continuing smooth motion had the point under his chin. The grin froze in place.

She pressed up with the blade. Very slowly and very carefully he got to his feet. She kept pressing, and he went all the way up on tiptoe. "What is this," she said, "a six-inch blade?" A bead of bright-red blood appeared, and he gave an inarticulate grunt. "I personally think your brain is too small for the blade to reach if I stick it in from under your chin." She pressed harder. "What do you think?"

His voice broke on a sob. "Jesus, Kate, don't, please don't."

Disgusted, she relaxed enough for him to come down off his toes. The point of the knife shifted, and he jerked back out of range. Blood dripped from his chin. He wiped at it and gave his hand an incredulous look. "You cut me! You bitch, you cut me!" He backed away from her as if he could back away from the blood, too. His heel caught on something, and he lost his balance and fell over the bank of the creek. It was short but steep, and momentum threw him into a heavy, awkward backward somersault. He landed on a fallen log. Kate heard the unmistakable crack of breaking bone from where she stood. The whiskey fire was high enough to show the white gleam of bone thrusting up through the fabric covering his left thigh.

Becoming aware of a low rumble of sound, she turned. Mutt stood in the middle of the airstrip, legs stiff, hackles raised, all her teeth showing as she stared into the trees. A steady, menacing growl rumbled up out of her throat. Kate followed her gaze. Five pairs of cold, speculative eyes met her own. Five muzzles sniffed the air, filled with the scents of burning whiskey, leaking hydraulic fluid, broken flesh, the rust-red smell of fresh blood.

Behind them Pete clawed his way up the creekbank and saw. "Kate." His voice sweated fear.

She turned her head to look at the man lying on the frozen creekbank, and she did not see him. She saw instead eight kids in Alakanuk, drunk and then dead drunk. She saw a baby drowned in Birch Creek, left on a sandbar by parents too drunk to remember to load him into the skiff with the case of beer they had just bought, and just opened.

She saw her mother, cold and still by the side of the road, halfway to a home to which she never returned and a husband and a daughter she never saw again.

Kate picked up the ax and took a step back. Five pairs of eyes shifted from the prone man to follow her progress. "Mutt," she said, her torn voice low.

The steady rumble of Mutt's growl never ceased as she, too, began to retreat, one careful step at a time.

"Kate," Pete said. "That thing with your mother, that was business. A guy has a right to make a living, you know?"

Her camp was already packed and stowed. The ax went in with it. The brush concealing the Polaris was easily cleared, and she'd left the machine pointed downhill for an easy start. She straddled the seat.

"Kate!" His voice rose. "Your mother would fuck for a bottle! Shit, after a while she'd fuck for a drink! Goddamn you, Kate, you can't leave me here! Kate!"

The roar of the engine drowned out his scream.

Gathering clouds hid the setting sun. It would snow before morning. It was sixty miles across country to her homestead. Time to go. Mutt jumped up on the seat behind her, and Kate put the machine in gear.

SALAD DAYS

An Angela Matelli story

Wendi Lee

FIRST APPEARANCE: *The Good Daughter*, 1994

Wendi Lee splits her time between the P.I. and Western genres, managing to forge a successful career in each. Most of her westerns are about Jefferson Birch, a P.I. in the Old West. Angela Matelli is her contemporary P.I., an ex-Marine living in Boston and beset by, among other things, a large Italian family, and all the adventures that entails.

"Salad Days" first appeared in the Winter '95 issue of *Noir Magazine*.

As I walked from the subway to the restaurant where I was working undercover, I kept feeling a draft up the back of my legs. I stared at my reflection in the glass front of the New Age vegetarian restaurant, Salad Days, and grimaced. My waitress uniform was bright green with a square neckline, puffed sleeves, a short, full skirt, and a bib apron with a vegetable motif. Oh, the things I did for relatives. On my little sister Rosa, the uniform looked cute. On me, an ex-Marine approaching thirty, it looked ridiculous.

When Rosa had been hired on a month ago at Salad Days, the hours had fit in perfectly with her school schedule. Then Joshua Cowan, manager of Salad Days, discovered that during the last month, someone had been systematically skimming fifty dollars a night from the dinner shift profits. Since Rosa was his newest employee, she was, in Cowan's eyes, the only suspect. He didn't want the publicity or the police, so he just let Rosa go.

"How could Mr. Cowan do this to me?" Rosa had sobbed.

After the initial shock wore off, Rosa got angry and decided to fight back. She suggested that I go to Cowan with a deal: I would find the real thief in exchange for Rosa being hired back. Since private investigation was my business, and since I had nothing in my appointment book for the next thirty years, I immediately agreed. Then the thought crossed my mind that Joshua Cowan might be stealing from Salad Days and covering for himself by firing Rosa. So I convinced Rosa to help me put an application together, under an assumed name, of course.

The next day, we concocted the perfect application, complete with high praise of my waitressing ability and glowing references to my reliability, all courtesy of an uncle in the restaurant business. I was hired on the spot and was told to report for work the next day.

Today was my first day. I stepped inside Salad Days and looked at the restaurant with new eyes. Paintings of eggplant, zucchini, tomatoes, and lettuce adorned the otherwise stark white walls. Square black tables each held a single red flower in a bud vase and place settings of white placemats and red cloth napkins. Ferns were hung from the ceiling in strategic places and rubber plants in large ceramic pots stood in corners and near posts. I took all this in before approaching a short, thin, woman in her thirties and introduced myself. "Hi, I'm Angie, the new waitress."

Her friendly smile told me that she was expecting me. "I'm Janice," she said. "I'll show you the ropes."

Mustering what little enthusiasm I had for wait-ressing, I replied, "Great. Let's get started."

Janice took me into the kitchen for introductions. Marcus, the cook, was a heavy man with a perpetual pout. "I do hope you can write clearly, my dear," he warned. "It would do well for you to remember that you are not a physician." I wondered if Marcus had any opportunity to steal from the till during or after work. I would be keeping my eye on the cash register all evening.

Next, Janice introduced me to Dennis, the dish-washer/busboy. He wore his dark blond hair slicked down and slightly long in back. The rest of him was pretty greasy as well, from his razor-thin, pockmarked face to his pointy-toed boots. When Dennis looked up at me, his eyes mirrored the boredom of his job, but he must have noticed my appraisal. "Nice to meet you," he said with a smirk. I noticed the gold Rolex on his wrist and wondered how he could afford some-thing like that. Chances were that his restaurant job didn't pay well enough.

The next hour was filled with mind-numbing instruc-tions such as how the tables were divided into stations, filling condiments, and how to make coffee and tea. While we were rolling the flatware into cloth napkins, Janice talked about herself.

"I just got divorced," she confessed, "and my kids are having a hard time adjusting." I had been shown wallet photos of her son and daughter during our break.

"It sounds rough," I replied sympathetically. "Are you still friends with your ex?"

She gave a bitter laugh and replied, "When I hear anyone telling me that they had a friendly divorce, I don't believe it. I don't think any couple can remain friends after divorce. It's hardest on me when he comes over to take the kids for a day, which is getting to be less often."

I changed the subject. "Where's the manager today?" I wondered why I hadn't seen Cowan yet.

Janice had begun to fill pepper shakers. She sneezed. "Oh, he rarely stays after three-thirty. He might drop in sometimes to see how we're doing, but he's usually here only through the lunch shift." Janice glanced at her watch and said, "We'd better move if you're going to get a chance to look at a menu before we open, Angie."

I attempted to memorize entrees and prices before Salad Days opened for business at five-thirty. By the time the first customers started trickling in, I had a pounding headache from trying to remember if the Eggplant Surprise was seven or eight dollars.

I kept my eye on the cash register as much as possible during my shift. Janice seemed to be the one who spent the most time at the till. As a new waitress, I had not been trained on the register yet. Dennis also worked in the front when business picked up. As the evening wore on, Dennis wore on my nerves. Whenever Janice called into the back for help, Dennis made sure to bump up against me on his way to the register. Despite this unpleasant distraction, I managed to notice that Marcus stayed in the kitchen all night. I don't think he even got a break. The hours went by swiftly and by the end of the evening, my feet felt as if I'd been on a fifty-mile march without a rest.

"So what do you think of this place? Is it anything like the restaurant you used to work at?" Janice asked as we wiped down the tables.

"I like it fine. The tips are better here than the last place I worked." I decided it was time to bring up

Rosa. "I heard that the girl who worked here before me was fired for stealing. How long had she been here?"

Janice's face darkened and she shook her head. "Poor Rosa. She only worked here about a month. It's hard for me to believe she did it." Her expression brightened as she added, "But Rosa's young and she'll find another job."

I shook my head grimly. "Being accused of stealing is going to make it difficult for her to find work. I know that at the last place I worked, the owner didn't hire anyone with even a hint of scandal in their past employment. Was there an investigation?"

"No. Josh didn't want the publicity. He told us that he was sure it was her and that he just quietly let her go."

"That doesn't sound fair," I replied. My tone had an edge to it. I was getting angry, so I changed the subject. "What about you, how long have you been here?"

"About two years. I didn't think I'd be here this long, but the tips are great. We've even gotten a few celebrities in here." She proceeded to name a couple of actors and musicians who had frequented the place in the past. Finally, Janice surveyed the dining room and nodded her head, satisfied. "We're almost done here, except for the register. Why don't I show you how to count it out. Besides, I wouldn't mind someone watching me after the incident with Rosa."

I followed her over and we counted it out, separated the checks, cash, and credit card receipts into bundles, and stuffed everything into an official bank bag. While Janice brought the bag back to the office safe, I went over to the coatrack. As I pulled my black wind-breaker down, a dark blue man's jacket fell to the floor. I stooped to pick it up. A small plastic bag fell out of a slash pocket. After a quick examination of the white powder residue in the bottom of the bag, I hurriedly stuffed it back into the jacket. The jacket had a recognizable label inside, the kind you would buy at a high-class store. I wondered if Cowan had left it behind this afternoon.

"That's mine," Dennis said. His voice startled me. He took the jacket from me and slipped it on.

"Nice jacket," I said, wondering how a dishwasher could afford a gold Rolex and brand-name clothes.

He smirked. "My brother owns an outlet." Dennis looked me up and down as if he liked what he saw. Small wonder, he'd spent most of the night up close and personal with me. If he weren't a suspect, I'd have knocked his lights out hours ago.

Dennis moved in closer. "I could get you some real nice designer clothes like what I'm wearing. And you wouldn't have to pay much for them. You free now?" He slipped an arm around my waist.

"No, I have to go home and feed my goldfish," I replied, moving away quickly as if I hadn't noticed his moves. I put on my shabby windbreaker. "But thanks," I added with a tight smile, "I'll think about it."

When I got home, I went directly to Rosa's apartment. She tried not to laugh at the sight of me in my waitress uniform, but her sense of humor finally got the better of her. "You look like a crazed leprechaun," she managed to say, wiping a tear from her eye.

"Right. Get it out of your system," I said crossly. "I'll be upstairs, changing. Come up when you can keep a straight face." I stomped out of Rosa's apartment, accompanied by the sound of my sister howling with laughter.

Ten minutes later, I was in comfortable clothes and Rosa had stopped laughing. I asked her about the people I was working with.

"Marcus badly wants to have his own restaurant," she said. "It's all he ever talked about when I was there. Janice, well, she's a sad case. Her husband was abusive and she took it for ten years. When he started taking it out on the kids, she packed up and left him. He's paying child support and she has a restraining order. He can't go near her, except to pick up or drop off the children."

"What about Dennis?" I asked.

"He's an interesting case. I never got to know him very well. During his breaks, he goes out in the alley for a smoke."

I nodded in understanding. Salad Days was a smoke-free restaurant. "What about that Rolex that he sports? How can he afford it on his salary?"

Rosa hesitated for a moment. "I've always suspected he sells drugs on the side."

More likely than he washes dishes on the side, I thought. As a drug dealer, he was a walking advertisement. A blinking neon sign around his neck couldn't have pointed it out more clearly. "What about Joshua Cowan?" I asked. "Do you think he might be in financial trouble?"

Although Cowan had accused Rosa of slipping the money out of the register while she was totaling checks, there was nothing to prove that Cowan couldn't have altered the bank slips before taking the night's total to the bank the next day.

"I don't know, Sarge," Rosa replied, shrugging. Ever since I left the Marines, "Sarge" was her affectionate nickname for me. "Digging up secrets is your department, right?"

I spent the next day getting information from Raina, the East Boston police dispatcher and my best friend.

"Wow, you sure don't ask for much, do you, Angie?" Raina said as she sat down in my office and slapped the manila folders down on my desk. "Do you know how difficult it was for me to get this information on my day off?"

"I know, and thanks, Raina," I said, sincerely meaning it. "If it weren't for Rosa . . ." I trailed off.

She made a dismissive gesture with her hand. "I know, I know. I've known Rosa almost as long as I've known you and I think she got a raw deal. Which is why I moved so fast on this request of yours."

I flipped through the folders. Janice had a few parking violations from a few years ago. Parking tickets were nothing new in a big city like Boston. Space was at a premium and after a while, the citizens begin to invent parking spaces. It was interesting to note that unlike most citizens, Janice had paid all her fines.

There was one more note of interest in Janice's file: the police had been called out to her home more than once for domestic violence. The reports always ended with "No charges filed" until the last one, about six months ago. Apparently Janice finally got tired of being beaten and filed for divorce. I caught a small notation in the report: "Evidence of battery on ten-year-old girl, Melissa." So that backed up what Rosa had told me. As in most cases of wife abuse, it had been all right if Dad beat up Mom, but when he turned violent with the kids, she suddenly found her backbone.

Dennis Holding's file was thick with arrest reports for selling and holding drugs. He never seemed to

spend any time in jail; he just got arrested a lot. I
would have loved to hang the restaurant's robbery on
Dennis, but I hadn't seen him near the cash register
more than a couple of times during my first night.
Still, he was a suspect.

Marcus Freeley's file contained one arrest report. I
scanned it, but found little to help me in my search
for the truth. The cook had been arrested once back
in the early seventies. He had been a college student
in possession of a bag of marijuana and had only been
given a slap on the wrist.

Cowan didn't have a file. He apparently didn't own
a car, so there weren't any tickets, and he didn't have
so much as a citation for spitting on the sidewalk. He
was, by all accounts, a model citizen. It would take a
little more digging on my part. I thanked Raina again
and we made arrangements to get together when I
was done working at Salad Days.

After she left the office, I started to make a few
phone calls to check on my suspects' financial background. I started with Joshua Cowan—his Victorian
house in Brookline, his family, his finances, everything. I discovered that he and his wife lived above
their means, taking at least one expensive three-week
vacation a year. Cowan also owned a cottage in Truro,
an exclusive community on Cape Cod. And I couldn't
figure out how he was paying for it all.

Although Cowan was still a suspect, I couldn't rec-
oncile the amount of money skimmed from Salad
Days with the lifestyle Cowan was living. The way
Cowan handled firing Rosa did not look good, but I
didn't see how skimming fifty dollars a night would
add up to the amount of money Joshua Cowan would
need to finance his extravagant lifestyle.

Marcus Freeley had been in serious financial trouble

a few months ago, but suddenly his bank account turned flush. Although it was mysterious, his good fortune could not be explained by the small amount skimmed off the restaurant's profits.

Janice Gardner's finances were about what I had expected for a divorced waitress with two growing kids. She was barely making ends meet. She was still a suspect, but if she was having such a hard time, why wasn't she skimming more money to make life easier?

Dennis had no bank account. On paper, he had almost no financial history. I would have to dig a little deeper tomorrow.

I looked up from the paper on my desk and glared at the perky green uniform hanging on a coat hook on the wall. It was almost time to go to work. I had pored over the files and dug into the backgrounds of the suspects, and had come up with almost nothing. The cook was last on my suspect list, and as much as I would have liked to pin the crime on the man who fired my sister, I couldn't see any serious motive on Cowan's part. Dennis and Janice were the only ones left—a drug dealer and a former battered wife with dependents.

I was beginning to form a picture in my head, something that I wasn't sure I liked. But I followed my instincts and made a couple of phone calls. After confirming my suspicions, I picked up the phone one last time and called a friend on the police force.

"Lee? This is Angela Matelli."

"Good to hear from you, Angie," Detective Lee Randolph said heartily. "What have you been up to lately?"

"Moonlighting," I replied, "at a restaurant called Salad Days. How would you like to make a drug bust tonight?" I bent over, opened my bottom left desk drawer, and took out a camera.

The dinner shift was busy for a Thursday night. Sometime during the evening, Joshua Cowan stopped in. When he saw how busy we were, he stayed and ran the register while Janice and I ran back and forth from the kitchen to the dining room until I was certain I'd worn an inch off my pump heels. By the time the last customers were getting ready to leave and Janice was putting the CLOSED sign in the front window, I slipped into the kitchen. Marcus was wrapping up left-over chopped vegetables. Dennis was nowhere in sight. The back door was open.

"Where's Dennis?" I asked.

Marcus looked up, then jerked his head toward the open door. "He's taking his break."

I went over to the coatrack and pulled my handy pocket camera from the pocket of my windbreaker. Then I walked over to the door and looked out. The alley was dimly lit and I hoped that what I was about to do would work. A few yards down, I spotted Dennis with a customer. It looked like a man, I thought, although the figure was too hunched over to get a clear picture. But that's exactly what I did. I fixed the camera on the two shadowy figures.

Just as money and drugs were being exchanged, I shouted, "Hey, Dennis!" He looked up at me, as did his customer, and I snapped the picture. The flash worked beautifully.

Dennis's customer turned and fled down the alley toward the busy avenue. Dennis's surprised expression turned into a snarl. He started toward me at a surprising speed. Before I knew what was happening, he knocked me to the ground. When I recovered my breath, I saw Dennis looming over me, a stiletto in his hand. He made slashing motions in the air before aiming the blade at my throat. I rolled out of the way, onto my side, and kicked him in the knee. Something snapped. He went down, howling and clutching his leg.

I picked myself up and brushed off my now torn and stained uniform. A big man, probably an undercover cop, helped Dennis to his feet. His leg wouldn't straighten out, but I figure he'd get treated at Mass General before being booked.

"What are you, a narc or something?" Dennis managed to growl at me.

I smiled and stood my ground. "No, but they are."

Detective Lee Randolph came up to us. I handed the photo to him before he started reciting the Miranda to Dennis. As I turned toward the restaurant door, I noticed that we'd drawn a crowd of three— Marcus, Janice, and Joshua Cowan.

"I think an explanation is in order," I said to all three. Once we were seated at a table in the dining room, I laid the whole story out for them. Cowan was irate when he found out that I had misrepresented myself, but he turned sheepish when I gently pointed out that he was the one who fired my sister without giving her a chance to prove her innocence.

"So Dennis was not only selling drugs out the back door during and after business hours, but was also skimming from our till," Cowan said when I was finished.

I nodded. "I can't prove it, but our boy has quite an arrest record. He served some time in jail, too."

Cowan's face went red. "He didn't mention it on his application."

I shrugged. "What's one more minor crime like lying on your application when you've got everything else stacked against you?"

Cowan rubbed the back of his neck. "I probably would have still hired him, but I wouldn't have let him near the till if I'd known about his record."

"That's why he didn't mention it, in the hopes that you wouldn't check into his background."

Marcus sighed and absently rubbed the table surface with a corner of his apron. "You must have suspected us all."

I nodded. "I did. But I checked into your backgrounds and you were all too nauseatingly normal to suspect for long."

Cowan got up. "Well, it's been a long day for everyone. Marcus, Janice, carry on and lock up. I'm going home." He motioned to me and I followed him to the front door. "Tell Rosa she can start back to work tomorrow."

I frowned. "That's all? You fire her, then hire her back so abruptly?"

He gave me a wry smile. "I do owe her an apology, so please convey that to her. When I see her in person tomorrow evening, I'll apologize again. Okay?"

I crossed my arms. "What about her lost work time?"

Cowan sighed. "You really drive a hard bargain. Okay, she gets two days' pay for her hardship."

"Including an average night of tips?"

"Don't push it, Matelli," he warned, then gruffly added, "plus some money to compensate for lost tips. By the way, what did you find out about me? Just out of curiosity, of course."

"You live way above your means. Your credit cards are maxed out. You do not have an A-plus credit rating."

Cowan studied me for a moment, then nodded. "Who does?"

"That's why I said you were all nauseatingly normal. You didn't have a good enough reason to skim such a measly amount of money."

After he left, I was approached by a sheepish Marcus. "I was wondering what you found out about me," he said.

With a sigh, I patted him on the back. "I hope your restaurant is a success, Marcus. But how did you come up with the money?"

He flushed. "I have a silent partner. I can't tell you who it is. He comes in here sometimes. He's in the music business." I remembered that Janice had mentioned that some celebrities considered Salad Days too chichi for words.

I held up my hand. "Say no more. Just send me an invitation for the grand opening."

After Marcus left, Janice and I were the only ones left. She was putting her coat on when I approached her.

"Janice," I began.

She averted her eyes. "I suppose Rosa will be back to work tomorrow. It sure was smart how you figured out Dennis did it all."

"But he didn't."

Her shoulders stiffened and her voice was timid. "He didn't?"

"Oh, he's guilty of selling drugs, but not of skimming. I was pretty sure that Joshua wasn't going to press charges once he found out who it was. After all, he fired my sister without an investigation." I paused, not knowing how to say it. "It was you who did it, right?"

She slumped over, suddenly looking very weary. "Yes," she said dully, "it was me. My ex is a deadbeat and I had no way of meeting all the monthly bills on just my salary. How did you find out?"

"I made a call to the county clerk's office to find out if you'd been getting your child support checks. Then I called your lawyer and he told me that you had contacted him when the checks stopped showing up a few months ago. And he'd told you that he didn't think he could help you."

"Because I didn't have the money to pay the lawyer," Janice replied bitterly. "And taking a second job would have meant less time with my kids. My ex, the vindictive son of a bitch, would have fought for custody, saying that I wasn't a good mother for leaving my kids alone."

"But he wouldn't have gotten custody, Janice," I pointed out gently. "He's on record as a child abuser."

"But his mother could have gotten custody," she replied in a hard voice. "I was going to pay it all back, every penny. I keep a running account. But I'm always behind on my bills. Something new comes along every month and, well . . ." A tear slid down her cheek and she turned her face away from me.

I put my arm around her. "I understand. And I think your lawyer was a snake not to recommend some recourse. You can get your ex's wages attached. I know a good lawyer, a cousin of mine, who'll help you file charges against him. Pro bono. But you have to promise me something."

"What?"

"Don't rob the till again. Dennis has taken the blame for this and I don't want my sister in trouble again."

"Agreed," Janice said with relief.

We locked up the place together and headed for the subway.

THE LAST PEEP
A Stephanie Plum story
Janet Evanovich

FIRST APPEARANCE: *One for the Money,* 1994

Janet Evanovich struck gold with her lady bounty hunter Stephanie Plum. Readers and critics alike hailed both their appearances on the scene with open arms and enthusiasm. Having appeared in five novels to date, Stephanie—and her creator—show no sign of slowing down and continue to forge their own path in the mystery genre, rather than follow someone who came before. Such originality is welcome, and refreshing.

This story first appeared in the Mary Higgins Clark anthology *The Plot Thickens*.

Uh-oh," Lula said. "There's something crawling on me. I think it's big and black and ugly. And it's not my boyfriend, you see what I'm saying?"

Lula is a former hooker turned bounty hunter in training. She looks like George Foreman with hair by Shirley Temple, and she has the disposition of a '54 Buick. Lots of power under the hood, headlights the size of basketballs, plus you can hear her coming a mile away.

I don't look at all like George Foreman. I'm more like Wonder Woman with a B cup. I'm the bounty hunter who's training Lula, but the truth is, I'm not exactly the bounty hunter from hell. A year ago, I blackmailed my bail bondsman cousin, Vinnie, into giving me this job, and now I'm going one day at a time, hoping the bad guys are all out of bullets.

"This is your fault," Lula said. "You're the one wanted to see what was in this dumb-ass cellar. Let's go down those rickety stairs and have a look, you said. Let's see if Sammy the Squirrel is down there. And then *slam* the door got closed and locked, and you drop your dumb flashlight and can't find it, and here we are in dark so thick I can smell it. Here we are standing on a dirt floor with things crawling on us."

"I told you to be careful of the door! I told you to make sure it stayed open!"

"Well, excuse me, Ms. Stephanie Plum," Lula said. "I was concentrating on not breaking my neck on the first step which happens to have a board missing."

"We should feel around for a light switch," I said. "There must be a light switch here someplace."

"I'm not feeling nothing. I'm not putting my hands to places I can't see."

"Then give me your gun. Maybe I can blast the lock off the door."

"I don't have no gun. I'm wearing spandex. I'm making a fashion statement here. I haven't got no room for gun bulges. I thought it was your turn to carry the gun."

"I didn't think I'd need it. I wasn't planning on shooting anyone today."

"Yow!" Lula said. "There's something just dropped on me again, and it's moving. Shit! There's another one. There's things all over me, I'm telling you. I bet they're spiders. I bet this place is filled with spiders."

"Just brush them off," I said. "Spiders won't hurt you."

I could be real brave as long as they weren't dropping on me.

"Ahhhh!" Lula yelled. "I hate spiders. There's nothing I hate more than spiders. Let me out of this place. Where's the door? Where's the freaking door?"

The door was at the top of the stairs, but the door was locked. We'd already tried the door.

"Outta my way," Lula said, somewhere in the blackness. "I'm not staying down here with no spiders."

Stomp, stomp, stomp. I could hear her on the stairs. And then *crash*! There was the sound of splintering wood and hinges popping. And a shaft of light cut through the dark.

I ran up the stairs and angled myself through the broken door.

Lula was spread-eagle on her back, on the floor, breathing heavy. "I don't like spiders," she said. "I got any on me?"

"Don't see any."

In all honesty, I wasn't looking too closely because my attention was diverted to a pile of rags on the other side of the room. We'd done a fast, room by room check of the house, but I hadn't looked under the soiled mattress or kicked around in the clutter. Some filthy blankets had been flung against the far wall, and from this angle I could see fingertips sticking out from under the blankets. I crossed the room in two strides, lifted the top blanket and found Sammy the Squirrel aka Sam Franco. He was dead. And he was naked.

The court wanted him for fleeing a charge of indecent exposure. I wanted him for the apprehension fee which was ten percent of his bond amount. Lula wanted him for her share of my share. And so far as I know that was the extent of Sam's being wanted. He was a societal dropout of the first magnitude.

"Uh-oh," I said to Lula. "Sam's turned up."

Lula opened her eyes and rolled her head to the side. *"Yikes!"* she shrieked, jumping to her feet.

The Squirrel had a hole in the middle of his forehead and a toe tag tied to his Mr. Happy. Someone had printed "Get a life" on the toe tag.

"Looks like ol' Squirrel flashed the wrong person," Lula said. "Someone didn't like him wagging his wonkie around."

Seemed like a high price to pay for wonkie wagging. "He wasn't shot here," I said. "No blood and brains on the floor."

"Yeah, and he's been dead awhile," Lula said. "He's pretty stiff." She took a closer look. "Most of him, anyway."

We were in a broken-down, boarded-up bungalow on Ryker Street in Trenton, New Jersey. The house backed up to the Conrail track and was a block from the old Milped Button Factory. There were scrubby fields on either side of the house and beyond that more abandoned bungalows. Very isolated. Excellent place to dump a body.

Everyone knew Sam lived in the house, and everyone knew he wasn't dangerous. Lula and I hadn't expected complications.

Lula cut her eyes side to side. "All of a sudden, this house is giving me the creeps. I don't like dead guys. I especially don't like them with their head ventilated like this."

There was a rattle at the back door and Lula and I exchanged glances.

"Probably the wind," I said.

"I'd go take a look, but one of us should call the police about the body. It's not that I'm afraid, or anything, it's just I got other things to do."

Unlike Lula, I was perfectly willing to admit I was spooked. No way was I staying there all by myself, waiting to get fitted for one of those toe tags using some innovative attachment process. "I'm sure there's no reason to be alarmed," I said. "But just in case, we'll both call the police."

"No need to panic," Lula said.

"Right. No need."

Then we whirled around almost knocking each other over trying to get out the front door. We scuttled across the yard of hard-packed dirt and weeds, to my black CRX and took off, laying rubber.

I usually carry a cell phone, but today it was home, recharging on my kitchen counter, so we drove around, looking for a place to make a call. I used to have one of those gizmos that let my phone charge in my car, but someone stole it, and I hadn't had a chance to get a replacement. If it had been an emergency I'd have stopped and rapped on a stranger's door, but I didn't think five minutes here or there would matter to Squirrel. All the king's horses and all the king's men weren't going to put Squirrel back together again.

I turned onto State Street, drove two more blocks and found a 7-Eleven with a pay phone. I put the call into police dispatch, identified myself and reported the body. Then Lula and I retraced our route back to the bungalow.

A blue and white was already on the scene. Two uniforms stood beside the car. One was Carl Costanza. I've known Carl for twenty-five years, ever since kindergarten. When Carl was nine he could burp in time to the "Star Spangled Banner." This was an accomplishment I unsuccessfully tried for years to emulate.

Carl gave me his long-suffering cop look. "Let me

guess," Carl said. "You were the one who made the call."

"Yep."

"Is this the right house?"

"Yep."

"Well, I don't know how to break this to you . . . but there's no body here."

"It's laying in the living room," Lula said. "You can't miss it. It's a naked body with a big hole in its head."

Carl rocked back on his heels, thumbs stuck in his utility belt. "I went all through the house, and there's no body."

Two hours later, Lula and I were eating french fries and sucking milkshakes in the McDonald's lot just outside center-city.

"I know what I saw, and I saw a dead guy," Lula said. "That Squirrel was dead, dead, dead. Someone came and snatched that body. And it wasn't the polite thing to do either, because that was our body. We found it, and it was ours." She crammed some fries into her mouth. "This whole thing is creeping me out."

I was creeped out, too. But more than that I was slack-jawed and bug-eyed with dumbfounded curiosity. What the hell happened to Squirrel? We'd been gone thirty minutes tops. Why would someone dump a body and then remove it?

"I had plans for my share of the recovery fee," Lula said. "I don't suppose Vinnie's gonna give us the money now that some loser came and took our body."

It seemed unlikely since we hadn't recovered anything.

"You know Squirrel?" Lula asked.

"I went to school with him. He was four years older than me. Stayed back a couple times and finally dropped out in junior high. I've only seen him in passing lately."

"He used to talk to me sometimes when I was on the corner doing my previous profession. Used to ride up on that rickety red bike of his. Bet that bike was a hundred years old."

I'd forgotten about the bike. Most street people never ventured farther than a couple blocks. Because Squirrel had a bike he was able to live in an abandoned house and range far and wide for recreational peeping.

"Do you remember seeing the bike at the house?" I asked Lula.

"Nope. That bike wasn't there. And we walked all over with the cops. We looked in the back and the front, and we looked all through the house."

We both thought about that for a moment.

"Squirrel wasn't a bad person," Lula said, serious-voiced. "Was just that his train stopped a few feet from the station. He liked to watch people. Liked to look in bedroom windows at night. And then one thing would lead to another, and pretty soon Squirrel wouldn't have no clothes on, and sometimes he'd get caught and get his bony white ass hauled off to jail."

Lula was right about Squirrel not being a bad person. He could be damn annoying. And seeing his nose pressed against your window at one in the morning could be scary as hell. But Squirrel wasn't mean, and he wasn't violent. And I didn't like that someone had killed him. And, I also didn't like that I'd lost the body. What were the police going to tell Squirrel's mother? *Someone said they saw your son with a bullet hole in his head, but we can't find him. Sorry.*

"This has gotten ugly," I said to Lula.

"Damn skippy. I'm feeling downright cranky about the whole thing. In fact, the more I think about it, the crankier I'm getting."

I finished my milkshake and stuffed the straw under the lid. "We need to find Sam."

"Not me," Lula said. "I'm not looking for no dead guy. I don't like dead guys."

"I thought you had plans for the recovery money."

"Well, now that I think about it I guess dead guys aren't so bad. At least they don't shoot at you."

Usually, I relied on the bond agreement to provide some leads. In this case it wasn't much help. Squirrel's brother, Bruce, had put up the bond to get Squirrel out of jail. Bruce worked at the pork roll factory and was an okay guy, but I didn't think he knew much more than we did about Squirrel. Squirrel was a brother who lived on the fringe. He was a thirty-four-year-old-man with faulty wiring. A man who related to people through panes of glass. A man who lived in an abandoned house, filled with treasures gleaned from the city's trash cans. A man who kept no calendar to remind him of holiday dinners. Squirrel and Bruce could have lived on different planets for all the interaction they'd had in the last ten years.

Myra Smulinkski had filed the indecent exposure charge. I knew Myra, and I knew Squirrel must have made a royal nuisance of himself for Myra to call the police. Myra lives on Roosevelt, in the heart of the burg. And mostly Squirrel is tolerated in the burg. After all, that's where he was born and that's where his family still lives.

The burg is a tight Trenton neighborhood of second- and third-generation Italians, Hungarians and Germans. It's roughly shaped like a piece of pie, and it exists only in the minds of its residents. Windows are kept clean. Numbers runners never miss mass. And at an early age, men learn to change their own oil in the alleys and single car detached garages that hunker at the back of their lots.

Like Squirrel, I was born in the burg and lived there most of my life. Four years ago, at age twenty-six, I moved into an apartment beyond burg boundaries. Physically I'm at the corner of St. James and Dunworth. Mentally, I suspect I'll always be anchored in the burg. This is an admission that caused my sphincter muscle to tighten in terror that someday I'll turn into my mother.

I shoved the last french fry into my mouth and cranked the engine over. "I think we should visit my grandma Mazur," I told Lula. "If there's anything going through the burg rumor mill about Sam Franco, Grandma Mazur will know."

Grandma Mazur moved in with my parents two years ago when my grandpa went to his final lard-enriched, all-you-can-eat breakfast bar in the sky. Grandma is part of a chain of burg women who make the internet look like chump change when it comes to the information highway.

My mother opened the door to Lula and me. She'd never met Lula, and she was making a good effort not to look dazed at seeing a huge blond-haired black woman wearing brilliant azure eye shadow speckled with silver sparkles, shocking pink spandex shorts and a poison green spandex tank top, standing on her porch. Grandma was jockeying for position beside my mother and wasn't nearly so circumspect.

"Are you a Negro?" Grandma asked Lula. "I didn't know Negroes could have yellow hair."

"Honey, we can have any color hair we damn well want to have. I've got yellow hair because blondes have more fun."

"Hmm," Grandma said, "maybe I need to make my hair blond. I could use some fun."

My father was in the living room with his nose pressed to the sports section. He mumbled a few words about my grandmother having fun on the moon and sunk lower in his chair.

"I've got a couple big thick steaks for supper," my mother said. "And I made a cake."

"We can't stay," I told my mother. "I just stopped around to see if you'd heard anything about Sammy Franco."

"What about him?" Grandma wanted to know. "Are you looking for him? Is this a case you're on?"

"He got arrested for indecent exposure again and didn't show up for his hearing."

"I knew he got arrested," Grandma said. "Poor Myra didn't have no other choice. She said he was always in her backyard. Said he trampled her marigolds into the ground."

"And that's it? That's all you've heard?"

"Is there more?"

"Sammy's been shot. Someone killed him."

Grandma sucked in air. "No! How terrible!"

My mother made the sign of the cross. My father went very still in his chair.

I told them the whole thing.

"I saw a TV show once on body snatchers," Grandma said. "The reason they wanted the bodies was so they could eat their brains."

"Don't mean to disrespect the dead," Lula said, "but those snatchers wouldn't make much of a meal on ol' Squirrel."

Grandma slid her uppers around some while she thought. "Maybe it was one of Squirrel's relatives that came and got him. Maybe he's downstairs at Stiva's on one of them grooved tables."

Stiva was the burg undertaker of choice, and his mortuary was the social hub of Grandma's universe. She read the obits like other people read the movie section.

"I suppose that's possible," I said. *Anything* was possible.

"I could check it out for you. I was going to Stiva's anyway. Big doings there tonight. Joe Lojak is laid out. There'll be a crowd on account of Joe was an Elk. I'm going to have to get there early if I want a seat up front. And don't worry about me. I can take care of myself. I'll go prepared, if you know what I mean."

I took Grandma aside. "What do you mean by 'go prepared'?"

"I'll take 'the big boy,'" Grandma whispered. "Just in case."

"No! No 'big boy.' No, no, no!"

My mother gave me an inquiring look, and I lowered my voice.

"No 'big boy,'" I said to Grandma. "I thought you promised to get rid of it."

"I was going to," Grandma said, "but I'm sort of attached."

"What's this discussion about?" my mother wanted to know, fixing her eyes on me. "Your grandmother makes a scene at the funeral parlor, and I'm holding you responsible. Last time the two of you huddled like this she set off an explosion and caused three hundred thousand dollars worth of damage."

"It could have happened to anybody," Grandma said. "It was an accident."

"Like your granny," Lula said when we were back in the car. "Bet she kicks ass at the funeral parlor. What's the 'big boy'?"

"It's a forty-five long-barrel she picked up at a yard sale."

"That the gun she shot the roast chicken with?"

"No," I said. "She shot the chicken with my thirty-eight."

Lula was looking through the bag of food my mother had sent home with me. "You got two cans of peaches, half a pound of sliced ham, some provolone and a tomato. And it looks like there's some walnuts in the bottom of the bag."

"They're for my hamster, Rex."

"Just like going to the supermarket only you don't have to pay."

"Actually, there's a price."

I turned the corner at Roosevelt and rolled to a stop in front of Myra Smulinski's home. There were six houses on the block, all duplex, all two-story. Each half of a house had its own personality, its own small front yard and rectangular strip of backyard. The backyards bordered a single-lane service road which everyone called an alley. Myra's house was fourth in from Green Street. It was July, and Myra had window boxes filled with begonias sitting on her front porch.

Lula looked at the house. "You think Myra whacked Squirrel?"

Myra was in her late seventies. She had seven grandchildren and a hundred-year-old schnauzer who was mean as a snake. She drove a ten-year-old Buick at a consistent twenty mph, and she was burg renowned for her sour cream pound cake. I didn't think Myra was the one who whacked Squirrel.

"Just thought it'd be useful to talk to her," I said.

Myra answered at the first knock. I wasn't sure word had gotten out about Squirrel being shot, so I simply said I was looking for him.

Myra shook her head. "That Squirrel is a pip. I called the police on him two weeks ago, and he's still coming around trampling my flowers. If you're looking for Squirrel, you've come to the right place."

"Have you actually seen him? Or is it just that the flowers are trampled?"

"I saw him the night I made the phone call. Naked as the day he was born. I heard this noise, so I put the light on the back porch, and there he was . . . shaking hands with the devil. It's a wonder the man isn't blind as a bat the way he was working at that thing."

"Have you seen him recently?"

"I haven't, but Helen Molnar said she saw his bicycle laying in the alley when she came home from bingo the day before yesterday."

"Any of your other neighbors see him?"

"Just Helen. She lives at the end of the block next to Green, and she said his bike was laying at the back of my yard. Don't know why he's singled me out. It isn't like I've got something to see."

"Is his bike still on your property?"

"Nope. The bike disappeared."

"You mind if we look around?"

"Go right ahead. Just try not to make too much noise. Lucille's husband, Walter, next door, worked a double shift last night, and he'll be sleeping. I'm getting ready to go out to the beauty parlor. Need to get a fast set to my hair for tonight. Did you hear about

Joe Lojak being laid out at Stiva's? He was an Elk,
you know. Gonna have to get there early if I want a
good seat."

"Gonna have to muscle Granny for it," Lula whispered behind me.

Lula and I walked the length of the street, turned
the corner and started down the alley. Helen and Lou
Molnar lived in the end house. The other half of the
duplex was occupied by Biggy and Kathy Zaremba
and their two little kids. Biggy worked for his father.
Zaremba and Sons Moving and Storage. There were four
sons and mostly what they stored were hijacked cigarettes and CDs. And mostly what Biggy did was play
cards with his brothers in the warehouse on Mitchell
Street.

Kathy Zaremba's sister, Lucille, lived three houses
down, in the other half of the house occupied by
Myra. Lucille worked at the hospital, and her husband,
Walter, was a security guard.

When we'd walked the alley in its entirety I made
my way back, cutting across yards, snooping into windows. All the houses had a back door with a small
stoop. The door opened into the kitchen, and there
was a room to the other side of the door which was
intended to be a formal dining room, but several people, including Myra, had turned it into a TV room.

Several houses had chain link fencing which deline-
ated the yard. Myra and Lucille had foregone the fencing in favor of a low hedgerow bordered with flowers.
It was this hedgerow that Sam had mutilated, probably
not able to see it in the dark. Neither Myra's house
nor Lucille's house had central air. Both had air condi-
tioners hanging butt-out from upstairs bedroom windows. Both had the downstairs windows open. Myra's
stoop was nice and tidy, but Lucille's stoop was clut-

tered with a bag of kitty litter, a rented carpet shampooer, a sponge mop that had seen better days and a
broken lamp which was probably on its way out to
the garage.

"A bag of kitty litter and a rug shampooer," Lula
said. "I bet Lucille's cat peed on the rug."

As if on cue, a gray cat poked its head out the
broken screen door. The cat was immediately pulled
back and scooped up by Lucille.

"Hi," she said, seeing us standing there.

"I'm looking for Sam Franco," I said. "I know he
hung out here sometimes. Have you seen him lately?"

Lucille stepped outside, leaving the cat in the
kitchen. She had a roll of red duct tape and a scissors
in her hand. She stood still for a moment . . . thinking,
lower lip caught between her teeth. "I saw him the
night the police came. Don't think I've seen him since
then. Sometimes I'd see him on the street, on his bike.
Not since that night though."

"You're not gonna be able to patch that door with
tape," Lula said. "You need a new length of screen."

"It's the cat," Lucille says. "Every time I put in a
new screen the cat pushes it out."

Lucille had a raised welt in the middle of her forehead that was surrounded by a brand-new bruise. I'd
been studiously trying not to stare. Lula, on the other
hand, was never lost to the dictates of etiquette.

"Boy, that's a beauty of a bruise you're growing,"
Lula said. "How'd you get that big goose egg on
your head?"

Lucille lightly touched the bump. "Wasn't paying
attention and ran into a cabinet. Caught the corner."

Lula and I left Lucille to worry about her door and
cut across two more duplexes, bringing us up to Biggy's house. Usually there was a Zaremba Moving and

Storage Econoline van parked in the alley. It was missing today, along with Biggy's Ford Explorer.

Kathy was in the kitchen, feeding the toddler cereal. I rapped on the kitchen window, and Kathy jumped in her seat and the spoon flew out of her hand.

"Jeez!" Kathy said, coming to the back door. "You almost scared me half to death."

I'd gone to school with Kathy, but we didn't see each other much anymore. She'd been the prom queen in high school. Lots of auburn hair and a fast smile. The hair was the same, but the smile was forced now and didn't reach her eyes. She was too thin, and her face was too pale, the only color being a smudge of a fading bruise high on her cheekbone. No point to blaming that bruise on a kitchen cabinet. Everyone knew Biggy smacked Kathy around.

"I'm trying to find Sam Franco," I said to Kathy. "I don't suppose you've seen him?"

She shook her head vigorously. "No!" she said. "I haven't seen anyone, and I can't talk now. I'm feeding Timmy here."

"That Kathy person is on the edge," Lula said when we were back at the car. "I guess babies'll do that to you."

Not to mention Biggy.

"Maybe we should talk to Biggy," I said. "Maybe we should mosey over to the warehouse and see if he's seen Sam."

The Zaremba warehouse was on the other side of Broad, down by the river. I drove to Mitchell, found a space at the curb at the end of the block and sat staring at the open bay doors. Open doors meant there was no business being conducted today. That was good. Most likely no one would want to talk to me if the warehouse was filled with stolen toasters.

Lula and I got out of the car and walked to the first bay. I flagged down a man wearing Zaremba coveralls and told him I wanted to talk to Biggy. A moment later, Biggy appeared. Biggy looked like a Polish knockoff of King Kong in clothes.

"I'm looking for Sam Franco," I told Biggy. "I know he spent time on Roosevelt Street. I was wondering if you've seen him recently."

Biggy grinned and jingled change deep in the pockets of his pleated polyester slacks. "I saw your picture in the paper when you and your granny blew up the funeral home. You're that twinkie bounty hunter."

"Twinkie?" Lula said, hand on hip. "Excuse us?"

Biggy swiveled his eyes to Lula. "Who's the fatso?"

"That does it," Lula said to me. "I'm gonna shoot him."

Biggy gave Lula a punch to the shoulder that knocked her a couple feet backward. "You aren't gonna shoot anyone, chubs. We don't allow shooting in this neighborhood. It lowers the property values."

Lula got her footing and leaned into Biggy, nose to nose, lower lip stuck out. "Don't you touch me," Lula said. "I don't like people to touch me. You touch me again, and I'll bust a cap up your ass. See what that does to property values, you bag of monkey slime."

Biggy pushed his shirt aside so we could see the 9mm. Glock stuck in the waistband of his pants. "Draw," Biggy said to Lula. "Let's see what you got."

"Hold it!" I shouted. "This isn't the gunfight at OK Corral!"

"He's just being a smart-ass," Lula said. "It's obvious I don't have no gun. Anybody could see I left my gun at home."

Biggy draped his shirt back over his Glock. "I don't like people snooping around this warehouse. I find either of you here again, and I'm going to get mad. And bad things happen when I get mad."

I grabbed Lula by the hand and pulled her away from Biggy, back toward the end of the street where the car was parked.

"I don't like him one bit," Lula said, shoe-horning herself into the passenger seat of the CRX. "And if you ask me, I think he did it. I think he shot the Squirrel. He wouldn't think nothing of it. He'd just go *bang* . . . squirrel season."

I did some mental eye rolling and stuck the key in the ignition. I returned to the burg and cruised Roosevelt for several blocks, looking for Squirrel's red bike. I took the corner at Liberty and made my way down Hunt, running parallel to Roosevelt, and kept enlarging the area until there was no more burg left.

"Maybe he wasn't in the burg when he was shot," Lula said. "Squirrel went all over Trenton on that bike."

"Okay," I said, "plan number two. You check the Stark Street neighborhood. I'll go home and make some phone calls."

I was halfway through my list of reliable gossipmongers when Eddy Gazarra called. Gazarra was another cop friend, and he was married to my cousin Shirley the Whiner.

"I heard you're looking for Squirrel," Gazarra said. "Dead or alive."

"You know where he is?"

"The boys just opened up a van on the corner of Wall and Perry. Someone called in a nuisance report. Apparently the van's been sitting there in the sun all afternoon, giving off a bad odor, drawing a thick fog of flies."

"Sam Franco?"

"Yeah. Strapped to a hand truck for easy transport. If you hurry you might still qualify for the recovery money."

I was on my feet and out the door before Eddie had a chance to say good-bye. Recovery of a felon wasn't sufficient grounds for a bondsman to get his bond returned. The bondsman's agent had to be present at the recovery. Considering the bizarre history of this case, I might still get the money back if I hustled.

I screeched to a stop behind a pack of cruisers on Perry Street and hit the ground running. I sorted through a gaggle of cops, looking for a friendly face and felt a wave of relief when I picked out Carl Costanza.

"Long time no see," Carl said. "At least four hours."

"Do you think I'm too late to get credit for the recovery?"

"What, weren't you always here? I was first on the scene, and I could have sworn you were already in place."

"I owe you a beer."

"You owe me a six-pack," Carl said. "And a pizza. Large. Pepperoni."

I glanced at the black lettering on the yellow Econoline. "Zaremba Moving and Storage."

"A clue," Carl said.

"Sort of an obvious clue."

Carl shrugged. "Maybe Biggy didn't think the smell would get bad this fast. Maybe he was waiting for it to get dark to dump the body."

"So you think it was Biggy?"

"It's his personal truck. The one he keeps in the alley behind his house. And he's the sort of hotheaded jerk who'd do something like this. I've been to his house twice this month on domestic violence. Never his wife who calls. She's too scared. Always the neighbor or Lucille, the sister."

I agreed with Carl. Biggy was a hotheaded jerk. Trouble was none of the events made sense. "This is all pretty strange," I said to Carl. "I saw this body in the abandoned house this morning. Why would Biggy take it back and put it in his truck?"

"Second thoughts," Carl said. "Happens all the time. You're in a rush to get rid of the body, so you drop it at the first place comes to mind. Then you get to worrying maybe your fingerprints are on his joystick, so you think the river might be better."

There were two suits from violent crimes in the van with Sam. The medical examiner's pickup arrived and backed in close to the truck. The ME drove a dark blue Ford Ranger with a white cap divided into compartments that reminded me of kennels. The ME got out, stepped onto the van's bumper and hauled himself up.

I sat on the curb and waited while everyone did their thing. By the time I got my body receipt signed, the sun was low in the sky. The medical examiner had placed the time of death around two A.M. Even better, he'd been able to ascertain that Sammy'd been killed with a .45 . . . as the slug had miraculously dropped from Sammy's head when one of the attendants lost his grip on the hand truck holding Sam, and the hand truck crashed to the floor, jarring the bullet loose. At least that's the story they told me.

I didn't feel like being alone with my thoughts, so I ambled over to my parents' house to mooch leftovers.

"Other women have daughters who work in banks

and business offices. I have a daughter who looks for dead people," my mother said, watching me eat. "How did this happen? What am I supposed to say to Marion Weinstein when she asks what my daughter does?"

"Tell her I'm in law enforcement."

"You could get a *good* job if you just put your mind to it. I hear the personal products plant has openings."

Just what I wanted to do . . . spend my days overseeing the boxing machine at the tampon factory.

A car door slammed shut out on the street, and Grandma hustled into the house. "You should have been there! That Stiva knows how to do a viewing, I'm telling you. The place was packed. Joe Lojak looked real good. Nice color to his cheeks. Real natural. He had on a red tie with little brown horse heads on it. And the best part was I beat Myra out for the best seat. She even had her hair done, but I got the seat in the first row next to the window! I'm telling you, I'm good.

"And everybody was talking about Sam Franco! They found him in Biggy's van. And that isn't all. Mildred Sklar was there, and you know Mildred's boy is a police dispatcher, and Mildred said it just came in that they went out to Biggy's house and found the murder weapon in Biggy's closet. Can you imagine!"

"I'm not surprised," my mother said. "Biggy Zaremba is a hoodlum."

"What about Biggy?" I asked. "Did they arrest Biggy?"

"Nope," Grandma said. "He clean got away."

I called Lula and left a message on her machine. "Found Sam Franco," the message said. "So that's the end of that. Give you the details tomorrow."

*   *   *

After two hours of television at my parents' house I still didn't feel comfortable with the Zaremba thing. Not that it was any of my business. My business was simple. Find the missing person. Deliver him to the court. Solving murders was a whole other ball game, and bounty hunters weren't on that team.

"Well," Grandma said, "guess I'm going to bed. Gotta get my beauty rest."

My father opened his mouth to say something, received a sharp look from my mother, and closed his mouth with a snap. My father, on occasion, had likened my grandmother to a soup chicken, and no one was able to deny the resemblance.

"It's late for me too," I said, pulling myself to my feet.

Late enough for me to act like an idiot and snoop along Roosevelt Street under cover of darkness. Don't ask why I felt compelled to do this. Sometimes it's best not to examine these things too closely.

I waved good-bye to my mother and drove down High Street as if I were going home. After three blocks I turned and doubled back and parked at the corner of Roosevelt and Green. The neighborhood was quiet and very dark. No moon in the sky. Downstairs lights were on in all the houses. The burg was a peeper's paradise at night. No one drew their curtains or pulled their shades. Drawn shades might mean your house wasn't immaculate, and no burg housewife would admit to having a dirty house. With the exception of Biggy's house. Biggy's curtains were always closed. Even now when Biggy wasn't in the house, the shades were drawn from force of habit. Biggy had enemies. There were people who might want to snipe at Biggy while he crushed beer cans on his forehead and watched Tuesday Night Fights. I traveled this street all the time, and I knew Biggy never left himself open for target practice.

If this was the movies there'd be a cop watching the Zaremba house, waiting for Biggy. Since Hollywood was a long way from Trenton, I was on the street alone. Round-the-clock surveillance wasn't in the Trenton cop budget.

I followed the sidewalk to the alley and hung a left. I'd only walked a few feet when a car cruised down Green and pulled to the curb. It was a red Firebird with rap music playing so loud the car seemed to levitate at standstill. The driver cut the music and got out of the car. Lula.

"Hah!" she said. "Knew I'd find you sneaking around here. Could hear on the phone you weren't satisfied."

"Curiosity is a terrible thing."

"Killed the cat," Lula said. "Biggy catches you in his yard it gonna kill you too."

"If Biggy has any sense at all, he's on his way to Mexico."

"Uh-oh," Lula said. "Don't look now, but we have company."

The company was Grandma Mazur. She was hustling across the street, waving at us, her white tennis shoes a beacon in the darkness, a distant streetlight reflecting off the big patent leather purse looped into the crook of her arm. I dreaded to speculate what was in the purse.

"I thought you might be coming here to do investigating," she said. "Thought you might need a hand."

What I needed was a parade permit.

"Bet you snuck out of the house," Lula said to Grandma.

"Was easy," Grandma said. "They don't pay attention to me. All I have to do is say I'm getting a glass of water and then walk out the back door."

"I wanted to go through the alley at night," I said. "I wanted to be out here like Sam. See what he saw."

"Then let's do it," Lula said.

"Yeah," Grandma chirped. "Let's do it."

We strolled forward in silence and stopped when we got to the house owned by Lucille and Walter Kuntz. We moved ten feet into the yard, and we could clearly see Lucille watching TV in the back room. She was dressed in a nightgown, her hair was slicked back, and I guessed she was fresh from the shower.

"Where's her husband?" Grandma wanted to know.

"Works the night shift at the stadium. Security guard. Gets off at twelve. Except last night he worked a double shift and didn't get home until eight in the morning."

We simultaneously swiveled our heads to Myra Smulinski's house when the downstairs lights blinked off.

"Myra goes to bed early," Lula said.

We turned our attention back to Lucille. Lucille stayed up late. Maybe she even fell asleep in front of the television.

"Squirrel wasn't peeping in Myra's windows," Lula finally said. "Nothing to see in Myra's windows. Lots to see in Lucille's."

"Nothing to see in Biggy's windows either," I said. "Biggy keeps his shades drawn. So why did Biggy kill Sam if it wasn't for peeking in his windows?"

"Could be anything," Lula said. "Sam could have seen Biggy unloading a van full of hot blenders."

"Maybe it's something homosexual," Grandma said. "Maybe Sam and Biggy were having an affair. And maybe Biggy wanted to end it, and Sam wouldn't hear of it. And so Biggy shot him."

We both just looked at Grandma.

"I was watching television last week and one of them talk shows was about homosexuals," Grandma said. "I know all about them now. And it turns out they're all over the place. You never know who's gonna pop out of the closet next. Some of those homosexual men even wear ladies' underpants. Must be hard to fit your ding dong into a pair of lace panties. Maybe that's why Biggy is so mean. Maybe his ding dong don't fit."

Sort of like the Grinch whose shoes were too tight.

"I gotta lot of theories," Grandma said. "Old ladies got a lot of time to think about these things."

A car swung into the alley and caught us in its headlights.

"Hope it's not the police," Lula said. "The police give me the hives on account of my previous profession."

"Hope it's not my dumb son-in-law," Grandma said. "He gives me the hives on account of he's such an old fart."

I wasn't nearly so concerned about the hives as I was about my life expectancy. I didn't have a good feeling about the car. Normally a driver would slow at the sight of three women walking in an alley. This car seemed to be accelerating. In fact, this car was flat-out aiming for us!

"Run!" I yelped, spinning Grandma around, pointing her at Myra's back door. "Run for cover!"

"Holy cow!" Lula shouted. "This dumb sonnova-bitch is trying to mow us down!"

We scattered in three directions. Grandma, having seen the last of her running days, did a fast shuffle to

Myra's side of the house. Lula ran to Lucille's side of the house. And for no reason other than dumb panic, I jumped behind the single garage that belonged to Lucille and her husband and sat at the back edge of their lot.

The car slid to a stop, spraying dirt and gravel, the door flew open, and Biggy lunged out and took off after me.

"You!" he yelled. "You set me up! I heard about the police report. You were the first one at the van. You found that body in the house and then you stole my truck and set me up, you pussy liar! I want to know who paid you to set me up!"

He didn't look like a man who would listen to reason, so I bagged the denial and raced for Roosevelt Street. He caught me with a flying tackle in Lucille's side yard, and we both went down to the ground, cussing and clawing. We rolled around without making much progress for a few seconds, and then I accidentally pushed his gonads into the space normally reserved for his pancreas.

"Ulp," Biggy whispered, releasing his grip on me.

"I didn't set you up!" I told him. "I had nothing to do with it."

He dragged himself to his knees. "This is what happens when I help someone out of a jam. I get goddamn screwed. I didn't even kill that little retard, but I'm going to freaking kill you. I'm going to cut you up into little pieces. I'm going to carve my initials in your tongue."

"*Help!*" I shrieked. I looked around. No one was coming to help. So I did what any intelligent person would do. I hauled ass out of there. I was moving so fast when I hit Roosevelt Street my feet were airborne. Biggy was thundering behind me. And in my peripheral vision I saw the Firebird rip around the corner and screech to the curb in front of me.

"Get in!" Lula hollered.

I dove into the backseat and the Firebird rocketed away.

Lula slowed after a block. "He's not handling this murder thing well," she said. "Good thing he's not a woman. He'd never make it through the monthly."

Grandma was in the front seat, holding her purse to her chest. "All them Zarembas are soreheads. The whole lot of them. Bunch of big babies."

"We need to call the police," I said. "Who's got a cell phone?"

"Not me," Lula said. "I don't make that kind of money."

"Not me," Grandma said. "I'm on social security."

I had one, but it was in my car, along with my gun and my pepper spray and my stun gun and my bulletproof vest. And unfortunately, my car was parked back on Roosevelt.

"We're only a block from St. Francis Hospital," I told Lula. "You can drop me off there, and I'll run in and make the call."

"Sounds like a good plan to me," Lula said. "That way if Biggy catches up to you, you're real close to the trauma unit."

Lula stopped for a light at Hamilton. High beams flashed in her rearview mirror, and we all swiveled to look.

"Oh, boy," Lula said. "I think I know this car."

I knew the car too. Ford Explorer with bug lights on the top. Biggy's car.

"You might not want to wait for the light to turn," I suggested to Lula. "You might want to move *now*!"

Lula stomped on the gas, and the Firebird jumped

forward. Biggy was less than half a car length away, hunched at the wheel, looking like the antichrist, eyes glittering red, reflecting our taillights.

Lula paused at a cross-street and . . . *wham*! Biggy slammed into the back of the Firebird. I felt my head snap, felt the Firebird accelerate again, away from Biggy.

"Did you see that!" Lula squeaked. "He hit my car! I have six more payments to make on this car."

Grandma had a hand braced against the dash. "You think he did that on purpose?"

Wham! Another jolt from behind.

"He's trying to kill us!" Lula said. "That crazy bastard is trying to kill us!"

Grandma leaned her head out the window and yelled back at Biggy. "You stop hitting us this instant! I'm an old lady. You can't go around whacking an old lady like this! I've got bones like a bird. Another crash and my neck could snap like a dry stick!"

Wham! Biggy didn't care much about old ladies' bones.

"Eeeeee," we all shrieked on impact.

Grandma sucked air. "If that don't beat all!" She fumbled in her purse. "I'll put a stop to this! I'll shoot out his tires. That'll slow him down!" She dragged the big .45 out two-handed, leaned out the window for a second time, and before I could reach her, she squeezed one off. A streetlight exploded and the kick from the gun knocked Grandma off her seat. "Dang," she said. "It looks a lot easier in the movies. Clint Eastwood never has this problem."

Biggy gave us another smack from behind, Lula lost control of the wheel, and the Firebird smashed into a parked car and stalled out.

"Okay, now I'm getting irritated," Lula said. "Now my car don't work at all."

We looked back at Biggy, and we gave a collective gasp when he sprang from his car with a tire iron in his hand and raced toward us.

"Yow!" Lula shrieked at Grandma. "Shoot him! Shoot him!"

Grandma examined her gun. "Looks to me like I only had one bullet." She rolled her window up. "Don't worry, he can't get to us in here."

Smash. The back window went out with one swing of the tire iron. *Smash.* Another window. I crouched to the floor, cowering and praying, and making promises to God, and safety glass chunked down on me. I should have listened to my mother, I thought. I should have gotten a job at the tampon factory. Hardly anyone got beaten senseless at the tampon factory. If I worked at the tampon factory I'd be home with my nose stuck in a thick book. A smutty romance with a half-naked man on the cover.

Red light flashed through the shattered windows, and I realized cops were shouting to Biggy to get off the car and drop his weapon. I raised my head and saw Carl Costanza looking in at me. "We've gotta stop meeting like this," he said. "People are gonna talk."

It took about an hour to complete the police report, get Lula's car towed away, and receive assurances that Biggy would be locked up and not let out anytime soon. It was a nice night out, and Lula, Grandma and I were only a couple blocks from my parents' house, so we decided to walk. We took a shortcut through the alley behind Roosevelt and fell quiet when we reached Lucille's backyard. Lucille was still watching TV in her nightgown. We stood there for a few moments, all of us lost in our own thoughts. I was the first to break the silence.

"I think Lucille killed Sam Franco," I said.

Lula smacked the heel of her hand against her forehead. "Unh!"

"I think Lucille woke up on the couch here, in the middle of the night, and saw someone looking in her window. I think she got all flustered and got a gun. Walter was a security guard. He would have had guns in the house. Lucille was alone every night. She would have known where the guns were kept. Maybe she kept one in the TV room . . . just in case. Then I think when she was rushing around to get the gun, Sam came into the house. Easy to do if Lucille only had the screen door closed so the house could cool off. Especially if the screen was already broken from the cat. I read through Sam's priors. He'd broken into a house once before. He said he'd been watching a lady get undressed and suddenly he wanted a soda."

"I could see that," Grandma said.

"Makes perfect sense to me," Lula said.

I agreed. I could see Squirrel doing such a ridiculous thing . . . walking into a house buck naked and asking for a soda. "Next thing you know, Lucille, who isn't in a lucid state of mind and isn't even very good with guns, has somehow managed to drill Sam Franco square in the middle of the forehead. He's stretched out in her den (after knocking her lamp over). He's obviously dead. And even more obviously he's unarmed. Walter is working, so Lucille calls the next person on her list. Kathy. And Kathy sends Biggy over to take charge. Biggy possibly having some experience in gangland body disposal, or at least having watched *Goodfellas* a hundred times, tags a message onto Sam and drives him home to the abandoned house."

"What about the part where we leave and the body disappears," Lula said. "You got that all figured out too?"

"The next morning Biggy goes off to the warehouse, and Kathy and Lucille get together and see the potential for getting rid of Biggy . . . who we all know beats the crap out of Kathy on a regular basis."

"Frame him for the shooting," Lula said.

"Exactly. So they hustle over with the moving van Biggy always keeps in his yard, not knowing two people have already seen Sam in the abandoned house, load Sam onto the hand truck, park him and the van in a place with foot traffic and plant the gun in Biggy's closet. Or maybe they don't even have to plant the gun. Maybe Biggy took the gun home with him."

"I think this is all a load of cockydoody," Lula said.

"I saw something like this in a movie," Grandma said. "On that Turner Classics station. I'm pretty sure it was Abbott and Costello."

"I'll tell you when I got this brainstorm," I said. "It was when Grandma fired off that first shot at Biggy and got knocked off her seat. The first time I fired a forty-five I had it too close to my face and the kick knocked the barrel into my forehead. I still have the scar."

"That little white mark?" Lula took a closer look. "Uh-oh, right in the same spot as Lucille's goose egg."

"*Yes!* And I bet the police can find trace evidence all over Lucille's den."

"You mean you think there might be some left after she shampooed her rug?" Lula asked.

I'd been so excited about my brilliant deduction I'd forgotten about the rug shampooer.

"No self-respecting burg housewife would leave brain gunk on her walls and floors," Grandma said.

"We keep our houses clean. Not like in some of them other neighborhoods."

This was bizarre but true.

"You think we have to tell the cops about your Lucille idea?" Grandma asked.

"It would be the right thing to do," I said.

"Yeah," Lula said. "And we always do the right thing. On the other hand, Biggy Zaremba is a real jerk. I don't like men who beat up on women."

"And kids."

I could feel Lula stiffen next to me. "He beat on his kids?"

"That's what people tell me."

"A man like that should be locked up."

"You could be wrong about Lucille," Grandma said to me. "You don't have any proof."

That was true. I could be wrong. But I didn't think so. Biggy had gone unglued when he saw me in the alley. And he said things he should have kept to himself. Like, how he'd done someone a favor, and how I'd been the one to transfer Sam from the house to the van. Biggy wasn't clever enough to orchestrate a scene like that for his own benefit. Biggy wasn't the killer. Biggy was an accomplice.

"Not only that, but you go telling the cops this theory about Lucille it's gonna take all the fun out of it for them," Lula said. "Homicide won't get no satisfaction if you don't let them figure this for themselves."

Jeez, I wouldn't want to ruin it for homicide.

Grandma shuffled one foot to the other. "There's all kinds of justice, you know."

"Fuckin' A," Lula said.

I thought justice looked like a real big gorilla. I wasn't in the business of determining justice. I was in the business of enforcing the law. But I had to admit, the thought of Biggy in jail sort of warmed by heart.

"Well, we could go to the police station and tell them Lucille's the one," Grandma said. "Or we could go back to the house and have some homemade chocolate cake."

This caught my attention. I'd forgotten about the cake.

"With vanilla ice cream," Grandma said. "The good kind with all them fat grams." She cut her eyes to me. "And hot fudge sauce to go on top."

Grandma wasn't above delivering a well-placed sucker-punch.

"Suppose homicide doesn't figure it out?" I asked Grandma and Lula.

Grandma took a moment to consider. "I guess if it would make you feel better, we could visit Biggy once in a while in the big house. Bring him some cookies."

"Yeah," Lula said, "or we could chip in for a TV. They let them lifers have TV sets."

"We can't just stand by and let a man spend the rest of his life in prison for a crime he didn't commit!"

"The hell we can't," Lula said

"And besides," Grandma said, "what about all the crimes he got away with? What about the stuff he stole and the people he beat up? What about evening the score?"

I pressed my lips together. "This isn't hockey."

We all shuffled our feet some more, and a drop of rain splattered on my bare arm. Then another. And another.

"It's a sign from God," Lula said, tilting her face heavenward, squinting into the rain. "God wants us to forget about all this shit and go eat some cake."

Wonderful. Now God was in on it.

"God's no dummy," Lula said. "He knows chocolate cake helps clear a person's head for making important decisions."

I thought about the bruise on Kathy's face. And then I thought about the way the oldest Zaremba kid always looked scared. And then I thought Lula might be right . . . that I wouldn't want to make a decision without the benefit of chocolate cake. In fact, to ensure that I wasn't making a terrible mistake, it might take me a very, very, very long time to make any decision at all.

ORPHANS COURT

A Tess Monaghan story

Laura Lippman

FIRST APPEARANCE: *Baltimore Blues,*
1997

In a short time Laura Lippman has made long strides in
the P.I. field. Out of three books she has won a Shamus—nominated for two—and is an Edgar Award winner with her third book. Her character Tess Monaghan
is a refreshing presence on the P.I. scene, and we are
proud to present her first short story appearance, written
specifically for this book.

T ess Monaghan was trying very hard to like the
  insurance agent who was buying her lunch at the
Polo Grill. She also was trying to like the Polo Grill,
which some objective part of her mind recognized as
worthy of its many "Baltimore's Best" awards. But
the restaurant had a preppie menace that made her
itch. Perhaps it was the dark green walls and the
framed prints, which tended toward horses and hunting. Perhaps it was the restaurant's very proximity to
a museum dedicated to the sport of lacrosse. She just
didn't feel as if she belonged here.

Then again, neither did her hostess, although she
was trying hard. Too hard. Kathleen Sawyer was only
a few years older than Tess, thirty-five at the most,
but she had a shellacked quality that made her seem
much older. Hair, face, clothes—everything about her
had a hard sheen, as if sprayed with some fixative.

She could have been pretty, in a Talbots kind of way. But with her black-rimmed eyes and painfully bright turquoise suit, Kathleen Sawyer—"It's Kathi, with an i"—was going for something else. Tess was still trying to figure out what it was.

"I even took up golf," Kathi-with-an-i was saying, as the waiter put down their appetizers, corn-crab chowder for her, a woodland mushroom tart for Tess. "Whatever it takes, right, to keep up with the boys? They want to schmooze on the greens, I'll schmooze on the greens. I play at Caves Valley."

A pause, as if she were waiting for Tess's reaction. And Tess would have been glad to have one, if only to be polite. But she wasn't sure what Caves Valley was suppose to convey, where it fell in the hierarchy of Baltimore's country clubs. The only thing she knew about local golf courses was that her Uncle Jules had once been mugged on the seventeenth hole of the municipal one, over on the northeast side, and never played again.

"You're not a golfer, eh? It *is* an expensive sport."

"I prefer solitary pursuits, which don't take as much planning," Tess said, poking at her mushroom. She loved mushrooms, and embraced the concept of huge ones, portobellos and the like. But then they showed up on her plate, and she was suddenly less enamored. Many of her relationships had run the same swift course. "Rowing, running, lifting weights."

"Oh, well, we girls have to stick together." It was the third or fourth time that Kathi had offered this little motto, always in the form of a non sequitur. She had said it when she called Tess to request this meeting, then shouted it again, as a kind of greeting, when they had met while waiting for the parking valet.

"That's a thought," Tess said now, her foolproof

response to the non-respondable. That's a thought, that's an idea, that's a concept. Not a good one, but undeniably an example of the noun in question.

"Rowing, huh? Did you 'crew' in college?" Her speech was full of such oddly emphasized words. "Where did you go to school?"

Kathi's hand went to the small charm she wore on a gold chain around her neck, a Phi Beta Kappa key. Her "tell," as a gambler would say, but what was she telling? *She's worried I went to an Ivy League school, and that she'll have to trump me by figuring out a way to introduce the fact she was an honors student wherever she went. As if I care.*

"On the Eastern Shore," Tess said, letting her off the hook. "Look, could I ask why we're having lunch today? You said you might have some work for me. But I assume a company as big as yours has investigators on staff."

"We do," Kathi said. She seemed relieved that Tess had ended the pretense that their lunch was anything but business. "Sometimes, it's better to go outside. It gives one greater leeway, if you know what I mean."

"I don't do anything illegal," Tess said quickly, if not truthfully.

"And I would never ask anyone to do something illegal. This is more about . . . temperament. I'm willing to pay someone a little extra for having the right attitude." Kathi named a price that was three times Tess's usual hourly rate, even the corporate one, which was largely theoretical, since no corporation had ever tried to hire her. "I did some research. I hear you're very direct, almost to the point of being blunt. That can be an asset at times."

Tess wasn't aware she had a reputation, not as a private investigator. "You're saying I'm rude."

Kathi waggled her soupspoon. "Don't take a compliment and turn it into an insult. It's one of the biggest mistakes a woman in business can make. Never draw attention to your deficits. Save your false modesty for dating."

It was a sanctimonious speech, but a shrewd one. Tess found herself warming to her dining companion.

"What's the case?"

"A month ago, I wrote a basic homeowners policy, for a woman I've done business with for years. She had purchased a house at auction, very cheaply. I'm not sure why it was so cheap. An estate sale, maybe a bankruptcy. It was a little rundown, because it had been vacant while it sat on the market, and a rental before that, but basically sound, and in a nice enough neighborhood. Do you know Aynesworth Avenue, over near Towson University? She said she was buying it as an investment. Forty-eight hours after closing, it burned to the ground."

"Arson?"

"That's the official ruling."

"But no arrest."

"No, and I don't expect one. Martha Pettigrew apparently had the good sense to contract it out. Most insurance fraud, the people are cheap—they try to do it themselves, and that's how we catch them, because they're not professionals. Or the arson investigators find the guy who set it, and they get him to turn on whoever hired him."

Tess had scraped the cheese and pastry from the tart, leaving behind a large, misshapen mushroom that looked very sad and startled on her plate, like a fat person caught naked.

"You think I can do what the Baltimore County

fire department failed to do, link the policyholder to the arson?"

"The case isn't a priority for the fire department. It is for me. I have something to lose. When a policyholder pulls an obvious scam like this, the agent looks stupid, or corrupt. I suppose I'm lucky that my district office just thinks I'm the former, a softie conned by a woman who's been nothing but a drain since I met her. Talk about your loss leaders—a little life insurance policy, a liability-only auto insurance policy. If all my clients were like her, I'd have closed my doors long ago. Now she stands to make money on this house fire."

"Where do I find . . . ?" She had already forgotten the name.

"Martha Pettigrew." Kathi took out a business card and wrote the name on the back, along with an address and a phone number. The card was printed with violet ink, Tess noticed, and Kathi had a pen to match. "She lives in a place on North Charles, behind GBMC."

"Behind the Greater Baltimore Medical Center? I didn't know there were houses back there."

"It's not a house." Kathi's spoon missed her mouth, and a few drops of pale yellow chowder fell on her turquoise suit, just above her right breast. "Shit. Excuse me. It's a kind of senior residence. You go through the main gates at GBMC, but don't worry, they validate. Now tell me about yourself. On your own, and just thirty years old. I bet you don't have half the coverage you need."

Tess sighed, remembering the adage about free lunches, the lack thereof.

*   *   *

Two hours and many female-bonding moments later, Tess turned into the long drive leading to GBMC, glancing at the small band of abortion protestors who gathered here most afternoons. Abortion protestors who happened to be middle-aged men, which Tess found amusing or infuriating, depending on her mood. Today, well-fed and on the clock, she was primarily amused. The parking attendant directed her to turn left and she soon came to a fairly new building in a little enclave. The stone-and-glass structure was smaller than she had expected. It might have passed for a private residence, albeit one owned by a millionaire. It wouldn't have been out of place in Italy, or the south of France. And, although it stood less than a half-mile from one of Baltimore's most congested suburbs, its setting was peaceful and bucolic, all meadows and wooded hills.

"This is beautiful," Tess told the desk clerk as she signed in. "But so small. I thought these retirement villages had to be huge. Economies of scale, that kind of thing."

"It's a hospice, not a retirement village," the young woman said, and her soft, neutral tone was more effective than an out-and-out rebuke. "Mrs. Pettigrew came to us a month ago. Were you one of her students?"

It was always nice when someone set the lie up. "Yes, yes I was."

"Well I'm glad someone's finally come to visit her. She doesn't have any family, and the only person who ever drops by is her lawyer, and that seems to be all business. She's on the terrace, outside her room. She's having a good day."

Good was clearly a relative term. Tess found a gaunt woman with gray-white skin and gray-blue eyes, lying in a hospital bed that had been rolled out into the warm June sun. Her eyebrows were white, but her hair was defiantly, admirably red, a banner of resistance in the face of imminent death.

"One of my students, eh?" Martha Pettigrew said, after Tess's escort had left. "I can't say as I remember you. But it's got to be at least twenty years since you were in the third grade."

"Twenty-one."

"I can't remember everyone." She sounded peevish, as if she expected Tess to challenge her on this. "I taught third grade in the same classroom for almost thirty years. I was still teaching up until this spring break, when I got sick."

"That's okay," Tess assured her. "It's something of a coincidence that I'm here, anyway. I've been hired to look into your house fire."

"Hired by who?" Tess thought a career teacher, even one who had never advanced past the third grade, should know it was "whom."

"Your insurance company."

Martha Pettigrew didn't look particularly surprised. But nor was there anything furtive in her expression, no sign of fright or guilt. "Those bloodsuckers. They think if they can draw this out, they won't have to pay me, because I'll be dead. But I have a will, I have an heir. You can pay me, or you can pay her, but you will pay."

Mrs. Pettigrew's voice carried well, and there were other patients out on their terraces, some with families. *Great—watch the private investigator interrogate a dying woman, so an insurance company can save a few bucks!* "No, that's not the situation at all," Tess said hurriedly. "But such . . . coincidences do draw scrutiny. You bought a house, very cheaply, and it burned down almost immediately. If you don't rebuild, you'll make money on the deal."

"It's not my fault that I know a bargain when I see one." Martha Pettigrew was younger than Tess had thought at first. Her body was frail, but the woman inside the body had not given up.

"Why would you buy a house when, when—"

"When I'm dying?" Martha Pettigrew's voice kept getting louder. People were clearly staring at them now, glad of the distraction from their own woes. "I don't see where that's any of your business. If dying isn't private, I don't know what is. You're just trying to get my estate kicked into orphans court. You're hoping I'll die, because then you'll be free to accuse me of all sorts of things, and gunk up the works. But it won't work. My will is tight as a drum. Tight as a drum."

Orphans court was where estates without wills, or contested inheritances, ended up. Tess couldn't see how it would apply here. "Mrs. Pettigrew—"

"Go away. I don't have to explain myself to you. That's the one good thing about dying. Pretty soon, I won't have to explain myself to anyone, ever again."

She squeezed her eyes shut, as if to make Tess disappear. It worked.

The county courthouse was less than two miles away. Tess sat on a bench on its lush grounds, watching rats scamper among the ornamental cabbages. The judges and the county employees were incensed that the courthouse had a rat problem, but everyone else saw it as an inevitable punchline.

She dialed Kathi Sawyer from her cell phone. "You didn't tell me Martha Pettigrew was in a hospice."

"Hospice, senior home—what's the diff?"

Tess thought it a rather large diff. "She's dying."

"Yes. Yes, she is." Kathi's voice was tentative, as if she was waiting to find out if Tess thought it was a bad thing, sending someone to hector a terminally ill woman over an insurance policy.

"She knew she was dying when she bought the house."

"*Exactly*. That's what raised my hackles."

Not the best image, perhaps—Tess envisioned turquoise scales rising from Kathi's back. "She said she's leaving the money to someone. Do you have any way of knowing who that is?"

"You don't have a beneficiary on a homeowners policy."

Tess sighed. "Not on the homeowners. On the life insurance policy you said you wrote for her. Martha Pettigrew has no family, and her lawyer is the only one who visits her, according to the hospice staff. But she spoke of leaving her estate to a single heir. That would mean the house goes to the same person named on the life insurance policy. Meanwhile, I'm going to check the property records here at the courthouse, find out who owned the house before Martha Pettigrew did."

"Why?"

"There's always a possibility someone torched it without knowing it had changed hands. Maybe the previous owner was trying to collect the insurance, but screwed up on his dates. Don't worry—it won't come to more than a quarter of a billable hour."

"Let me put you on hold." Kathi Sawyer was too smart to have Muzak, but not smart enough to know that fusion jazz was just as annoying. "She listed some-one named Annie Greene for the life insurance policy.

Described her as a 'friend.' You want the social security number?"

"It would help," Tess said. "It's not the most unusual of names. Besides, women still have a habit of being tricky to find. They use initials, they hide behind husbands."

"You married?" It was the first time Kathi Sawyer had asked Tess a personal question in which she seemed genuinely interested in the answer.

"No."

"Boyfriend, though." It was more diagnosis than question.

"Well, yes."

"You look like the type."

"What type is that?"

"The type of woman who always has a boyfriend. The funny thing is, it's not even about being pretty, is it? Oh my God—I'm not saying . . ."

"I think I know what you were trying to say." The thing was, she did. "I'm not that type, though. I've had plenty of downtime. You know, those long fallow periods where you eat ice cream from the carton and get your eyebrows waxed."

"Oh, what does it matter?" Kathi's voice had lost its chirpy edge. "We all end up alone. You know that, don't you? Women invariably die alone. The gap has narrowed, but it's still there. Actuarial tables don't lie."

"Everyone dies alone," Tess said. "Even if you're on a jet, spiraling into the ocean, with 250 other people on board, you're alone."

"Well, thanks. Now I feel much better."

But Tess wasn't paying attention to Kathi's sarcasm. She was thinking of Martha Pettigrew.

*   *   *

The courthouse told Tess nothing. For want of anything better to do, she drove to Aynesworth Avenue and sat outside the ruins of the house, feeling an odd sense of déjà vu. Only it couldn't be déjà vu, for the house was gone. She was missing what had once been there, yet she had never seen it. Try to explain that. A demolition crew had been there, and cleared the debris from the lot. All that was left was a picket fence, blackened by smoke, and a garden that had gone to ruin long before the fire.

Her cell phone rang from the depths of her knapsack. Dorie Starnes, her computer specialist, had done a rush job—at rush job prices. Tess wondered if she would ever dare suggest to Dorie that girls had to stick together. No, Dorie would just double her rates.

"Annie Greene is a twenty-three-year-old woman whose address has changed three times in the last year. No phone in her name, but she's probably got a roommate. Probably can't get a phone in her own name. She's cycled on and off unemployment for the last few years. Just cycled off a few months ago, when she took a job at a deli in Towson. Scooter's. She has the kind of credit card debt you'd expect—overdue at Penney's and Hecht's, a Visa maxed out at $1,000."

"Please don't tell me you pulled her credit history, Dorie." As the systems manager at the local newspaper, the *Beacon-Light*, Dorie had long ago learned how to tap into the business-side computers.

"Fine, I'll never tell you what you don't want to hear," Dorie said. "For all I care, you can walk around with spinach in your teeth and your fly open. Will that make you happy?"

Scooter's called itself a deli, but that didn't make it one. It sat on the ground floor of one of Towson's suburban skyscrapers, a bland place with flimsy furniture and a few framed railroad prints, which bore no relationship to anything in the restaurant. Tess, still full from her lunch at the Polo Grill, took a seat in one of the molded plastic booths and asked for a Coke.

"You don't need me for that," the waitress told her. "You can grab one from the case and just pay up at the register."

"I suppose I could." Tess slid a ten-dollar bill across the table. "But then I couldn't tip. Does a woman named Annie Greene work here?"

The young woman looked at the bill wistfully. She was small, with dark hair and dark eyes. A young twenty-three, but a definite possibility. "Why?"

"I just want to ask her a few questions."

"You a bill collector?" Clearly Annie Greene.

"No. I'm an investigator, and she's sort of tangential to what I'm trying to find out."

"What's that?"

"What I'm trying to find out? I'm sorry, that has to be confidential." There was nothing like the prospect of someone else's secrets to lure someone into a conversation.

"No, that word you said, tangential. What does that mean?" The young woman's face was soft with yearning, and not just for the ten-dollar bill.

"Related, but not central to the matter at hand."

"Like coleslaw, or potato chips. They're tangential to the corned beef sandwich, right?" The waitress had a crooked, unhappy smile. "I guess I know something about being coleslaw. I'm Annie Greene."

"I thought you might be."

"You're looking for me, but you don't know me?"

"Only as a name, and a social security number. Should I know you?"

"No, I guess not." She slid into the booth opposite Tess. "What am I . . . tangential to?"

"There's a woman, a woman named Martha Pettigrew. She's dying, and you're the beneficiary on her life insurance. She indicated to me that you stand to inherit her entire estate."

"Why?"

"I don't know. I thought you might. I do know that she bought a house, well below market value, and it burned two days after closing. If the insurance pays off, you'll get that money, too. Assuming I'm right about you being her sole heir."

"Martha Pettigrew." The waitress allowed herself to touch the edges of the ten-dollar bill. "The name is familiar, for sure."

"Even if the insurance company doesn't have to pay for the house, you stand to inherit the lot when she dies. Assuming I'm right about you being her beneficiary in all things. It's a nice little neighborhood. Nothing fancy, just solid old homes, near Towson University." It occurred to her that she had spent much of the day in just a few square miles. Martha Pettigrew, the courthouse, the burned house, even Scooters, were all so close to one another. "The house is on Aynesworth—"

"Aynesworth. *Aynesworth.*" Annie Greene slid from the booth and pushed the ten-dollar bill back at Tess. "You can't make me take that house. I'd drive twenty miles out of my way to never go down that street again. I won't have anything to do with it. Or Martha Pettigrew. I remember her now. You bet I remember her. So she's dying? I hope it's painful. I hope it's slow."

"Miss Greene—"

"Tell your insurance company I don't want any of

it. Not the house, and not the money. Martha Pettigrew doesn't get off that easy."

"Weren't you here yesterday?" Martha Pettigrew asked Tess.

"This afternoon," Tess said. "It's June. The days are getting longer."

"Not mine," Martha Pettigrew said.

"Even yours. You may have fewer of them than I do, but they're still longer than they were a week ago, not so long as they'll be in another week."

"Were you always such a smartass? I think I'm beginning to remember you."

"You're good at remembering people when it's too late, aren't you? As it happens, I was never in your class."

"So why are you here? Oh, the money. Of course. It was about the money."

Martha Pettigrew's bed had been rolled in from the terrace, into a lovely room, not at all institutional, with pretty furniture and bright wallpaper. If you had to die, and the word was that everyone did, you could do worse than this room, catching the last minutes of light from the day, one of spring's last. But Tess doubted that Martha Pettigrew noticed much about her surroundings, except the button on her morphine drip.

"I talked to Annie Greene today. Your beneficiary, although she didn't know it."

"She doesn't have to know." Martha Pettigrew's voice was weaker than it had been this afternoon, her eyes duller. Even the dyed red hair seemed to be fading, but maybe that was a trick of the light. "It's still legal. I talked to my lawyer. He knows where she is, and how to find her, when the time comes."

"She doesn't want to be found, now that she knows who you are, and what you're bequeathing her."

"Is she doing so well that she can turn her nose up at $500,000 in life insurance, plus the settlement from the fire?"

"No." *Five hundred thousand?* But Kathi had said it was a small policy, barely worth her while. "Still, she said she doesn't want it."

"Then she's not very smart, is she? The truth is, her sister Helen wasn't particularly smart, either. But that's a truth we weren't suppose to tell."

"Yes, Annie Greene was Helen Greene's sister, wasn't she? Her name didn't mean much to me, but I remember Helen Greene."

"Remembering Helen," Martha Pettigrew said, "is practically a pathology in this town. But Helen's gone, beyond our help. Annie was there, too, you know. Annie suffered, too. Her name was never publicized, because of the sexual abuse. The media downplayed that, what the father did to her. It made the story messy. Helen was a more perfect victim. She was dead. But it's for our suffering when we're alive that courts give us money. Not our deaths."

"Helen was your student, though, not Annie."

"I see you've spent part of the afternoon reading old newspapers."

"And looking at Helen's picture. Remember it? It stared out of the newspaper for weeks, after the murder and during the trial. Do you remember her face, Mrs. Pettigrew? Do you remember the little girl who was starving to death in your classroom? But I suppose you do. That's what the legacy to Annie Greene is all about, trying to make up for her sister's death. The thing is, Annie Greene doesn't want to let you off the hook so easily."

On the defensive, Martha Pettigrew found some new reserve of energy. "It's not as if she was emaciated. That's another thing people don't understand. She was skinny, yes, but she didn't look like those African children you see on the news. And children get cuts, don't they? She told me she fell down on the sidewalk at home." Tess saw Martha's thumb reach for the morphine drip, then back off, as if she were testing herself. "I had thirty-five children in my class that year. Thirty-five, in a classroom built for twenty. Don't ever let anyone tell you that good school districts don't get overcrowded. They're the worst."

"Why did you buy the Greenes' house?"

"It was a bargain."

"Then why burn it?"

"I didn't do anything."

"Yes, that would seem to be the point."

"What?"

"Never mind."

Martha Pettigrew's thumb moved to the button again, and this time she did push it. Several seconds passed, and Tess stood to leave. She was almost out the door before Martha Pettigrew spoke again.

"That was an evil place, that house. The landlord couldn't sell it, because people in the neighborhood remembered what happened there, and it always got back to prospective buyers. No one wanted the house where Helen Greene died. She spent her last night on earth tied to a bed, so she wouldn't pick at the scab on her chin. And now I'm tied to my bed, in a fashion, and I'm dying as slowly as she died. Things even out."

"Not always."

"Always," Martha Pettigrew said firmly, and Tess suddenly saw her as the teacher she had been, a tall, plain woman with too many students, her feet swollen, her head aching, yet ultimately full of love for what she did. Thirty-five children. Would Tess have noticed the one with the scab on her chin?

"I guess I'll be going."

"Miss—I've forgotten your name."

"Monaghan."

"I didn't burn the house on Aynesworth, or arrange for anyone else to burn it. Why would I complicate things like that? It's true, I bought it, right after I was diagnosed. And I'm pleased to think that it's gone. But that's one thing I don't have on my conscience. You realize there's only one person with a motive to burn that house, don't you? I was right from the very first. This is headed for orphans court. Poor Annie Greene won't have the stomach for that."

And Tess felt her own hackles rise.

The next and last time that Tess and Kathi Sawyer met, it was on Tess's turf, in a long, narrow bar above the Brass Elephant.

"Very classy," Kathi Sawyer judged, still playing mentor, oblivious to the fact that Tess had resigned as her protégée. "A good place to meet clients. Although some people might be put off by the fact that the bartender knows you so well."

"You'll never be able to link that fire on Aynesworth to Martha Pettigrew," Tess said.

"Oh well, it was worth a try." Kathi smiled over the rim of her wineglass. Merlot, of course. One of the bland, bodiless Merlots that had overwhelmed the market since Kathi Sawyer and her kind had begun chasing fads through the wine world. Tess was drinking a martini. In the case of the martini, they could concoct horrible versions, but they couldn't ruin the real thing.

"You don't seem surprised."

"I knew it was a long shot."

"I suppose so. It would be awfully hard to prove that Martha Pettigrew burned the house, when you're the one who had it torched."

Kathi Sawyer made eye contact with her Merlot. "Martha Pettigrew," she said in a slow, even tone, "was a pain in the ass."

"A pain in the ass because she expected more than a Christmas card and a calendar every year? Or because she had the bad form to try and cash in on her life insurance?"

"She was forty-nine when she took out that policy. According to actuarial charts, she should have lived another thirty years. Instead, she gets lung cancer and she doesn't even smoke. Or so she said. At any rate, I can't stay in business, writing policies for unlucky people. That might sound cold, but it's a reality. I've had a streak of bad luck lately. It evens out, over the long run. But I wasn't so sure I was going to have a long run, at the rate I was going."

It evens out. Martha Pettigrew had said much the same thing. "So she's dying, and you're seething about it. Then she comes to her friendly insurance agent, insisting on buying a house, confiding how she plans to leave it to a young woman. Did you hire another private investigator to uncover the link between Martha, Annie Greene, and Aynesworth Avenue?"

"I did it myself." Kathi Sawyer allowed herself a smile. "And much faster than you, too. All I had to do was call the former owner and find out why the house had gone for so little money. Once it had gone to closing, he was happy to tell me all about Helen Greene. It didn't take a genius to figure out who

Annie Greene was, and why Martha Pettigrew wanted her to inherit everything."

"It also shouldn't have taken a genius to make some link between the two, but I guess the arson investigators let you down on that front. You were counting on them to find Annie Greene, and implicate her in the fire. Were you hoping she'd skip town, or that the criminal charges would keep her from collecting the life insurance policy? At any rate, when that didn't work, you hired a private detective whose people skills aren't the best, someone guaranteed to drop the news so casually, so carelessly, that Annie Greene would explode, just as she exploded on the witness stand eight years ago."

Kathi Sawyer actually looked pleased with herself. "And it worked, didn't it?"

"More or less. One more question. You told me the first time we met that amateurs get caught, because they're too cheap to hire professional help. Did you have help with the fire, or did you do it yourself?"

"Let's just say there's no one out there who can help you corroborate your little crackpot theory."

"That's what I suspected. So I settled for tracking down Annie again and convincing her that forgiveness has its own rewards. She's going to accept her inheritance. As for the house on Aynesworth, the land will be donated to the community, for a playground in Helen's name."

"As if anyone will remember or care who Helen Greene was five years from now," Kathi said. "As if the world lost anything, except another stupid girl to work the lunch shift at Scooter's."

Tess picked up her martini glass so it was safe in hand when she rocked the table's base with her foot, sending Kathi's wineglass into her lap. The red stain showed up beautifully on her bright yellow linen suit.

"I'm not paying you," Kathi Sawyer said.

"That's okay," Tess said. "When I explained everything to Martha and Annie, they agreed to pay my fee. After all, I really ended up working for them. Besides, you know what they said?"

Kathi, patting at the red wine stains with a napkin soaked in water, refused to play along.

"They said we girls really have to stick together."

AN AFFAIR OF INCONVENIENCE

A Lady Vespasia story

Anne Perry

FIRST APPEARANCE: *Mary Higgins Clark Magazine,* **1998**

Anne Perry's two famous, bestselling Victorian series are the William Monk series and the series featuring Inspector Thomas and Charlotte Pitt. While there are no short stories featuring these characters, Ms. Perry did pluck one of her more popular secondary characters from the Pitt series for this story featuring Lady Vespasia Cumming-Gould.

I t had been quite distinctly the sound of breaking glass, once, sharply, and then silence. Lady Vespasia Cumming-Gould sat up in bed. It had come from the room next door, the only unoccupied guest room in the house.

On a long country weekend such as this, when the London season was over and the Queen and Prince Albert had retired to the late-summer pleasures of Osbourne, it was not unusual for there to be a number of romantic affairs conducted with discretion but distinct relish. An assignation in the middle of the night was not of itself remarkable. But it should not entail the smashing of glass. That sounded more like an accident, or even an intruder.

Vespasia fumbled in the dark for a moment, found the matches and lit the lamp on the table beside her. She rose and pulled her ivory silk robe over her shoul-

ders without bothering to straighten the cascades of
lace or arrange her hair carefully. She picked up the
lamp and walked softly across to the door and
opened it.

The corridor outside was dimly lit from the gas
bracket halfway along, turned down as low as possible
until it burned yellow. There was no one there and
total silence.

She tiptoed along to the next door and put her hand
on the knob. She turned it slowly and pushed. It
swung open.

Lady Oremia Blythe was standing in the center of
the room, her abundant fair hair streaming around her
shoulders, her yellow peignoir with its gleaming satin
and extravagant ribbons hanging open over her nightgown. In her right hand was the brass base of an oil
lamp. The splintered shards of its mantle lay on the
floor around the recumbent body of Sir Ferdinand
Wakeham. The crown of his bald head was bleeding
a little. He was wearing a paisley robe and a striped
cotton nightshirt. Oremia was ashen-faced, her eyes
wide with horror.

Vespasia glanced automatically at the bed. The
four-poster had been made carefully but not with the
skill or the neatness with which a chambermaid would
have done it. The corners were uneven. The coverlet
was not smoothed under the pillows. Its recent use
was apparent.

What was far less apparent was why Oremia should
have struck Ferdie senseless, or in fact why she had
been with him at all! Vespasia had been observing the
gathered company all weekend. She had seen the covert glances and smiles, the twitching of skirts, the
dropped handkerchiefs, the unnecessary errands, the

laughter and lingering moments. She was well aware that Ferdie's interests lay elsewhere.

She gazed at Oremia with raised eyebrows.

"Oh . . . er . . Vespasia . . ." Oremia began awkwardly, blinking at last. Her hand holding the remnants of the lamp was trembling very slightly. She licked dry lips. "I . . . er . . ." She swallowed. Her voice cracked. "Vespasia! What am I going to do? For God's sake . . . help me!"

Vespasia closed the door behind her softly and turned to face Oremia, whom she was not particularly fond of. But she would help for Oremia's husband's sake. Toby Blythe was not merely an old friend who deserved better than the scandal and the mockery this would cause, he was a man with a public reputation to preserve, upon which his position depended and his power to do a great deal of good—good about which Vespasia cared profoundly. He was a man ahead of his time in seeking to widen the franchise, an altruistic but unpopular cause among his peers. Ridicule would be the most potent of weapons against him.

"What happened?" she inquired, not entirely sympathetically. Certainly she was curious.

Oremia was torn between the desire to defend herself and a need to enlist Vespasia's help. Self-preservation won. "I . . ." She steeled herself, her expression reflecting her dilemma. "I had an . . . assignation here. My lover"—she said the word with a brightness in her eyes and the flicker of a smile on her lips—"my lover had not yet left when Ferdie came in. I had no choice!" She raised her shoulders in an elegant shrug. "I could not allow him to find us here! I did the only thing I could. I had the lamp in my hand . . . I used it."

"I see," Vespasia said dryly.

"For heaven's sake, what am I to do?" Oremia's

voice was rising, and there was a note of panic in it.
"Help me!"

Vespasia forced herself to think of Toby and stifle
the response that came naturally to her tongue. Toby
had been not unadmiring of Vespasia in the past. She
had most agreeable memories of him. She could smile
even now as she thought of them. Her mind raced.
How many believable explanations were there for this
rather ridiculous scene?

"It's not amusing!" Oremia snapped, her face pink.
"Have you any idea—"

"A very vivid idea," Vespasia said coolly. "A great
many ribald jokes, none of them flattering." She had
no knowledge who the lover might have been and did
not choose to ask. The solution was now fully formed
in her mind. "Put that lamp down, or what remains
of it . . . there!" She pointed to the floor about a yard
from Ferdie's head. "And go back to your bed. Close
your door. As far as the rest of the world is concerned,
you slept through the night without waking. You
heard and saw nothing at all."

Oremia stared at her as if she hardly dared believe her.

"Go on!" Vespasia ordered. "Before Ferdie comes
to his senses and it's too late!"

"Oh! Yes. Yes, of course. Vespasia . . ." Still, she
hesitated, breathing heavily.

"No, I won't tell Toby," Vespasia said, answering
the unspoken question. "Now hurry, and do exactly
as I told you."

"Yes. I will." And this time she swept past Vespasia, who caught her by the arm as she was about to
fling the door open.

"Watch!" she hissed. "Make sure there is no one
there! You can't afford to be seen!" She nearly added

"you fool!" and bit her tongue only at the last moment. Vespasia was still the most beautiful woman in the house, perhaps even in England, but she was twenty years older than Oremia Blythe, and she had learned a little wisdom and perhaps a little regret.

Oremia caught her breath in a sob, keeping her back to Vespasia, her shoulders stiff. Possibly it was embarrassment, but more likely it was anger. She put her hand on the doorknob and turned it very slowly. The latch freed, and she pulled it open no more than three inches, then four, then a foot. "There's no one here," she said with satisfaction, as if she had known it all along.

"Then go quickly," Vespasia commanded. "And stay in your room unless something happens that would waken the dead."

Oremia swung around. "Such as what?"

"An explosion or a fire alarm!" Vespasia said tartly. "I don't know!"

Oremia disappeared along the corridor and around the corner.

Vespasia turned back into the room. Mercifully, Ferdie Wakeham was still insensible. She wondered if she ought to hit him again, just to make sure he remained that way. She still had a considerable amount to do, for which she required his mental absence. But she did not wish to injure the poor man beyond what was absolutely necessary.

She paused only a moment. She would trust to luck. Besides, what she planned to do must be done immediately, and there was no other weapon readily on hand.

She went over to the window and opened it, gave him a last swift look to make sure he was still showing no signs of returning to consciousness, then slipped out the door herself and went along the corridor to the linen cupboard. She opened the door and whisked inside, pulling it almost closed, and waited, her eye to the crack.

She was just in time. She had barely arranged herself when a figure passed by—a lush, feminine figure, all gleaming skin and rustling silk, most inappropriate for a discreet assignation. It was the Honorable Mrs. Leonora Vickery—fourth bedroom on the left, east wing.

As soon as Leonora had passed on her way to the spare room—and passed Ferdie Wakeham, whom she would expect to be there awaiting her—Vespasia came out of the linen cupboard, picked up her skirts and ran down the corridor, across the landing and into the east wing. She passed the first door, second, third and opened the fourth. She went in, swung around, closed the door silently and immediately turned up the gas, which was so low as to be barely burning at all.

She looked around the room. The bedcovers were thrown back where Leonora had climbed out. The brushes and combs were set out on the dressing table, the chair askew where she had sat arranging her hair before leaving. There was her jewel box. That was what Vespasia needed. In half a dozen strides she passed to the window and threw up the sash. The night air was warm and faintly scented with cut grass. One of the gardeners had trimmed the croquet lawn in the afternoon.

She went back to the dressing table and picked up the jewel box, making sure all the drawers were closed, then took it to the window and threw it out, sending it as far as she could. She closed the window, as quietly as possible. Even so, it made a slight click.

She turned down the gas again and opened the door a crack. Thank heaven there was no one else about. She could not afford to hesitate even an instant. Leonora would have found Ferdie by now and with any luck would have realized she could not afford to be discovered in the west wing at this hour of the night. Even if he had cried out, she could not possibly have heard him had she been in her own room, or anywhere else for which she could provide a reasonable explanation. And a glance would tell her Ferdie needed some medical attention.

The only disaster would be if Leonora panicked, or if Ferdie had not enough sense to realize he needed assistance, or conceivably if Leonora were so in love with him that she threw caution and both their reputations to the wind and summoned help on the spot. Mercifully, not likely!

Vespasia came out of the east wing onto the landing and passed the foot of the stairs leading up to the attic, where the servants had their rooms. This flight of stairs was for convenience, for valets and ladies' maids to come as soon as summoned. There was a large vase of flowers on a table. It was crooked, as if someone had knocked it in the extremely dim light.

She turned into the west wing and stopped abruptly, her heart beginning to beat violently. Someone was moving at the far end! Leonora! Vespasia had meant to be back in the linen cupboard by now. She had been too slow! If she were caught here, Leonora would be bound to leap to the conclusion that Vespasia was out of her bed for the same purpose she was herself!

Vespasia would greatly prefer not to give Leonora such a weapon in her hand. Should she turn the landing light down so far that she would not be seen?

Yes!

No! Then Leonora might fall over something in the dark and possibly raise the house. Vespasia could just imagine the scene if Leonora knocked over the vase of flowers at the bottom of the servants' stairs. Or the jardiniere by the banisters. How could she possibly explain that? Inebriated—at the very kindest! But on the landing in the middle of the night?

More likely, Leonora would turn up the gas again, and certainly see Vespasia, and wonder what in heaven's name she was doing. Then there would be only one conclusion—and not a charitable one.

She was coming. Vespasia could hear the rustle of silks. Stupid woman!

Vespasia flattened herself against the wall next to the potted palm and stood rigid, almost breathless.

Leonora came out of the corridor and passed within a yard of her. Her almond-flower perfume was sweet in the air. She was tiptoeing, watching where she was going. She was breathing heavily. Not surprising. She had just found Ferdie senseless on the floor and debated what to do. Vespasia had relied on the shock causing her to pause at least a few moments before leaving.

Now Leonora was going back to her own room. She passed by the newel post of the main stairway down, safely negotiated around the jardiniere and then the table at the bottom of the servants' stairs. A moment later she was into the east corridor and back in her own room.

The instant the crack of light disappeared from under Leonora's door, Vespasia swung around and ran along the west corridor past her own room and into the unoccupied room where Ferdie Wakeham still lay amid the shattered pieces of the lamp. He was just beginning to stir.

"Oh, Ferdie!" Vespasia exclaimed with horror. "How incredibly brave of you!"

"Wha . . . What?" He blinked, opened his eyes and winced sharply as the light caught them. "Ooh! Ooooh." He put out his hand and caught it on a piece of broken glass. He swore loudly and snatched his hand away, putting it to his lips to stop the blood. "What in hell happened?"

"You must have caught him," Vespasia said, as if it were the only possible answer.

"Caught him?" He remained motionless, acutely aware of the glass around him.

"The burglar! You heard him and came to tackle him. You caught him right here, only he seized"—she looked around, then down at the floor—"the lamp and struck you over the head." She let her expression convey her admiration for his courage and quick action. "No doubt he fled, leaving you here." She glanced meaningfully toward the window. "Please allow me to help. We owe you so much." She bent down and very carefully began picking up shards of glass and putting them in the wastebasket.

He sat blinking uncertainly.

She put the last of the pieces into the basket. "There. Now you may rise without further injury. You may be feeling a little dizzy." She looked at his head earnestly. "He appears to have struck you rather hard. I daresay he was a very large person, a complete ruffian."

"Yes . . ." Ferdie agreed. "Yes, he was rather large."

"Allow me." She offered him her hand, and he took it, climbing to his feet rather shakily. Poor Ferdie was looking very much the worse for wear. Yet had he regained his senses any sooner it would have been most unfortunate.

"Thank you." He accepted her help, swaying a little. "Yes . . . a real ruffian. I am most obliged to you. I assume you heard the . . . the lamp breaking?"

"Yes," she said quite truthfully. "I sat in bed some minutes, gathering my wits before I realized there must be something very wrong. I think I was deeply asleep."

"Yes." He nodded, and winced, standing suddenly very still. It had not been a good idea to move his head. He groaned involuntarily. "Yes, of course," he whispered.

"I think we had better raise the servants and see what damage he has done," she said. "And perhaps get some ministration for your head. That cut looks rather unpleasant. I don't doubt you will have a severe headache in the morning, if you have not one already."

"I have," he said ruefully. "I've never had a hangover like it." He smiled at her. "This is worse than rough cider . . . or at least as bad."

"Come." She offered her arm again and, when he took it, led him to the door and back along the corridor to the landing. She sat him in the only comfortable chair and turned up the gas in all the brackets. There was still no noise in the house. If anyone was awake, he or she was being remarkably discreet, assuming the movement was all illicit and better unobserved.

Vespasia went to the foot of the servants' stairs, ready to go up if necessary and waken one of the valets to minister to Ferdie. She noticed the crooked vase again. It was exactly where someone would have caught it on the way up if passing in a hurry, or in the dim light. Who would be going up there in the half dark and not want to straighten a vase he or she had knocked?

Oremia's lover! Because he did not want to be seen and feared he might be—after Ferdie had intruded into the bedroom he presumed not occupied, only to find a previous pair of lovers about to leave.

And the lover would go up there rather than to his own room, unless his own room were indeed up there. Oremia had been sleeping with one of the servants!

Vespasia knew which one it would be—the remarkably handsome young footman with the dark hair and the curving lips and fine legs. Really, how could Oremia be so—so incredibly, monumentally stupid? To betray Toby with one of his friends was bad enough, with a footman was appalling! If it became known, Toby would be mocked or pitied, or both. His effectiveness to do good, his life's goals, would be nullified. Who would take him seriously?

Vespasia was so furious she could hardly swallow. All for the sake of a few moments' utterly selfish gratification! Oremia had known the wretched man barely a week, and she had used him simply for her own enjoyment. He was hardly in a position to refuse her. She could ruin him with a word, and if rejected might well do so out of spite! Vespasia felt the anger settle inside her like a stone, but she was helpless to do anything about it. She must protect Oremia for Toby's sake, and because she had said she would.

She marched up the stairs, fists clenched, and knocked lightly and firmly on the butler's bedroom door, and then again, in case he should doubt what he had heard.

It was opened after several moments, and a very

anxious face appeared in the crack, his nightcap askew. He blinked before he recognized Vespasia.

"Lady Cumming-Gould! Is something amiss, my lady?"

"Yes, I am afraid so, Harcourt. It seems Sir Ferdinand has disturbed an intruder and been attacked when he tried to apprehend him. He is not very seriously hurt, but he was knocked insensible for some few minutes and has a very nasty cut on his head. We are not aware of anything that has been taken."

"Oh, dear." Harcourt gathered his wits very quickly. "That is dreadful. Are you all right, my lady?"

"Yes, thank you, Harcourt, I am quite unhurt. Perhaps you might call whoever on the staff is best able to minister to injury and a severe headache, and then see if anything is missing or anyone else disturbed. Although I have heard no other sound."

"Certainly, my lady. That would be most wise. I shall come straight down," and he retreated behind the door. Vespasia assumed he was arranging his clothing with a suitable dignity. After all, he was the principal among the servants and must always appear to be in command.

She went downstairs again and found Ferdie still looking pained and very groggy, propped up by the chair rather than sitting in it. "I think you need a stiff brandy," she observed. "Or perhaps one of my maid's herbal preparations against headache and a brandy afterward."

"I think I'll take the brandy," he said with more decision than she had thought him capable of.

Vespasia smiled. "You don't surprise me," she murmured. "Although, Ferdie, I do think the herbs might have a more lasting result."

"I'll have the brandy," he repeated.

She smiled very slightly. "I think next time you hear burglars in the night, you would be wise not to involve Leonora," she said casually.

"Oh . . ." He looked nonplussed, then suddenly blushed deeply. "Oh, yes . . . of course. I . . ."

She turned away, so as not to witness his embarrassment. She had said enough. He knew she knew.

Harcourt came down the stairs looking purposeful, with two ladies' maids and a valet behind him. The brandy was sent for, and the herbs, plus a bowl of hot water, ointment and plaster.

Within minutes doors were knocked on, and people began to appear in various stages of sleepiness and disarray.

A full ten minutes passed before Leonora Vickery came stumbling out of her room, wailing loudly that her jewelry had been stolen—all of it, even including the case in which she kept it. It was monstrous! She had been robbed of everything!

"Not quite everything," Vespasia observed in an aside. "I rather fancy something of it you were willing to give." But fortunately, no one heard her, or if they did, they were too stunned and generally dazed to take it in or question her meaning. Not that people often questioned Vespasia, in any event.

By three o'clock in the morning Ferdie's wound had been seen to, and he had been returned to his bed. Leonora had been comforted and assured that every possible avenue would be pursued in order to recover her jewels. Finally, everyone else in the household had gone back to their rooms.

At nine o'clock in brilliant sunlight Vespasia came along the corridor to the landing, ready to go downstairs for the day. By now, no doubt, the garden staff would have found Leonora's jewel box and everything would be returned to her. Ferdie would have a resounding headache, but it would eventually go, and he would be little the worse for the adventure. At least he could pose as the hero. He would certainly never deny that.

On the whole, Vespasia felt rather pleased with herself, and as always she looked magnificent.

Toby Blythe was going down the stairs. Vespasia watched his straight back and dark head, now definitely touched with gray here and there, and smiled with delightful memory.

Then Oremia swirled out of the east corridor, her skirts flying in an enormous bouffant of rose-pink and wine. Her face was sickeningly pale and her eyes like sockets in her head.

Vespasia was startled and her composure completely shaken. "What is it?" she gasped. "Oremia!"

"My diamonds, Vespasia!" Oremia said in a dry whisper, so quiet Vespasia barely heard her. "My diamonds have been stolen!"

Vespasia drew in her breath, her hands flew to her lips and she stifled a laugh. "Oh, my dear!" she said with only the merest shred of sympathy. "If you will sleep with the footman, you must expect a certain inconvenience!"

Oremia glared at her, then whirled around and sailed down the stairs after her husband.

Vespasia sighed, and smiled, then followed her down, her head high, her ivory skirts touching the banister rails on both sides.

SIGNET

Praise for the *FIRST CASES* series:

"[A] smashing concept."—*Mystery News*

"A mystery fan's fantasy."
—*St. Louis Dispatch*

Edited by Robert J. Randisi

BESTSELLING DETECTIVES.
GROUNDBREAKING CASES.

First Cases
❏ 0-451-19016-5/$5.99

First Cases, Volume 2
❏ 0-451-19017-3/$5.99

Prices slightly higher in Canada

PENGUIN PUTNAM INC.
Online

Your Internet gateway to a virtual environment with
hundreds of entertaining and enlightening books from
Penguin Putnam Inc.

*While you're there, get the latest buzz on
the best authors and books around—*

Tom Clancy, Patricia Cornwell, W.E.B. Griffin,
Nora Roberts, William Gibson, Robin Cook,
Brian Jacques, Catherine Coulter, Stephen King,
Jacquelyn Mitchard, and many more!

**Penguin Putnam Online is located at
http://www.penguinputnam.com**

PENGUIN PUTNAM NEWS

Every month you'll get an inside look at our upcoming
books and new features on our site. This is an ongoing
effort to provide you with the most up-to-date
information about our books and authors.

**Subscribe to Penguin Putnam News at
http://www.penguinputnam.com/ClubPPI**